Recovering
Alice

To Alison,

Thanks for your
support!

love,
Cattie

Catherine Morrison

C M x

For Mum and Daz

Chapter One

Alice Patterson stood at the closed door, adrenaline pumping through her veins. It was fight-or-flight time. Oddly for Alice, they meant the same thing. For her to fight, she had to run away, but her feet felt as if they were fixed to the ground. She stared at the door and tried to recall some of the strategies and techniques she had been taught during almost eight months of counselling and cognitive behavioural therapy. But all she could think about was what was behind that door. She tried to rationalise her intentions. *It wouldn't be a relapse, just a little slip. One drink to calm my nerves – medicinal, really. It's no big deal. I can stop again tomorrow.*

As if on autopilot, she opened the door and stepped inside. Desperate not to draw attention to herself, Alice did a quick scan of the busy wine bar for any familiar faces. She wasn't thinking clearly enough to do a thorough search, but she convinced herself she was in the clear so that she could sit down before her trembling legs gave way beneath her. All of the tables were occupied but there was one free seat at the bar. *That'll do. I'm only staying for one anyway.*

She clambered onto the bar stool, which was slightly too tall for her to claim gracefully. Cursing her wardrobe choice, she shifted on the stool and tried to pull her short skirt further down her thighs. *If I'd known I'd end up in a bar tonight, I would have chosen a different outfit.* But truthfully? She would have just stayed in bed.

"What'll it be?" the bartender asked. *What'll it be?* She hadn't given a thought to what her first drink might be. A glass of wine might be nice, or prosecco – that was all the rage these days. She used to kid herself that she had a sophisticated palate, but by the time she'd hit rock bottom she was guzzling down the cheapest, nastiest vodka or gin. It had been all she could afford. Spirits would be the only thing to settle her shaking hands and give her some relief. Gin? Yes, it was definitely gin she needed. That usually packed a real punch. And it had the added bonus of being the healthiest of the spirits. Those juniper berries were a godsend.

"Bombay Sapphire and tonic, please," she said, surprised at how easily the words rolled off her tongue. "Make it a double … and hold the tonic," she added quickly. *After all, I'm only having one. I'd better make it count.*

The bartender nodded and reached for a glass. "Ice and lemon?"

Don't even think about it! "Um, no, thank you."

She watched with bated breath as he poured the first shot into the glass. Saliva pooled in her mouth as he poured the second. By the time he had placed a cocktail napkin in front of her and set the glass down, she was nearly off her seat with anticipation.

Snaking her shaking hands round the glass, she cradled the precious liquid inside. She slowly raised it to her nose and inhaled the smell of the alcohol. It was familiar and comforting, yet she felt her stomach tighten. Tears welled in her eyes.

What am I doing?

She set the glass back down on the bar and stared at it.

Am I really going to drink this? Undo everything I've done for the last eight months? She sat on her hands to stop them shaking. *But … it would help with the shock. Numb the pain. Perhaps make me forget what I've just seen. But will I be able to stop after one?* She clutched the glass. *Fuck it. There's only one way to find out.*

She knocked back a large mouthful and regretted it instantly. Not only was straight gin disgusting, but it also stung the back of her throat and triggered her gag reflex as it burned its way down. She fought to stop herself bringing it back up, then set the glass down and steadied herself on the bar. After a few deep breaths, she drained the remainder and signalled the bartender for another.

While she waited for her refill, she questioned her decision. *I said one drink and I've had it. I should go home, climb into bed and try to forget this happened. Or I could get a tonic for this one, make it last a bit longer. Really savour it, as it will be the last drink I ever have.*

The bartender set down a fresh glass with two measures. Alice smiled at him. "Could I get a slimline for this one, please?"

He placed a bottle of Schweppes on the bar.

She poured the tiny bottle into the glass and took a sip. That was better; exactly what she needed. It was already starting to warm her insides. She examined her hands to see if they had stopped shaking. They hadn't. But they would soon. She'd be calmer, relaxed, and less devastated about what she had just seen.

She took another sip, then a large gulp.

Noticing that she was more than halfway through her drink, she placed it on the bar and surveyed the contents. She tried to calculate roughly how long it would last if she sipped it. Would she be feeling any better by then? Probably not, she thought. I'll need a third.

"Rough day?" a voice said.

She turned to face the man who was sitting on the next bar stool to hers. "Yeah, you could say that." She focused back on her drink.

"I had a pretty crappy day, too."

Rather than react, Alice took another sip.

"It's still early. Maybe you should pace yourself."

She rolled her eyes. She was thirty-two, not thirteen, and a stranger spewing out unsolicited advice was the last thing she wanted to hear. She'd heard it all before, anyway: 'the answer's not at the bottom of that bottle' – bullshit – or 'you can't drink away your problems' – nonsense. No one knew what *she* was going through. Especially not this bloody middle-aged man in his expensive suit, sipping his pretentious bottled beer.

"Pace yourself, asshole," she muttered under her breath.

"What did you say?"

"Nothing." She flashed him a sweet smile.

"You called me an asshole."

"Oh, so you did hear me."

He recoiled. He was about to speak when his mobile phone rang in his pocket. He turned away from her and answered it.

Alice caught the bartender's attention and pointed to her now empty glass. He brought another drink, and with it the bill. "Can you settle up? Can't have a tab unless you're eating."

She grimaced when she saw the total. Whether she liked it or not, this would definitely have to be her last drink. She'd go home after this one. Or maybe to the Wetherspoons around the corner... She got her debit card from her purse and waved it at him. While she waited for him to return with the card machine, the man beside her finished his call and placed another one. She sipped her drink while she tried not to listen. It sounded like he was arranging something, and whatever it was, he was definitely in charge. There was an air of authority in his voice, and confidence, which she usually found attractive. Maybe it was the two double gins starting to take effect, but she felt a bit bad that she'd been rude to him. It wasn't his fault that her ex-husband was such an insensitive asshole.

He finished the call and put his phone back into his pocket. He stared straight ahead, sipping his drink occasionally. Alice sipped hers too. After a few minutes she couldn't bear the tension any more. She tapped him on the arm. He turned to her and shrugged. "What did I do now?"

"Nothing." She sighed. "I'm sorry I snapped. I've had a shitty day, and it just got so much worse."

"How so?"

"Because I've been sober for two hundred and forty-three days." She put the glass to her lips and downed the rest of the third double gin.

"You're an alcoholic?"

"I prefer to say that I have alcohol use disorder."

"But you don't look like someone who has alcohol use disorder."

"Oh!" She looked down at herself. "Hey, maybe I don't. God, I really shouldn't have wasted all that time in rehab."

"Rehab? I've never met anyone who's been to rehab before."

"Then this must be exciting for you," she said dryly.

He sighed and pointed to her empty glass. "Listen. I

know it's a cliché and you've probably heard it a million times, but you're not going to find any answers in there."

And there it is. Bingo. She sighed again. "Thank you for your concern, but all I want is a quiet drink. If I'd wanted to talk, I'd have gone to a meeting."

"I don't know how to break this to you, but people in bars like to talk. Especially men like me to women like you. If you didn't want to talk, you should have bought a bottle and taken it home."

"Chance would be a fine thing. If Tam caught me drinking, she'd march me right back to rehab before the tonic was flat."

"Who's Tam?" His phone rang again. He took it from his pocket and looked at the caller ID. "Excuse me. I need to get this."

"Go right ahead. Whoever's on the end of that phone *wants* to talk to you. I just sat down beside you and now I regret it." She turned her back on him, but she could hear exactly what he was saying.

"Hey, you're late. What?" He sighed. "It's fine. I said, don't worry. We'll do it another time. OK. Bye." He ended the call and put the phone back in his pocket. "There goes my night..." He took a swig from his bottle.

Alice wasn't sure whether or not he was talking to her, so she ignored him.

Another swig emptied the bottle. He took out his wallet and placed some money on the bar, then pushed back his stool to get up. He tapped Alice on the shoulder. "I'm leaving now, but before I go, is there anyone you want me to call for you? Tam. Is that your sponsor?"

She held up her glass, "I've got everything I need."

"OK." He shuffled his feet. "Well … get home safe."

"You too." She turned away from him.

As he walked towards the door, he spotted a crowd of men, who were pretty rowdy for so early in the evening. One of them had clearly noticed him get up and had pointed to Alice. They were all looking at her – and why wouldn't they? She was a slim, attractive young woman and she was wearing a very short skirt. She was also getting drunk. Alone. At a bar in Greenwich. He knew there was no way she'd get the quiet drink she wanted with that lot around. And how much was she intending to drink? What if something happened to her? He knew he wasn't responsible for her, but something compelled him to try and help her. Knowing it probably wasn't a good idea, he went back over to the bar.

"Listen. I know it's useless to try and get you to stop, but I don't think you should be drinking alone. Let's help each other out. I had dinner plans but I've been stood up. How about you join me?"

She squinted at him. "Are you asking me out, mid-relapse?" She had initially meant it as a joke, but it wasn't the worst idea. There was no rule to say you couldn't enjoy yourself while relapsing. The three double gins in quick succession had already started to loosen her inhibitions, and she knew her own MO only too well. After a few more drinks she'd probably try to find a man to hook up with. This one wasn't bad-looking, and he was well presented in a nice suit, with clean, shiny shoes. After a few more drinks her judgement would be further impaired, and she could end up with far worse.

"I'm not asking you out. You're intent on getting

hammered – God knows what trouble you could get into all by yourself. You need someone to keep an eye out for you while you get … whatever this is out of your system. Come with me. You don't even have to order food. You can tell me about your shitty day while I eat. Then I'll make sure you get into a taxi and home safely."

She was tempted. *I'm definitely not ready to go home. I suppose I could set myself a limit. One, perhaps two more drinks. Be tucked up in bed before Tam and Cameron get back from that gig.*

"Come on," he coaxed. "I'm dying to know what happened to you that was so bad that you couldn't make it to day two hundred and forty-four."

"You really think I'm going to pour my heart out to a total stranger?"

He held his hand out to her. "I'm Bob."

She rolled her eyes as she shook his hand. "I'm Alice."

"Interesting to meet you, Alice. Come on. I've reservations in that new fusion place down the street."

"OK, I'll come with you, but only because you didn't reference that Roy Chubby Brown song." She slid down off the stool and gathered her stuff.

"You don't look like you're in the mood for jokes."

"I'm never in the mood for that joke."

He helped her with her coat and led her out of the bar.

Once seated in the restaurant, Alice questioned her decision to come. She looked around the chic, contemporary dining room and realised that not only was she underdressed, but the plain white blouse and black skirt she wore made her look like she should be working there, not eating. She ran her fingers through her long brown hair, pulled it into a bunch and draped it over her left shoulder.

As if sensing her unease, Bob took off his suit jacket and hung it over the back of his chair, then loosened his tie and undid his top button. "That's better. Now we can relax."

The waiter arrived at the table and handed them each a menu. "Would you like to see the wine list?"

"Lady's choice. Alice, would you like some wine, or do you want to stick to gin?"

She mulled it over. *A glass of wine wouldn't go amiss – just the one. Unless Bob wants some wine too. I'd better order a bottle.* "A bottle of the house white, please."

The waiter nodded and left to get the wine.

Bob read through the menu. "I'll just have a main course. I don't want to keep you out too late. Why don't you have a look too? You should probably have something to line your stomach. It's been two hundred and forty-three days. And you'll thank me tomorrow." He scanned the page. "Oh look, chicken skewers with fresh tomato and vodka sauce. It's meant to be."

She couldn't figure him out. One second she thought he was coming on to her, and the next – was he mocking her? She squinted at him. "So, Bob. What's your story?"

"I don't have a story."

"Yes, you do. Who stood you up, and why?"

"Just a friend. A male friend," he added quickly.

She giggled. "Is that your way of telling me that you're single – or that you're gay?"

"Neither. I'm married."

"Married? And what would your wife say if she knew you were here having dinner with me?"

He held up his left hand. It was bare. "She'd probably be OK with it. We've been separated for months, and there's no way she isn't sleeping with somebody else by now."

Just then the waiter arrived to pour the wine.

"I'm not sleeping with you, Bob. It's just dinner." Alice took a sip while the waiter poured Bob's glass. "Although, a few more of these and I might just change my mind..."

The waiter looked at her, wide-eyed. "Um, are you two ready to order?"

Bob flushed. "A few more minutes, please."

The waiter scurried off.

"So, did you cheat?"

He frowned at her. "Why do you automatically assume I cheated? There are plenty of other reasons marriages don't work out."

"I'm well aware of that," she whispered.

"Are you speaking from experience?"

"Yup. I was married. Now I'm divorced, and I don't want to talk about it." She took a long sip of wine.

"Yeah, let's not do that. So, tell me why your day was so bad that it tipped you off the wagon."

"I can't. We just agreed not to talk about it."

"Oh. OK. The waiter's glaring at us, so let's talk about the menu."

Bob asked for the bill while Alice was in the ladies' room. He thought about the evening. The food had been great, and so had the company. Conversation had flowed naturally, even though it was mainly just small talk and nothing of a personal nature. He could tell that Alice was smart, funny and, despite her initial rudeness, had a nice personality. He was definitely attracted to her and wanted to see her again. Then it hit him. He had been so busy enjoying her company that he had forgotten the purpose of the dinner. He started to regret his actions. Was he enabling her by letting her drink? Was he using her as an escape because he had been stood up by a friend and was feeling lonely and wanted someone to be miserable with? Just then, he saw her wobbling back to the table. She'd drunk two bottles of wine, apart from the glass the waiter had poured for him at the beginning of the evening, which he hadn't touched. He knew he had to keep his wits about him to get her to stop drinking and agree to go home. It was time to call it a night.

Alice tried to look sultry as she stumbled back into her chair, then pouted when she saw the bill. "No next bottle?"

"I think two was enough."

"Nah." She dismissed him with a wave of her hand. "Let's go clubbin'."

"I don't think they'd let you into many clubs in the state you're in. I should get you home."

She raised her eyebrows at him. "For what?"

"Nothing. You're drunk. I just want to make sure you get home safely."

"I'm not druuunk," she slurred.

"OK, then. Prove it by walking in a straight line to the taxi I've ordered."

"Certainly, sir." She saluted. She slammed her palms onto the table and gripped the tablecloth to pull herself to her feet, but as she turned she caught her foot in the strap of her bag and stumbled towards the next table. Bob leapt up to catch her before she fell into the lap of an elderly diner. He held on to Alice while she retrieved her handbag from the floor, then steered her outside to the taxi.

He held her arm as she lowered herself into the back seat, then helped manoeuvre her feet over the sill and into the footwell. She threw herself back in the seat and closed her eyes.

"Budge over," he instructed.

She turned to look at him and licked her lips. "Oh good, dessert."

He flushed again. He was really attracted to her. If she had been sober, he'd love nothing more than to take her to bed. But there was no way he was going to go inside her house. He just wanted to make sure she got home safely. And to find out where she lived so he could perhaps see her again. When she was sober, of course.

She tried to budge but only moved about a centimetre. He sighed and went around to the other side of the taxi and climbed in beside her. She rested her head against his shoulder and closed her eyes. He nudged her. "Go ahead. Tell the man where you live."

"London," she said through a yawn.

"Can you be a bit more specific?"

"Eight … Eat-on … Road. Lon-don."

The driver looked into the rear-view mirror at Bob. "Is she going to throw up?"

"Are you?" Bob asked.

She lifted her head briefly to shake it, then snuggled back against Bob's shoulder, pressing one of her breasts against his arm. In an effort not to stare, he looked at the floor of the taxi, but he couldn't stop his gaze roaming up and down her bare legs. They looked silky smooth and longer than they should have as her short skirt had crept up her thigh.

When the taxi stopped abruptly at a set of traffic lights, Alice instinctively put her hand on Bob's lap to steady herself. When she didn't move it away, he looked up at her, to see that she had fallen asleep. His eyes were drawn to the sliver of the baby-pink bra that poked out from under her tight white blouse. He was wondering why she'd done up so many buttons when he realised he was staring. He turned away and looked out of the window for the rest of the journey. When the taxi stopped at a line of old three-storey townhouses that had been converted into flats, he groaned. "What are the chances she lives on the ground floor?"

The cabbie grimaced.

Bob tried to stir her. "Alice, wake up. You're home."

She lifted her head and looked out of the window. "I don't live here."

"But this is where you said."

"I did? Wait..." She pushed Bob up against the back of the seat and looked out of the opposite window to the other side of the street. "I live over there."

Bob got out of the taxi and went around to her side to open the door. He held out his hand to help her, then had to practically drag her out and onto her feet. She collapsed against him and rested her hand on his chest. "You're really handsome."

Bob rolled his eyes, then leant in to speak to the driver. "Leave the meter running. I'll be two minutes."

"Just two minutes?" Alice giggled. "No wonder your wife left you."

"Hey!"

She slapped her hand to her mouth. "Kidding! Come in. Nightcap."

He shook his head.

"Coffee?"

She was swaying so badly he was afraid she'd fall once she was inside. He'd better get her settled.

"One cup." He propped her up against a wall and paid the driver, then helped Alice up the steps to her front door, which was on the first floor. She leant against the door for balance while she fumbled for her keys, giving Bob a smug look when she got the key into the lock on the first try.

"See, I'm not as think as you drunk I am. Slept it off in taxi." Then she fell through the door.

He helped her back to her feet and into the living/dining area, where she collapsed onto the sofa and snuggled into a cushion. Bob shook his head. He wasn't sure whether to leave her alone or try to sober her up a bit before he left. He draped his suit jacket over the back of the sofa. "Do you live here alone?"

"No, itsh my friend's place. She lets me live here. She's so nice." Alice put her finger over her lips and whispered, "Don't tell her I've been drinking. She'll kill me."

"Is she at home?"

Alice shook her head. "Nah. Best we're in bed before she gets back."

His eyes widened. He wasn't going anywhere near her bed. Although he could use the bathroom; he'd had a lot of water to drink at the restaurant. "Do you mind if I use your bathroom?"

She pointed down the hall and waited until he was

gone before dragging herself off the sofa and staggering to the kitchenette. She opened the cupboard under the sink, shoved a few bottles of cleaning products to the side and took out a bucket. "Yes!" she exclaimed when she saw there was a bottle of red wine inside. She was carefully pouring two glasses when Bob returned from the bathroom.

"That's funny-looking coffee."

"Ssh!" She stumbled towards him with a glass in each hand, and held out one to him.

"No, thank you."

"Take it." She forced the glass into his hand, spilling a few drops onto his white shirt. She gasped and reached for his shirt with her free hand. "That needs to come off..."

He took a step backwards. "It's OK. I'll keep it on."

She pouted, then took a long sip of wine, swaying from side to side.

He set his glass down on the coffee table and guided her back to the sofa. He sat down, maintaining a reasonable distance. Alice set her glass down beside his and moved closer to him. He shifted uncomfortably when she put her hand on his knee, and then, before he knew it, her lips were on his. She kissed him hard, thrusting her tongue into his mouth. He pulled away, leaving her sulking. Then she got a mischievous look in her eye, and he knew he was in trouble. She grabbed his tie, pulled him close and kissed him firmly. This time it was harder for him to pull away. Her lips were too soft and warm. He met her tongue with his own, enjoying the sweet taste of wine as he raked his fingers through her long brown hair. He pulled her onto his lap so she was straddling him and kissed her hard, running his hands down her back to her backside and squeezing it tight.

She moaned as she arched backwards, letting him trace his lips down her neck, but when he reached her chest, she climbed off his lap. She stood in front of him and held his gaze while she slowly unbuttoned her blouse, revealing the baby-pink bra underneath. She let the blouse slide off her shoulders and onto the floor.

He stared at her, desperately trying to subdue the urge that was building inside him.

She held her hand out to him and gestured to the hallway behind her, presumably to her bedroom.

Just as he was about to take her hand, his gaze darted to the wine on the coffee table. He was stone-cold sober and she – well, she was not. He cleared his throat. "I don't think this is a good idea, Alice."

She nodded suggestively.

"You're drunk."

"Not *that* drunk..." She beckoned with her index finger, turned and staggered down the hall.

He was aroused, and contemplating giving in to her. Was she really so drunk that she didn't know her own mind? But the voice in his head told him that if he had to ask this, it meant she was. He leapt up from the sofa and grabbed his suit jacket. "Alice, I'm going to go."

There was no answer.

"Are you OK?"

Again, no answer.

He crept down the hall, expecting to find her passed out on the bed, but instead he found her sitting on the side of the bed, struggling to undo the strap of one of her heels.

"Be right with you..."

"Um, I'm going to go."

She glared at him. "Why? Don't you find me attractive?"

"Incredibly."

"Then why don't you want to sleep with me?"

"I do, but I can't. You're drunk."

"Not drunk... Tipsy."

"Either way, it's not a great idea. Would you like me to make you some coffee before I go?"

"No. I want you to fuck me before you go."

He shook his head.

"Then get out," she hissed.

"You're not in a good place. Sex isn't the—"

"Get out!" she yelled. She finally pulled her high heel off and threw it at him. He didn't need to dodge, as her aim was off, but there was force behind her throw and the shoe hit the wall beside him with a thud.

The situation was out of control. He wasn't going to stick around for her friend to come home, in case he was accused of something. Shame washed over him at how he'd let things get so badly out of hand. He was glad he hadn't left her in the bar, but now that she was safe in her own home, it was the right time to leave.

"Goodnight, Alice," he said softly, then hurried up the hall towards the door.

She dragged herself off the bed and stumbled down the hall just in time to see the door close behind him. She banged her fists on the door.

"Fuck you, Bob. Fuck you!" she screamed. Tears rolled down her cheeks as she made her way to the sofa and threw herself down on it. She spotted her blouse and slid onto the floor to retrieve it. She wiped her eyes with the blouse, then noticed the wine on the coffee table. She crawled over and lifted a glass, propped herself up against the sofa and drained it in a few gulps. Then she took the other glass and sipped it between sobs. When she had finished the second glass, she got up and stumbled into the kitchen. She grabbed the wine bottle and took it with her back to the sofa.

Chapter Two

It was after eleven when Alice woke the next morning. She was relieved to find herself tucked up in her own bed, alone. Even if she wasn't entirely sure how she'd got there. She tried to piece together the events of the night before. She remembered going to the bar and drinking the gin, meeting a man: Bob, if she remembered correctly. Then the restaurant, dinner, but it all got a little sketchy after that. She vaguely remembered a taxi journey home, and she had flashes of taking her blouse off and straddling Bob on the sofa. But now she was in bed. *Oh my God, did we have sex?* A quick glance under the duvet revealed she was naked, but for her underwear. She relaxed, but only briefly; that didn't mean anything. Slowly she ran her hand down to check herself – it had been a long time since she'd had sex, so surely if she had, it would feel like she had. It did not.

Her feeling of relief was short-lived. Her head throbbed and the light streaming through the cracks in the blinds assaulted her tired, bloodshot eyes. She pulled the covers over her head and tried to go back to sleep, but it was no use. The room was spinning, and she was nauseous as hell. *And why does my body ache? Was I in a fight?* She wanted to die.

After a few minutes she summoned the energy to sit up. It was only then that she noticed the glass of water and two tablets, presumably paracetamol, waiting on her bedside table. She took a sip of water to wash down the pills, but still gagged on them, making her heave. Bile rose into her throat. She lay back down again, filled with dread. Tamzin must have left the tablets. Alice had hoped to hide this from her, but it was obvious that she'd been found out. She prayed that Tamzin would go easy on her. After all, no one could hate her more than she hated herself at that moment. She took another few sips of water and pulled her pyjamas on. It was time to face the music.

Alice shuffled to the kitchenette to find her best friend Tamzin at the table with her fiancé Cameron. It was their flat, but Alice had been staying in the spare bedroom for the past few months. After her stint in rehab, she had gone back home to live with her parents, but her tumultuous relationship with her mother had been driving her insane. Cameron was on a two-year work secondment in Edinburgh and lived there most of the time. But the rent on his flat there, combined with the mortgage on the flat in London, was straining the couple's finances. Alice had suggested that she rent their spare room for a few months to help out, but also so she could escape her judgemental, overbearing mother. Tamzin had jumped at the chance to live with her best friend while her fiancé was away, and had said that the extra money was just a bonus.

They stopped talking when they saw her. Cameron stood up and offered Alice his seat. "I've got to see a man about a dog." He tucked Alice into the chair and squeezed her shoulders. He kissed Tamzin on the cheek then left the kitchen. A few moments later, they heard the front door close.

Alice braced herself. *This is going to be bad.*

Tamzin got up from her chair and threw her arms around Alice. She hugged her friend tight then, without a word, went to the counter and poured her a cup of coffee. She sat back down at the table beside her. "How are you feeling?"

Alice shrugged.

"We came home about three. You were passed out on the rug."

"You should have just left me there."

"We couldn't. I thought you might vomit, then asphyxiate. No one wants a corpse on their living-room floor. Cameron carried you to bed and I finished undressing you." She pointed to the empty wine bottle on the kitchen counter. "Do you want to tell me what happened?"

"I'll replace the wine," Alice whispered.

"I don't give a shit about the wine. What happened to you?"

The events of yesterday evening came flooding back. Alice tried to choke back her tears. "Dylan." She sank her head into her hands and sobbed.

Tamzin jumped up and hurried round the table to comfort her. She didn't speak, just held her while she cried. "Oh, Alice," she murmured, stroking her hair. "It's OK. It's OK."

Alice tried to catch her breath. "It's not OK. It'll never be OK." She continued to sob; her heart was breaking all over again. She'd never felt so hopeless, so betrayed. Tamzin didn't speak but let her friend cry until she had no more tears.

By then the coffee had gone cold. Tamzin made a fresh pot and made some buttery toast for Alice. They took it to the living room and curled up on the sofa together, like they'd done since they became next-door neighbours when they were four years old.

"I'd just finished work. I was on my way to the bus

stop and … then I saw her."

"Who?"

The memory brought new tears to Alice's eyes. "A woman. She was pregnant, and she was … with Dylan. Holding his hand."

Tamzin gasped. "Oh, Alice. I'm so sorry."

"I couldn't believe it. He even tried to talk to me. I've thought about that moment a thousand times. I had rehearsed what I wanted to say to him. But when I saw him my mind went blank, and when I saw that baby bump … I just turned and walked away. I practically ran. What could I have said? That woman had my husband, and she was having his baby. It should have been me. Why wasn't it me?" She began to sob again.

Tamzin held her and tried to soothe her.

"At least I didn't break down in front of him. That's something, right?"

"See, every cloud has a silver lining."

"Not that silver. All the feelings, the hurt and anger – they all came flooding back. I felt so hopeless. All I wanted to do was have a drink. I thought it would have been harder – you know, once I had the drink in my hand? – that it would have been harder to take that first sip. Turns out, I didn't even hesitate. And now everything I've been through these past eight months has gone to waste. Because of one weak moment."

"Don't let it be a waste, Alice. It's a bump in the road, and it's my fault. I shouldn't have had wine in the house."

"No, Tam. This isn't your fault. It's not even Dylan's. It's mine. It was my decision to drink, and I was drunk long before I got home." She offered it as a comfort to her friend, but Tamzin still looked defeated. "Don't feel bad – you're allowed to have wine in your own home. Just do me a favour and hide it better from now on."

They laughed.

"I can't believe he's having a baby. I hope it's really ugly."

Tamzin's jaw dropped. "Alice Patterson, how could you say such a horrible thing?"

"Like there's any way that baby is going to be ugly. She was really pretty, and Dylan – he's gorgeous."

"He's not gorgeous. He's a cruel, heartless, ugly-on-the-inside man who ruined my best friend's life. Promise me these are the last tears you'll shed over him?"

Alice nodded.

"That's my girl. Now, do you want me to find you a meeting today? I'll go with you."

Alice sighed. She hated AA meetings and hadn't been to one in ages, thinking she didn't need them any more. She'd thought the same about her sponsor, and had been dodging her for months. If she hadn't, she might have been able to stick to her recovery plan and not abandon it completely when she saw Dylan. Clearly, she still had a long way to go. "No. I can't face a meeting. Not hungover. I promise I'll find one for tomorrow. I'll have a shower, then I'm going back to bed and sleeping until tomorrow. Start day two."

Tamzin hugged her tightly. "I'm so proud of you."

"Proud? Do you need me to get you a dictionary?"

"Last night's performance aside, I've seen you at your lowest. Back then, you'd be drinking already, or at least planning to. Not thinking about day two."

Alice rubbed her temples. "I can't go backwards. I've got to get my head straight for this job on Monday."

When she got out of rehab, she couldn't face going back to her job as an actuary. The stress, the hours, even the thought of talking to people – it was too much to entertain. So she took a job washing dishes in a hotel kitchen. It got her up and out of the house, and she could switch off at the end of the day and not take any pressure home with her. But now she felt that it was time to slowly build herself back up to more professional work. She had signed up with an agency and made herself available for temporary accountancy and clerical work. On Monday she would start her first assignment from the agency, and she wanted to be in a good headspace.

"Oh, and by the way..." Tamzin pointed to the two wine glasses drying on the side. "Was there someone here with you last night?"

Alice screwed up her face. "Bob."

"Who's Bob?"

"A guy I met at the bar."

"I'm going to need more than that. Did he get you into that state? Did he try to have sex with you?" Her voice was getting higher.

"No. I told him about my *problem*, and he stayed with me while I drank to make sure I was safe. He made me eat something. Then he brought me home."

"And did he expect any reward for his efforts?"

Alice had a sudden flashback of the sofa, then her bedroom, and then her flinging her shoe at him. "No. I wanted to sleep with him, but he left."

"A guy actually said no to a drunk woman who wanted to have sex with him? Sounds promising. Are you going to see him again?"

"Absolutely not. My days of getting drunk and

sleeping with random men are over." She walked off to the bathroom. *Well, until my next little slip, at least.*

After her shower, Alice climbed back into bed and pulled the covers up over her head. The shower hadn't been effective at eliminating the stale smell of alcohol. And she was sweating badly; the alcohol was seeping out of her pores. *When am I going to start feeling better?* She rolled over and tried to go back to sleep.

She was sleeping when the doorbell rang. She prayed it wasn't her sister; it would be just her luck that today would be the day she chose to call over unannounced. She lay and listened, but she couldn't hear any voices. She glanced at the clock and saw it was nearly five – perhaps Tamzin had ordered an early dinner. She was settling back onto her pillow when there was a knock at her bedroom door, then the door opened.

"Psst! Are you awake?" Tamzin pushed the door open and walked in holding a huge bouquet of flowers. "These just arrived for you."

"Oh my God." Alice groaned. "That is so typical of Dylan. Rubbing salt in my wounds."

"Sadly, I thought the same thing. I didn't want to put you through that, so I opened the card. They're not from Dylan." She was beaming as she held out the card.

Alice took it and read the message. *Hope these make the headache a bit easier. Call me. Bob x.* She tossed the card onto the bed. "Throw them in the bin."

"What? No! His mobile number is on the bottom. You have to call him."

"No, I don't."

"Come on, look at these. They must have cost at least a hundred pounds. And same-day delivery – that costs a premium. This guy's not shy about spending money, and he wants to spend it on you. Is he good-looking?"

Alice tried to picture him, but her memory was fuzzy. "He's all right, I suppose, but I'm not calling him."

"You can't *not* call him."

"I'll text him to thank him for the flowers, but that's it. I'm a mess. I'm not ready to date."

"I'm not telling you to marry him. Call him and see what happens. You need to get out of the house more."

"I go out."

"I meant to places that aren't the gym. Alice, if you spend another Saturday night there, or curled up on that sofa watching chick flicks, I'm going to kill you. And if I hear you sobbing your way through *Hopelessly Devoted to You* one more time, I'm going to kill myself."

"I'm *trying* to get my life back. That's why I quit the job at the hotel and I'm starting a proper one on Monday. I'll save up a few quid and get my own place. But I don't need to date. I'm done with men."

"Done with men? You're only thirty-two. This guy, Bob, seems nice so far. Just see what he has to say. And I don't want to hear you talking about moving out. You can stay here as long as you like."

"You guys are getting married in October. Cameron will be back from his secondment not long after the wedding. You two can't start your married life with me under your feet."

"We're your friends. We want you here. I'm worried about you going back into the big bad world."

"I've got to sometime."

"Not until you're ready." Tamzin looked over at the flowers again. "What are you going to text him?"

26

"Who?"

"Bob!" Tamzin grabbed Alice's mobile from the bedside table and handed it to her.

Alice sighed and typed a quick message. Then she took the card and keyed in Bob's number. She pressed send and set the phone on the bed.

"What did you say?"

"I said, 'I'm sorry about last night. Thank you for the flowers. Take care. Alice.'"

"That's it?"

"That's—"

Alice's phone beeped. She lifted the phone and angled it so that Tamzin could see the message.

You're welcome. Fancy meeting for a coffee this evening? I have a sneaking suspicion you might need one.

Tamzin nudged her. "Do it."

"I don't want to go out for coffee."

"It's what normal people do. If you go, I'll butt out."

"Promise?"

Tamzin made a cross over her heart with her index finger.

"Ugh, OK. I should apologise. I need to own up to my mistake. But just coffee." She held up the phone so Tamzin could see what she was typing.

OK. Do you know Dean's by the park? Meet you there at 7?

It's a date! X

It's not a date.

☹

"I can't believe you talked me into this." She checked her phone. It was just after 5 p.m. "Oh shit, I probably look like a dog's dinner."

"You've looked better. Have another shower. Put on your black jeans or leggings, and your grey tunic-jumper-top thingy. Casual, but flattering."

Alice had another flashback to the night before. Drunk, stripping off in front of him, throwing herself at him. Neither casual nor flattering. This was going to be embarrassing.

Alice pulled open the glass door and looked around the coffee shop. She was afraid that she might not even recognise Bob, but she soon spotted him at a table in the corner. He was already sipping a coffee. He looked better than she had remembered. Not devastatingly handsome, but not unattractive either. And there was no sign of the suit he'd worn the night before. He was wearing a dark-grey sweater with a casual white shirt underneath. She met his eye and he grinned when he saw her. He stood up as she approached the table.

"Good evening, Alice. You're looking lovely. What can I get you to drink?"

"An Americano. Thank you."

"Snack?"

"No thanks."

"Take a seat. I'll be right back." He hurried off to place her order.

She took off her jacket and draped it over the back of

her chair, then sat down and watched him at the counter. If this had been an actual date, he'd already have scored some points. Punctual, polite, attentive. And now that she was sober and paying attention, she could see that he was good-looking, but not in a conventional way. A bit off-handsome, if that was a thing. A few grey flecks in his thick brown hair and the odd wrinkle around his hazel eyes told her that he was older than her, but probably not by much. Her ex-husband had been the same age as her, so someone more mature might be a nice change of pace. She stopped herself. *You're done with men, remember?*

Bob arrived back with the coffee and pointed to the straws of sugar in the middle of the table. She shook her head.

"So, how was your head this morning?"

"Awful."

"Good."

"Why is that good?"

"OK, maybe good isn't the best word. But it's good that you're here with me on a Saturday night, sober and drinking coffee. It's important to me that you stay on the path to recovery."

She was taken aback by his concern. "I wish it was as simple as that. But yes, I'm taking baby steps. Why is it important to you that I recover?"

"I feel responsible for allowing you to get so drunk. It's been eating me up all day. I should have tried harder to get you to stop. Instead I bought you two bottles of wine. It was really irresponsible. But I'm glad I got you home OK. If I had just left you, something awful could have happened to you."

"Please don't beat yourself up about it. You did the

right thing. Nothing would have stopped me from drinking. So thank you for keeping me safe. And feeding me. And thank you for the flowers – they're beautiful. But you really shouldn't have. I'm the one who should have sent you flowers. To apologise for my behaviour."

"You've nothing to apologise for."

"Of course I do. I got drunk and made a complete show of myself. I'm suitably ashamed and embarrassed. And I might have been a bit rude when I asked you to leave..."

He choked on his coffee. "Asked? Told, more like. But if it's any consolation, I really did want to sleep with you. It's not every day a beautiful woman gets half naked and throws herself at me. I had to muster every ounce of my self-control to make myself walk out of there."

She tried hard not to blush. No one had called her beautiful in a long time, and it was nice to hear.

"What do you say we start again? Soberly. Would you like to have dinner with me sometime?"

"No. I'm sorry."

His face fell.

"I just came here to thank you for everything. You've been really sweet. But I'm not interested in seeing anyone at the minute. Last night proves I'm not recovered yet. I need to focus all my energy on that."

"You still need to eat."

"You don't know what you'd be getting into. You seem like a decent man – there's got to be someone more conventional for you out there. Someone who doesn't have any problems."

"We've all got problems, Alice." There was sincerity in his eyes. "I like you. You're pretty. Interesting to talk to. And when you pushed me back on the sofa and climbed on top of me – well, I'd be lying if I said I didn't enjoy it."

She cringed at the memory. "But I'm a mess."

"I don't think so. Your life might be a bit of a mess. But it's obvious that you're trying to turn that around. You seem determined. I find that a very attractive quality."

"You do?"

He nodded.

"Anyway, I couldn't go out with you even if I wanted to. You're married."

"Only on paper until the divorce is final. Besides, it didn't seem to bother you last night."

"I was drunk and distressed."

He sat to attention. "Who distressed you?"

"No one." She was overwhelmed by his concern for her. He knew that she was divorced and had a problem with alcohol; most men wouldn't be so eager to date her. And he was good-looking and seemed to be decent. Maybe she should give him a chance...

"OK, let's compromise. How about you hold on to my phone number and when you're actually divorced, give me a call? Hopefully I'll be ready to date by then. I should go." She pushed back her seat.

"But you just got here. At least stay and finish your coffee."

Alice didn't want to stick around any longer than she had to. She'd already thanked him and apologised; there was no point in prolonging the agony. "I shouldn't, really. It'll keep me up all night and I've got an early meeting tomorrow."

"A meeting – on a Sunday?"

"AA."

"Oh, shit. Sorry."

"That's OK. All part of my hectic lifestyle. It was lovely meeting you, Bob."

"You too, Alice. Take care of yourself."

"I'll try. Bye." She wasn't sure whether to shake his hand or give him a peck on the cheek, so she patted him gently on the shoulder as she passed him on her way to the door.

Once outside, she wanted to stop and catch her breath. She hated the 'making amends' part of the recovery process, but she had to keep walking and put some distance between her and the coffee shop before she could relax. Although it had gone better than she had expected. Usually she wasn't comfortable talking to new people, but there was something about Bob that made her feel at ease. *Is Tam right? Should I be dating? Bob seems nice so far and he's easy to talk to.* She was distracted by a raindrop landing on her face, then one on her forehead, and another. Then the heavens opened.

Typical, she thought. The February evening was unseasonably mild, so she only had a light jacket and no umbrella. She jogged to the bus stop and groaned when she saw it was thirteen minutes until the next one.

She wrapped her arms around herself and waited. The rain was getting heavier, and it was still seven minutes until the bus was due to arrive. She was accepting her current situation as karma paying her back for her behaviour the night before when an electric-blue Jaguar saloon with tinted windows pulled up at the bus stop. The window rolled down, and she looked in to see Bob behind the wheel.

Of course it's him. She was soaked to the skin.

"Get in!" he shouted.

"No, it's OK. I'm already drenched. The bus will be along in a minute."

He looked up at the sign – six minutes until the bus was due. "You'll be washed away by then. I'll drive you home – I know the way."

"Honestly, it's fine."

The driver's door opened, and Bob jumped out and hurried around to the passenger side. He opened the door and pointed inside. "Now get in before I get drenched too."

Alice looked around at the other people waiting for the bus, feeling as if their eyes were boring into her. She threw Bob an exasperated look, then climbed into the passenger seat. He slammed the door shut and hurried around to his side.

Inside, he tutted and wiped the rain from his face. "It's raining and I'm offering you a lift. There's no need to be so stubborn." His voice was stern.

"I'm sorry. Thank you."

He started the car and pulled away from the bus stop. The journey back to Alice's was silent but for the radio. She kept her eyes forward and was very conscious of dripping all over the car's expensive upholstery. She knew her eye make-up would be halfway down her cheeks, and her hair was sopping, yet she couldn't shake the feeling that he would ask her out again. *What will I say?* she wondered.

When he stopped the car outside her flat, he turned and smiled at her. "All the best for your meeting tomorrow."

"Thanks. And thanks for the lift."

"You're welcome." He started the car.

That's it? Disappointed, but also relieved that he hadn't tried to ask her out again, she slipped out quietly and climbed the steps to the front door. She didn't dare to look back. She had just turned her key in the door when she heard the car drive away. *That's that.* She sighed and went inside.

Tamzin met her at the living-room door. "Nice car."

"Were you spying on me?"

"No. I thought you were the pizza … which we haven't ordered yet. Why were you so quick, and when are you seeing him again? Did you have a kiss in the car? Was it just a peck or a full-on snog?"

"Neither, and I'm not seeing him again."

"Oh no! Is he hideous without your beer goggles on?"

"He's not hideous." Alice sighed.

"Then what's your problem? The flowers, that car – not hideous. What more could you want?"

Nothing, really. If she was ready to date, he would probably be the type she would go for.

"Look. You said if I had coffee with him, you'd let it go. I had coffee with him. So…"

Tamzin scowled at her. "Do you want your own pizza, or do you want to share a large pepperoni?"

"Pepperoni, please. I'm going to dry off and put my PJs on." Alice sulked off to her bedroom, wondering if she had made a mistake saying no to Bob.

Chapter Three

When Alice woke the next morning, the impending AA meeting was not her first thought; it was Bob. Talking to him in the bar the night they had met had been easy because the alcohol had reduced her usual anxiety and increased her sociability, but seeing him at the coffee shop when she was sober hadn't been as awkward and awful as it should have been. He seemed sincere, and she felt genuinely at ease with him. It was the first normal thing she'd done since rehab that didn't involve work, the gym, or doing something with Tamzin or her own family, and it felt good. *Is Tam right? Am I ready to date? Or at the very least, make a new friend and get out of the house from time to time?* She suddenly remembered the AA meeting and pulled the covers back over her head.

Alice timed her arrival at the church hall perfectly; the meeting was about to start. That meant she could avoid any potential small talk. She'd never made friends with anyone at a meeting before, and she didn't want to. In some way she felt it made her seem more normal, not to have other addicts as friends, but truthfully, she just didn't like talking to people she didn't know. It made her anxious. She didn't have any close friends other than Tamzin, and since rehab she had chosen to take on temp work as she didn't want the responsibility of a real job, or the pressure to form relationships with co-workers. When she was younger, she had used alcohol to help her cope in social situations, and she always drank way more than she should have as a result. The irony was not lost on her; it was a cruel and vicious circle. Just as she was about to open the door, she heard a voice behind her.

"Is this your first time?"

Alice turned to see an older woman with a friendly smile. She was plump, with greying hair, and probably a few more wrinkles than she deserved.

Alice returned the smile. "No. I used to go to meetings all the time. I just haven't been to one in a while."

"Welcome back. You picked a good one. Everyone here is really friendly. I'm Joan. Come on, you can sit next to me." Joan held the door open for Alice and they followed the signs to the meeting room. There were already about two dozen people there, standing around talking. Joan pointed to the refreshments table in the corner. "Let's get a coffee."

They had just poured their coffees when people began to take their seats in the circle. Alice and Joan sat down next to each other. Alice looked around at all the faces. Men and women of all ages and backgrounds, with no obvious connection to one another. There wasn't a smile in sight. Well, apart from one guy.

"Good morning, everyone," he said cheerfully. "I'll start, shall I?" Without waiting for an answer, he began. "I'm Karl, and I'm an alcoholic. I've been sober for eleven years, four months and nine days."

Alice listened as Karl told his story. His achievement of eleven years sober was impressive, but he admitted to a few false starts. After he had finished, they went around the circle, each person taking their turn to speak. Their stories were very similar.

Soon they came to a man who was a bit detached from the circle. He shook his head; he didn't want to speak. Although she was dreading it, Alice was next in line. She placed her coffee on the floor and gave everyone a wave. "Hi, I'm Alice and I'm an alcoholic."

"Hi, Alice!" everyone replied in unison.

"I *had* been sober for two hundred and forty-three days ... until Friday." She stopped and looked around. There were a few sympathetic nods. "I came face to face with my biggest trigger. It was totally unexpected, and I wasn't prepared. Instinct took over and the only thing I wanted to do was have a drink. And not just one drink. I thought, seeing as I'd started..." She took a deep breath. "I woke up yesterday morning with a terrible hangover. But that wasn't the worst thing. The shame and regret I felt were unbelievable. I was so angry with myself. But this time last year, my solution would have been to start drinking again. The one thing I was certain of yesterday was that I didn't want to drink. I went back to bed and pulled the covers over my head. I woke up this morning and here I am."

The tear that slipped from the corner of her eye caught her off guard.

"Good for you, Alice." Karl initiated a round of applause. "Triggers can catch you off guard. Even when you think you're prepared for them."

"Totally. But I haven't been helping myself. I have to admit that this is the first meeting I've been to in months. I thought I didn't need them any more. That I was strong enough to go it alone. I guess I was wrong."

"That's very honest. And we've probably all felt the same way. Meetings like this aren't for everyone, and they don't help everyone. But by coming along this morning you are giving yourself a better chance of long-term sobriety. Every meeting increases your odds. And it's a safe space. There's no judgement, and there's free coffee. So why the hell not?" There was a ripple of laughter.

Alice turned and signalled to Joan that she was finished. Joan drew breath to speak.

Later that evening, Alice was at the gym lifting weights. While she worked out, she replayed the AA meeting in her mind. It had been OK. The people seemed nice and she had enjoyed the absence of judgement and the sense of camaraderie. She vowed to go again. Not every day, though – once a week wouldn't be too soul-destroying.

She finished her set then stood up to increase the weight on her bar. She settled back on the bench and struggled with the first few lifts, but soon found her rhythm. Her mind turned to Bob, and she wondered again if she had made a mistake. Having dinner with him wouldn't have to mean anything; it didn't have to lead anywhere if she didn't want it to. But she'd missed her chance. There was no way he would ask her out again. *But I have his number. I could ask him out...* She shuddered at the thought. *Even if I had the courage, he probably hasn't considered the implications of dating someone like me. I'd be holding him back. Judging by his car, the clothes, the fancy restaurant he took me to, he obviously likes the good things in life. And would he drink in my company, or would he have to give up too? That wouldn't be fair on him. And what if things got serious and we ended up together and he wanted to have a family? That's something I can't give him.* An image of Dylan and his pregnant girlfriend flashed before her eyes. All of a sudden the weight bar was heavier. It was getting harder and harder to continue, but she pushed on regardless. Her heart was beating overtime and sweat was dripping off her, but she couldn't stop. Then the weight disappeared. Her arms dropped down to her sides and she tried desperately to catch her breath. She felt like she was about to throw up, and she was so dizzy that she couldn't turn her head. Someone shoved her water bottle into her hand.

"Alice! What are you thinking?" Marco, one of the personal trainers, was standing over her, shaking his head. "Too much. I was watching you – you looked like you were in a trance. You can't lose your focus with these weights. It's dangerous."

"Sorry. I was in the zone," she gasped.

"Zoned out, more like. You've had enough for today."

She tried to sit up, but it was too soon. She hadn't realised how hard she had been pushing it. "I think you're right. I'm going to lie here for a few minutes."

He held his hand out to her and helped her to her feet. "Hydrate and walk it off. I'll see you tomorrow." He walked away, shaking his head.

After wiping her sweat off the apparatus, she got herself a protein bar from the vending machine and refilled her bottle at the water fountain. After that she felt much better, if not a bit embarrassed for getting so carried away.

When she left the gym and walked into the car park, Alice's gaze was drawn to a familiar car – an electric-blue Jaguar. Bob looked great leaning up against it, as if he was in a photo shoot for a car catalogue. She, on the other hand, was a sweaty mess, but there wasn't much she could do about it except own it. She slinked up to the car.

Bob bit his lip when he saw her. "I was thinking of joining this gym, and that clinches it."

She narrowed her eyes at him. "What are you doing here?"

"I went to your flat. Your friend told me you were here. On a Sunday night? You must be dedicated."

"The best way to break old habits is to form new ones. This is my new addiction. But why were you at my flat?"

"I've been thinking about you all day." He shrugged. "I just wanted to talk to you."

She tried to subdue her grin. She had been thinking about him all day too. "About what?"

"Dinner."

"I thought I said no last night."

"You did. But I can't get you out of my head."

That makes two of us. She blushed.

"And I'll leave you alone, but only if you can honestly say that you haven't thought about me at least once today."

She looked away.

"I knew it."

"OK. I've thought about you, more than once. But I don't know if I'm ready to date. And I don't mean to be rude, but I don't have time for this right now. I'm starting a new job tomorrow and I need to get home to get organised."

"A new job? That's great. How about I take you out to dinner tomorrow night and you can tell me all about your first day? I don't even know what you do."

"I'm an actuary."

He squinted at her. "What does an actuary do?"

"Recently? Washes dirty pots and pans in a hotel kitchen. But when I'm doing what I'm trained for, I use

40

maths and statistics to analyse the financial consequences of risk."

"Pardon me?"

"I work with statistics, analysing and forecasting."

"Sounds complicated."

She shrugged. "Not really. It's fascinating. I had a promising career with one of the biggest firms in London, but my drinking ruined it. When I got out of rehab I couldn't face it again, so I took a job in a hotel kitchen. I finished my last shift on Friday, and tomorrow is my first professional job. It's a three-week temporary placement doing books in a tiny company that I'm hideously overqualified for, but..."

"It's a start. I wish you all the best with it. So, what about dinner?"

She was torn. She did want to – so much so that she had even considered asking him out. But he was asking her again, and this could be the last time he asked her. Maybe she should just say yes, take things slowly. "All right. But can we just have dinner, not a date, and see how it goes?"

He smiled. "Like you reminded me last night, I'm still married. I don't want to rush into anything either. Not a date, just dinner. Sounds fine to me. Do you like Chinese food?"

She nodded.

"Do you know the Purple Dragon?"

She nodded again.

"If it was a real date, I'd pick you up at your flat. But it's not, so I'll meet you there. Half seven OK?"

"Yes."

"Great." He offered her his arm. "Then I'll walk you to your car."

"Oh, it's OK. I ran here."

"You ran here? To the gym?"

"Yes. It's my warm-up. Then I lift weights or do a yoga or spin class, and I use the walk home as my cool-down."

"It must be at least two miles."

"Actually, it's nearly three."

"Well, this one time, may I offer you a lift home?"

"What about my cool-down?"

"You can do some stretches now, if you want. I'd love to watch."

She whacked him on the arm.

"Oh, come on. Just because we're not going on a date doesn't mean I can't fancy you." He opened the car door for her. "Get in."

Unlike the uneasy silence the night before, they shared friendly chit-chat on the short journey home. Alice kept looking at Bob out of the corner of her eye. She fancied him too and was looking forward to getting to know him a bit better. When the car pulled up outside the house, Bob jumped out, ran around to the passenger side and opened the door. He helped her out of the car.

"Thank you," she said with a smile.

"My pleasure." Gently he kissed the back of her hand before he let it go. "I'll see you tomorrow night." He got back into the car, but waited until she had ascended the steps and put her key in the front door before driving off.

Tamzin was waiting in the hall. She clapped her hands with delight. "You could have cut that sexual tension with a knife."

"Do you spend all day spying on me? Why the hell did you tell him I was at the gym?"

"Cupid doesn't answer to mere mortals. Now, tell me you're seeing him again or I'll kick your butt all the way back to that gym."

"We are having dinner tomorrow night ... but it's not a date."

"Not a date, my ass!" Tamzin scoffed.

Alice tugged on her sweat-stained top. "I'm surprised he even asked me. I look terrible."

"You look great. You don't smell great, though."

"I'd better take a shower. Is Cameron gone?"

Tamzin pouted and nodded.

"Grey's Anatomy?"

Tamzin's eyes lit up. "Popcorn or ice cream?"

"Both." Alice winked. She headed off to the bathroom, a spring in her step.

Chapter Four

The next day, Alice was at her new job, working on her second batch of invoices. But she was barely concentrating on work; she was wondering what to wear for her non-date with Bob that evening. He'd already seen her in plain clothes, no clothes, and sweaty clothes. Each time he had been impeccably dressed, so she thought she'd better make an effort. Her wardrobe was full of nice stuff, but nothing fitted any more. She used to be at least a dress size heavier but had lost weight when she'd been drinking and, thanks to her new exercise regime, had never regained it. Working at the hotel for minimum wage over the last few months meant she could only afford to buy a few necessities – nothing she considered suitable to wear out for dinner, date or not. She had a nice maxi dress hanging in the wardrobe – it might be loose, but the style permitted it. She was deciding on shoes when she heard her phone buzz. She smiled when she saw it was a text from Bob, but her smile soon faded when she read it.

I'm so sorry. I have to postpone tonight. Can we reschedule for tomorrow? Same time & place? x

She couldn't believe her eyes. *Talk about blowing hot and cold! He's spent all weekend hounding me for a date and now he's blowing me off with no explanation?* She threw the phone onto the pile of invoices.

After sulking for a few minutes, she thought about it more rationally. *I've cancelled things before, even things I was looking forward to, because sometimes life happens. Plus, I did stress that it wasn't a real date, so maybe he thought it was all right to postpone it.* Deep down, she wondered if she was only annoyed because she had actually been looking forward to it. Perhaps she was being too hard on him, but she wasn't going to be messed around. *I'll let this one go, but if it happens again, that's the end of it.* She picked up her phone and typed out a text.

If it was a proper date, I'd be fuming. But since it's just dinner, it can wait until tomorrow. See you then.

He'd obviously been waiting for her reply, as the ellipses started bouncing immediately. It didn't take long for his text to come back.

Thank God it's not a proper date. See you tomorrow x

She smiled at the kiss in his reply, but frowned at the absence of a second apology. He obviously wasn't one to grovel for forgiveness.

Alice spent most of the next day watching her phone, waiting for another text from Bob. She was half expecting him to cancel again. But when he didn't, she hurried home after work and started fretting about her hair and make-up. She wanted to look stunning, but not in an obvious way. Tamzin approved her make-up and offered to do her hair in a French plait. But Alice preferred to keep her hair down or draped over her left shoulder – to conceal a scar behind her ear.

Alice timed it perfectly, and arrived at the restaurant at

exactly seven thirty. Her hand was shaking as she reached out for the door. *Why am I so nervous? It's just dinner.* She took a deep breath, then heard a voice behind her.

"Hold the door, please, miss."

She turned to see Bob arrive beside her. He wore a dark-grey suit and a crisp white shirt. He'd already removed the tie and undone his top button. He looked great, and she was over the moon to see him, but she narrowed her eyes. "I wasn't entirely sure you'd show up."

"Boy, am I glad I did. That's some dress. Are you sure this isn't a date?"

"I'm sure."

"Shame... Suppose we'd better get on with it then." He held the door open and slid his arm around her waist to guide her into the restaurant. Even though it was the gentlest of touches, it excited her. The waiter directed them to their table. Bob kept his arm around her until they made it to the table, then pulled out a chair and invited her to sit. She tried to calm her breathing and watched him take his seat. If he had the same nerves, he was good at hiding them. He looked completely at ease as he settled into his chair.

"What can I get you to drink?" the waiter asked.

"Soda water and lime please," Alice said.

"That sounds good. I'll have the same."

The same? Alice sighed. *This is awkward already, and we've only just sat down.* She waited for the waiter to leave. "What are you doing?"

"Ordering a drink."

"You can have a proper drink if you want one. I'm not going to grab it from across the table."

"I don't want to have a drink right now. I'm not saying I'm never going to drink again, but I don't want to drink when I'm out with you. It wouldn't be fair."

"Oh my God. I just had a flashback to my first family meal in a restaurant after I got out of rehab. It was me, my parents, my brother and sister and their other halves. The waiter asked if we wanted to see the wine list, and my mum said, 'My daughter is an alcoholic. Just bring us all some water.' It was loud enough for the whole restaurant to hear."

Bob grimaced.

"Oh, it gets worse. I said it was all right if anyone wanted to have a drink. My brother – he's a total asshole, by the way – chimed in. 'See, Mum, I told you she's fine with it. I'm ordering some wine. Who's in?' My mum started to huff, and it was all picture and no sound until the waiter had the balls to come back to the table. My dad was the first to speak. He winked at me and ordered a half pint of Guinness, which he nursed all night. My brother ordered a bottle of wine for himself and his wife. My sister and her wife, who were both on call for work, ordered Coke. Mum got the water she wanted."

"What did you order?"

"Nothing. I was trying to make a point. But I ended up cutting off my nose to spite my face. It was an Indian restaurant; I ordered a madras. It was a tough meal to get through."

Bob laughed.

"Stop! It's not funny. It was the most embarrassing moment of my life – and I've done some pretty dodgy things. But my mum is always finding new and exciting ways of making my life hell. She hates me."

"I'm sure she doesn't hate you."

"She does. She wanted a boy. She's been disappointed in me from day one."

"I'm sure she wasn't disappointed. Some people have a hang-up about wanting their firstborn to be a boy. I know my dad was relieved to get his boy first; my sister came four years after me."

"But I wasn't the first," Alice said. "I'm the youngest of *three*. My brother was first. Then my sister. I'm the second girl and their biggest disappointment."

"I'm sure that's not true."

She counted out on her fingers. "Alcoholic. Divorced. Childless. Career in tatters. As if having a professional career and 2.4 kids is the only measure of success. My life seems to have gone wrong at every turn, and it all started the day I was born. The day she gave me the name Alice."

Bob cocked his head. "I'm pretty sure that Roy Chubby Brown song came out *after* you were born."

"It's nothing to do with the song. My mum loves classic literature and named each of us after a character in a book. My brother is David, after David Copperfield. My sister is Elizabeth, after Elizabeth Bennet from *Pride and Prejudice*. And I got named Alice, after some schizophrenic. I was doomed from the get-go."

"I don't follow…"

"Alice. In Wonderland. She's a schizophrenic."

"What? I thought that was a children's book."

"Yes, it is. But when I read it, it was obvious to me that nearly all the characters had some sort of mental health issue. The Mad Hatter had PTSD; the rabbit had generalised anxiety disorder. Alice may not be schizophrenic, but she's got some sort of psychosis.

There's even a real-life neurological condition named after her. I've really lived up to my namesake. I suffered from anxiety as a teenager. I've battled with depression – it contributed to my alcoholism. And my therapist agreed with me about the Alice thing. Although she said it was more of a self-fulfilling prophecy than my mother trying to hurt me. But she did. Nothing I ever did was good enough. My brother, on the other hand, could do no wrong. He got away with murder as a child. He never had to lift a finger around the house – Mum made me and Elizabeth pick up after him. He was lazy at school too, did the bare minimum, but the jammy git somehow always managed to scrape through his exams. He's married now with three kids, and his wife does everything for him. He's been spoiled rotten his entire life. No wonder he's a total deadbeat."

"What does he do for a living?"

"He's a solicitor."

"A deadbeat solicitor. How is that even possible?"

"He had to repeat most of his exams. When he finally qualified he couldn't get a job with a reputable firm, so he works for one of those awful 'no win, no fee' companies. He's a glorified ambulance-chaser. But my mum thinks he's Amal Clooney, saving the world one bogus whiplash claim at a time. But I used to work for Deloitte, one of the biggest companies in the world. I worked on a project for Microsoft, for God's sake. And she tells people I'm a bookkeeper."

Bob tried to suppress a laugh. "Wow, your parents had smart kids. Are they professors or something?"

"My dad's an ex-professional boxer. He coaches teenagers now. And my mum's a school dinner lady."

"What does your sister do?"

Alice smiled fondly. "We're all really proud of her. She's a paediatric orthopaedic surgeon. And her wife is an anaesthesiologist. Their eyes met over the operating table, and it was love at first sight. It's the cutest story. But keep that to yourself if you ever meet my granny. She wasn't invited to the wedding because she's incredibly homophobic. She thinks Elizabeth and Katie are 'good friends' who just never met the right guy."

Bob laughed. It was a nice laugh, and Alice enjoyed hearing it. Although she winced when she realised it was her life they were laughing at; she hadn't shut up since they'd arrived. She'd been talking about herself, and quite candidly. That was a first for her. Usually she didn't give too much away, but she found Bob so easy to talk to. Easy to be with. Maybe it was his acceptance of her, warts and all, so to speak, but she saw something in him that she really liked.

"I'm so sorry. I thought I was in therapy there, you're so easy to talk to. You must think I'm a horrible person."

"No. I think you're a little crazy, but I found that out when you threw your shoe at me."

"I'll throw my other shoe at you if you ever call me crazy again."

"I'd prefer it if you threw yourself at me..."

She couldn't remember too much about that night at her flat, other than that she'd been drunk and forceful. But the intense look in his hazel eyes sent a shiver down her spine as she imagined how good it might feel to do that again. She fiddled with her hair. "So, Bob. Tell me more about yourself. Do you have kids?"

"No." He shifted in his seat. "I..."

Alice winced. *Why on earth did I ask that? I hate being asked that. If he had kids, surely he would have volunteered that information at some point?* She tried to think of a way to change the subject, but then the waiter arrived and did it for her. He set their drinks on the table.

"Are you ready to order?"

"Sorry, we haven't looked yet. May we have a few more minutes?" Alice pointed to the menu in Bob's hand. "Looks like they have a huge selection here. Best get looking."

They discussed the menu and settled on two main courses to share, and after they had ordered Alice tried another one of her 'getting to know you' questions. "You said you had a sister. Are you close?"

"When we were younger, yes, but we grew apart. Her name was Rebecca. She ... passed away a few months ago."

"I'm *so* sorry. There I was, complaining about how much I hate my brother, when the truth is, I couldn't bear it if something happened to him. Was she sick?"

"No. She had a car accident. It was a real shock. And what came after was so..." He shifted uncomfortably again.

Alice wanted the ground to swallow her up. Usually she was the one who felt uncomfortable talking about her life. She reached over the table and put her hand on top of his. "I'm sorry. You don't have to talk about it. What's a safe topic – work? I don't even know what you do."

"I run my own company. A cleaning business. Not very fancy, I'm afraid."

"Everyone's got to make a living. And judging by the car you drive, you must be doing well. I'll bet I've heard of it. What's it called?"

"Christine Cleans."

Alice swallowed. She'd heard of it, all right. Their vans were a familiar sight around the city, and they had one of those chatty advertisements on local radio: the husband-and-wife cleaning team, a local business makes good.

"Don't worry. The business turns twenty next year, and I'm planning a total rebrand."

Alice was impressed. To have run a business for nineteen years was a huge achievement. For her to have done that, she would have had to start it at the age of thirteen. She had known that Bob was older than her, but how old was he?

"Do you mind if I ask how old you are?"

"I recently turned forty."

"Forty? I'm only thirty-two. Is eight years a big age difference? You know, just in case we ever go on a proper date."

"I don't think so. We're both adults. We've both been married."

"*You* still are."

"That's just a matter of paperwork. Contract gone bad. Soon to be dissolved."

Alice sat back in her seat and observed him. He had said that very coldly, which suggested that the split wasn't amicable. He had also said he didn't cheat, so had Christine cheated on him?

As if he could tell what she was thinking, he said, "We just got to a point, and we couldn't go any further. Rebecca's death changed everything. Christine — well, let's just say she didn't like who I became." He rubbed his eyes and gave her a little smile. "I like who I became. That's what matters, right?"

"Right." Alice nodded. Even though she didn't know exactly what he meant by that. But she did know that during her deepest depression, she had hated herself. She had been convinced that she wasn't good enough to deserve a normal life. She knew now that it wasn't true, but she'd had to hit rock bottom and have a hell of a lot of therapy before she accepted it. She looked over at Bob. They both had a lot going on. Perhaps instead of dinner, what they both needed was to sit and have a good cry. But no good ever came from wallowing in self-pity, so she leant forward and smiled. "This is getting depressing. Let's stop talking about our exes. There's no need at this point. What about hobbies? You already know I love going to the gym. What do you like to do when you're not working?"

"Nothing out of the ordinary. Christine and I used to go out for dinner, parties, the theatre, weekends away. Now I mostly just stay at home. I've become boring in my old age."

"Well, you weren't boring on Friday night. You had plans – weren't you intending to have fun?"

"I was. That was my first night out in months. A friend and I were meant to have dinner, a few drinks, then hit the casino. But one of his kids had a bad fall. He had to stay at home with the other one while his wife took their son to hospital."

"Oh my goodness, was he OK?"

Bob smiled. "Yeah, he was OK."

"Well, it sounded like an awesome plan for a night out. Was it a special occasion?"

"It was my birthday."

She beamed. "Aw, happy birthday. Wait! Your birthday? You said you just turned forty. Are you saying that the night we met was your fortieth birthday?"

"Yup. And it was set to be the most depressing birthday ever. No wife to make a fuss of me. My parents had invited me for dinner, which would have been even more depressing, but luckily a friend took pity on me and arranged a guy's night out. Then he bailed. I was feeling lonely, a little down. Then a beautiful woman sat next to me, and it turned out she was feeling pretty awful too. Maybe I was being selfish, but you know the saying 'misery loves company'. We didn't have a bad night, all things considered."

"It wasn't bad at all. If you don't count my slip back into the abyss."

"But you're doing OK at the minute, aren't you?"

She nodded. "Four days and counting."

"That's a great start."

After dinner, Bob offered Alice a lift home. When they reached his car, she ran her hand over the bonnet. "I'd love to get behind the wheel. My dad would too. He loves cars. For his sixtieth a few years ago, me and my siblings took him to one of those track days. It gave me a real thirst."

He offered her the key. "Do you want to try her out?"

"Um, I can't. I've lost my licence."

"That's OK. You don't need to have it on you. And you can get a form at the post office to get it replaced."

"No. I mean, I've *lost* my licence. As in it's been taken away for driving under the influence."

He recoiled. "You didn't hurt anyone ... did you?"

Her mind raced back to his sister. Alice really hoped she hadn't been killed by a drunk driver. "No. Thank

God. I didn't even crash. It was a morning after the night before thing. A routine police stop, can you believe it? The officer smelt alcohol on me. I told him I'd been drinking the night before, but that I thought I was OK to drive. He put me in the back seat of his car and breathalysed me. That was the first test I'd ever failed. I got arrested and taken to the police station where they breathalysed me again, on the official machine. I blew 61. The legal limit is 35. I was nearly double the limit at nine o'clock in the morning. They kept me in a cell for a while then charged me. I had to go to court a few weeks later to receive my sentence. My solicitor, the deadbeat, really wound me up about it. He said they would probably make an example out of me, but all I got was an eighteen-month driving ban and a £450 fine. I thought I got off pretty lightly. Although the real punishment was the begging I had to do so my brother wouldn't tell my parents about the conviction. He kept my secret, but only for a while. He didn't realise at that time that my drinking was so out of control. If he had, he would definitely have told them, and maybe things would have been different." She took a deep breath. "I really should stop talking. If you weren't already having second thoughts about me, then you should be by now. Aren't you glad this isn't a real date?"

He shook his head. "No. It's in the past. You can't change it and it's made you who you are. You paid for your mistake and you're still paying. And now that you're sober, you won't be driving under the influence again when you get your licence back."

"That's for sure. I'm never driving a car again."

"Oh, don't be so dramatic."

"I'm not being dramatic; I'm being an actuary. My

insurance premiums will go through the roof. There's no way I would be able to afford it."

He clicked the car open. "Looks like I'm driving."

Back at her flat, Bob jumped out of the car and hurried around to the passenger side, then opened the door and offered his hand. She blushed as he helped her out. Dylan had never opened a car door for her; he had barely held her hand either. He was never one to show affection in public; he thought his mates would think he was a sap.

Bob caressed her hand. "You know, if this was a proper date, this is the part where I would kiss you goodnight."

"Then it's a shame it's not a date." She cosied up to him and ran her hand down his arm as she stared into his hazel eyes. "You know, Tam is probably watching at the window. If I go in there without kissing you, I'm never going to hear the end of it." She gazed at his mouth and ran her tongue over her bottom lip. "You'd be doing me a huge favour..."

Without hesitation, he slipped an arm around her waist then cupped his other hand around the back of her neck and pulled her close. He leant towards her but stopped short, leaving her to close the distance. She took a breath then pressed her lips against his, feeling an unexpected rush of emotion as he kissed her back. All the feelings of loneliness and sadness that she'd had for so long were suddenly silenced by feelings of happiness. She felt safe and comfortable in his arms. Their tongues curled around each other's, and when his hand moved from her waist to her backside and he caressed her gently, she moaned with pleasure. It had been so long since she'd felt desired that she had to fight the urge to give herself to him, right there in the street.

She broke the embrace but, as she pulled away, he pulled her back against him for another firm and urgent kiss. Then he whispered against her mouth, "Goodnight, Alice." He left her standing there, breathless, and got back into the car. "I'll call you tomorrow." He closed the door and started the engine.

Flushed and with her legs feeling a little weak, Alice made it to the top of the steps and put her key in the door. She turned to wave at Bob and waited until he had driven away before she went into the flat.

She smiled to herself. She'd known full well that Tamzin wasn't at home.

Chapter Five

Over the next few weeks, Alice and Bob saw a lot of each other. Sometimes it was lunch, the occasional dinner, but they mostly met for a quick coffee when they could squeeze it into Bob's busy schedule. Although she was determined not to, Alice did relax her rule and was happy to agree when Bob rearranged their dates or cancelled at the last minute, but only because his diary was full, with appointments for quotes for cleaning contracts and site inspections. And they were still meant to be keeping things casual. But 'casual' now included a kiss at the start and the end of their dates, as a way of saying hello and goodbye. And their 'goodbyes' were getting longer and much steamier.

Alice was on cloud nine. Her life was really starting to turn around and she felt normal for the first time in nearly two years. She'd made it back into an office and was interacting with people in a professional capacity again. She was enjoying going to the gym and making new friends there – the physical benefits were just a bonus. She looked and felt great. And now there was Bob. Even though the fear of getting hurt again was at the forefront of her mind, she was glad that she'd given him a chance and was excited about where their relationship might go.

To celebrate their two-month 'anniversary' Bob sent Alice another beautiful bouquet of flowers, and with it an invitation to dinner at the fusion restaurant where they'd had their first meal together. Alice treated herself to a new dress for the occasion, and made a special effort with her hair and make-up as she didn't want to be recognised after her drunken escapades the last time.

After they had ordered, Alice surprised Bob with a belated birthday gift. "I ordered it ages ago – it just took a long time to get here."

His eyes lit up as he accepted the book-shaped gift. "You didn't need to get me anything. That beautiful dress you're wearing is present enough." He tore off the paper to reveal a copy of *Alice in Wonderland*. "Um, thank you."

"It's an early edition. Pretty rare. I thought, when you're sitting around being old and boring, you could read a book."

"No one has ever bought me a book before. Not since I was a kid."

"Oh, don't you like to read? That's OK. I'll give it to my mum. She can add it to her collection." She held her hand out for the book, but he held it close to his chest.

"I read. Usually spy thrillers or Stephen King, but I can try a classic. It's just that no one has ever bought one for me before. Christine always bought me clothes or aftershave, or surprised me with fancy meals or weekends away. But usually the holidays were something she wanted, so they were more of a gift for her. And the clothes..." – he gestured to his expensive suit – "were usually what she wanted me to wear. I would never spend so much on clothes. The Jaguar was her idea too, but I liked that one."

Alice laughed.

"Thank you for the book. I look forward to reading about your childhood."

Playfully, she kicked him under the table.

"And I'm definitely not sitting at home as much any

more." He reached across the table and stroked the back of her hand. "I've enjoyed our meals and coffees together, but let's get a bit more adventurous. Do you like the theatre?"

"Yes. And I haven't been in ages. I'm dying to see *Hamilton*."

"Great." He took his mobile from his pocket. "I'll book it now. When do you want to go?"

"If there's any last-minute tickets available, I'm free this Friday night."

"No can do. I'm quoting for a job in Manchester on Friday afternoon, so I won't be home until late."

"Manchester? Are you thinking of branching out?"

"I already take on work all over the country. This is a big one. It's a couple of weeks' work, and there's always the prospect of repeat business and referrals if it goes well."

"Then I hope you get it. But would that mean I'd lose you to Manchester for a couple of weeks?"

"Would you miss me?"

She avoided his eye as she nodded.

"Good. Then no, you won't lose me to Manchester. I have a second in command, Kristof, and a couple of supervisors that I trust to do a good job. When we do a job like this, I send one or two staff up there with a van full of supplies, put them up in a guest house or cheap hotel. Then I hire local temps and equipment. Keeps costs down."

"Smart."

"I thought you'd like that. Hey, I just had a great idea. Do you want to come with me? I would really enjoy your company for the drive. And we could make the most of it – spend the night and drive back on Saturday.

An old friend of mine just opened a fancy restaurant up there. It's tipped to get a Michelin star. If he finds out I've been in Manchester without eating there, I'll be in trouble."

Alice was sorely tempted. She and Dylan used to go to fancy restaurants all the time, and they had enjoyed frequent city breaks much further afield than Manchester. But she couldn't afford to live that sort of lifestyle at the minute. "That sounds amazing. But I can't."

He frowned. "Why not?"

"I have to work on Friday."

"Phone in sick."

"I can't. I'm a temp. If I phone in sick, I don't get paid. Money is kind of tight for me at the moment."

"Please don't worry about money. Dinner will be my treat, and I can write a *nice* hotel off as a business expense. And I'm not being presumptuous – I'll get us separate rooms."

Separate rooms hadn't even crossed her mind. She'd love to spend the night with him. They had great chemistry, and she was falling for him. She knew that it was only a matter of time before they took their relationship to the next level. So what better way to do it than to make a real night of it?

"OK, I'd love to join you. I've been working for the agency for two months now, so I'm bound to have accrued a day's leave. But Bob…" She locked eyes with him. "Don't waste company money on separate rooms."

On Thursday evening, Alice rushed home after work to get ready for the trip. The restaurant they were going to was tipped for a Michelin star, so it was bound to be fancy, but did she have anything fancy enough to wear? She couldn't wear her new dress again so soon; it was hardly appropriate anyway. She remembered the red designer dress she had stashed away at the back of the wardrobe. Even though she'd spent a fortune on it, she had only worn it once to a gala event held by Dylan's company a few years ago. She'd had to go on a crash diet for two weeks beforehand just to get the zip up, but she'd lost weight since then, so it was worth a try.

Alice stepped into the dress. Much to her delight, the side zip slid up effortlessly. She posed in front of the mirror but, as she arranged her hair around her shoulders, she felt a pang of sadness. The last time she'd worn the dress she'd been happily married, with a successful career and plans to start a family. All of that was gone. Now she was just a mess in a pretty dress. She continued to stare at herself in the mirror until she realised: *I'm not as much of a mess as I used to be. I'm sixty-two days sober, working again, and dating. Bob mustn't see a mess either. In fact he makes me feel desirable.* She studied the dress again. It did look fabulous, and it fitted like a glove. *OK, I'll wear the dress, not to impress Bob – although I hope it knocks his socks off – but because it makes me look and feel great.*

Just then, Tamzin popped her head around the bedroom door. Her jaw dropped when she saw the dress.

"Too much?"

"No way. I'd do you. What shoes are you going to wear?"

Alice rummaged through the pile of shoes at the bottom of her wardrobe. She stood up, holding one hand behind her back, and brought the other up to show Tamzin a pair of red strappy sandals. "I wore these last time because the dress was so tight I needed comfy shoes to offset the misery. But..." She produced a pair of black stilettos from behind her back. "...these are way sexier."

"Go with the sexier."

"At least I'll be wearing *something* sexy." Alice groaned and opened her underwear drawer. "There's nothing nice in here." She held up a red bra and her sexiest pair of pants, which were black. "I need to wear this bra with that dress, but I've no matching knickers. And don't I need a negligee or something?"

"Why?"

"Isn't that what people wear as PJs when they go on sexy nights away?"

"Yeah, but just wear what you would have worn to seduce Dylan."

"That was never difficult. All I had to do was bend down or reach for something on a high shelf and he was all over me." She sighed. "We were together forever. And we were each other's firsts. We were so comfortable with each other, we didn't need to do all that sexy underwear stuff."

"Don't worry about sexy underwear, just get naked. If Bob really likes you, he's not going to care what you're wearing. Or not." She winked.

"I'm worried about that too."

"What?"

"About him liking me. I mean, really liking me."

"Wouldn't that be a good thing?"

"What if he wants to settle down and have kids?"

"He's forty. He was married for years. If he had wanted to have kids, he would have had them by—"

Alice threw her hands up in the air.

Tamzin cringed. "I'm sorry. That was insensitive."

"Yes, it was. But when do you tell someone you're dating that you're infertile? Should I casually drop it into conversation? *Hey Bob, isn't the weather awful? Oh, and by the way, I can't have kids.*"

"I don't know how you should tell him. But listen, just go and have sex. And then come back and tell me all about it."

Alice cracked a smile.

"Good girl. You're going to have a great night." Tamzin checked the time on her phone. "Shops are still open. Let's jump in my car and go get you something nice and sexy. You're only going for one night, so you can get away with one bra, two matching knickers and a nightie. Something not too expensive, so he can rip it off you. Now, talk to me about grooming. What have you done so far?"

"Um, I've done my nails, hands and feet. Plucked my eyebrows, waxed my top lip. I'll do my legs and bikini line in the shower in the morning. Do you mind if I borrow your new perfume? I know it was expensive but it's so lush."

"Of course you can." Tamzin clapped her hands. "Oh, I'm so excited for you. You need this, girl. You need to get laid."

Chapter Six

On Friday morning Bob picked Alice up at her flat and they set off on the long drive to Manchester. Bob filled Alice in on his friend Jack, whose restaurant they would be eating in that night. They'd known each other since secondary school, when they had spent their weekends playing football and chasing girls together. Bob warned Alice that Jack could be quite brash, and apologised in advance for any embarrassment he might cause.

An accident on the motorway just outside Birmingham had caused a huge traffic jam, so Bob only had time to check Alice into the hotel and rush back out again to get to his meeting on time. Unfortunately, the meeting and site inspection took longer than expected, so Bob only had time for a quick change out of his hard hat and hi-vis vest before they headed out for the evening.

"This is so cool," Alice exclaimed, watching dozens of chefs, waiters and porters fuss around the kitchen. They were seated in the middle of the chaos, at the chef's table.

"Isn't it? I can't believe this is all his. I have to hand it to him – he's paid his dues, honed his craft and worked his way up the ranks. He's been saving for years and has put everything he has into this business. I hope it takes off for him, I really do."

"Aw," Alice cooed. "I haven't seen this side of you yet."

"What side?"

"The sensitive side."

"I'm a pretty sensitive guy. And while we're on the

subject, I've not seen this sexy temptress side to you. Have I told you how amazing you look?"

"I think that's the fourth time."

"Just four?" He reached across the table and took her hand. "I'm so sorry we had no time together at the hotel. I hope you were OK without me. What did you do?"

"Just ... sat around."

"You went to the hotel gym, didn't you?"

"How did you know?"

"I know you better than you think. Oh, and you left your hoodie there. Reception phoned up when you were—"

They were interrupted by a loud voice. "This is meant to be a classy place. Who let this riff-raff in?"

The voice belonged to Jack, the executive chef. Bob jumped up and they shook hands, then gave each other a manly hug and slapped each other on the shoulder.

"Well, what do you think?"

"Looks great, Jack. Congratulations." He gestured to Alice. "This is Alice."

"*Enchanté.*" Jack took her hand and kissed it softly.

She pretended to swoon. "It's nice to meet you too. I love this place. The dining area is understated elegance, but this kitchen... I love the island-style layout. You've got a great flow, and so much floor space."

Bob scratched his head.

Jack grinned. "You know your kitchens, Alice."

"I'm an ex-kitchen porter."

"Great! If old Robert can't pay the bill, you can work off his debt." He winked. "Then afterwards, you can wash some dishes."

Bob covertly stuck his middle finger up at him.

"So, let me tell you what I have planned for you two

lovebirds. A tasting menu the likes of which you will never have experienced before. I had to make adjustments for your medication, Robert, so everything is alcohol-free. The bar staff have been working hard on the accompanying beverages. We've enjoyed the challenge!" He looked around and summoned one of the waiters to the table. "This is Jay. He is at your service while I'm in service. So sit back, enjoy the food but, more importantly, enjoy the show." He curtseyed and backed away, bowing.

"Wow. He's a real showman."

"He always has been. But he doesn't just talk the talk; he can back it up."

"Good to know. Oh, by the way, what medication are you taking?"

He groaned. "I'm sorry. I knew there would be copious amounts of alcohol forced in our direction, and I didn't want to make you feel uncomfortable. I told Jack that I have a bacterial infection and can't drink because of the antibiotics I'm on, and that you're abstaining to support me because you're so wonderful. But I need to make it clear that I'm not embarrassed by you. I just... It wasn't my business to tell people your business."

"He's not a stranger. He's your friend. I don't mind if he knows. I don't need you to lie for me. But thanks for trying."

"Does it get hard for you? Being in places like this when there's people drinking around you?"

Alice sighed and looked around. She pointed to a couple in the corner, sharing a bottle of champagne. "That's hard for me. Knowing if I had a special occasion, I wouldn't be able to celebrate like that. But mostly I try not to think about it. I try to remember all the positives about being sober. How about you? We've had a few meals together – do you miss not having a beer or a glass of wine to go with your food?"

"Actually, I don't. I enjoy your company too much."

"Me too." She blushed. "OK, I'm going to go and freshen up. I wonder where the loos are."

Bob pointed to Jay. "Ask him. He's at your service."

"Oh, I like the sound of that." She winked at Bob then headed over to talk to Jay.

Jack had seen her leave, and made his way back to the table. He sat down in Alice's chair. "Nice catch, man. Age?"

"Thirty-two."

"Nice! How long have you been tapping that?"

"It's not like that. We met a couple of months ago and we're taking it slow. But I've got a really good feeling about her. She's amazing and unbelievably smart. And isn't she gorgeous?"

"That she is. Which begs the question, what the fuck is she doing with you?"

"I don't know. But I'm not complaining."

"But seriously..." Jack frowned. "What's wrong with you, mate? You said you had an infection, but I don't believe you. I've seen you suck back a six-pack when you were on amoxicillin for your adenoids. It's not cancer, is it? That's why you got such a hot girlfriend. It's pity sex before you die."

"No, Jack. I don't have cancer. Truthfully, it's not me who can't drink. It's Alice. She's a recovering alcoholic. I don't drink when I'm with her."

"She's an alcoholic? That explains it."

"Explains what?"

"What she's doing with you. I knew she was too good to be true. She seems nice, but come on, man – you don't have to settle for the first girl you meet. Especially one who's an alcoholic. You're single for the first time in years. Play the field, sow your oats. My Leah says you're not bad-looking. It shouldn't be too hard to find yourself a normal girl."

"Alice is a normal girl."

"I meant one you can have fun with. God knows you deserve it."

"I have fun with Alice."

"Fun like you used to! Go out, get drunk, do the odd line of coke. All the shit you used to do with Christine. Now, there's a woman who liked a good party. She still does, by all accounts. Leah said—"

"I don't want to hear about Christine! My priorities have changed. I'm not interested in doing that sort of stuff any more. I don't need someone to party with; I need someone I can talk to. Someone who doesn't expect anything from me." He checked over Jack's shoulder to make sure Alice wasn't on her way back. "Oh, and by the way, Alice doesn't know about Sam yet. So don't mention him."

"How long do you intend to hide him away for?"

"I'm not hiding him away. I just wanted time to see how I felt about Alice before I introduced him into the mix. I'll tell her. Just not yet. I'm working up to it."

"Where is the little man anyway?"

"At my parents' until Sunday."

"So you got a weekend pass. You'd better make tonight count."

"That's the plan." Bob's eyes lit up when he saw Alice making her way back to the table.

Jack noticed and shook his head. "I definitely see the attraction, but an alcoholic? Just when I thought your life couldn't get any more fucked up."

Jay also arrived at the table, carrying the first course.

"Just in time, Alice." Jack got up from her chair and tucked her into it. "Please sit and prepare your palate for the time of its life." He bowed and left the table.

"Chef definitely saved the best course for last. That was delicious."

Jay cleared away their empty plates. "Chef will be pleased to hear that. I'll be right back with the first of your desserts."

Alice picked up the menu. "First of ... three. Ugh, I don't mean to sound ungrateful because it's all delicious, but I can't eat three desserts, even if they are tiny."

"Me neither. It's all so rich. Don't worry, I'll get us out of it. I had my own ideas about dessert..."

The way he spoke suggested that he was about to sweep his arm across the table, send everything crashing to the ground, and take her in the middle of the restaurant. She fanned her face with the menu.

Jay arrived back at the table. "May I present to you a coffee-and-walnut soufflé with clotted-cream ice cream."

"Sounds amazing, Jay. Thank you." Alice waited until he had left the table before groaning, but she grabbed her spoon when she saw Jack coming over.

"I'm so sorry. I feel like I've abandoned you tonight, but it's been manic in here. Just how I like it. So, how are you enjoying your meal?"

"It's been outstanding," Bob said.

"I've never had food like this before. Everything was delicious. And the truffles in the pasta dish were expertly sliced."

Jack threw his arms around Alice and kissed her on the cheek. Then he turned to Bob. "She's a keeper!"

"Thanks, Jack. It's all been amazing, but could we get the next two courses to go?"

Jack glared at him. "No! You may not. I didn't spend all day slaving over this intricate menu for you two to skip off early. You'll sit and eat the food I have so painstakingly prepared for you."

Bob loosened his tie. "You're right. Sorry. It's just been a long day, with the drive up here and then I had to work. It's kinda late."

Jack narrowed his eyes and looked at Alice, then back to Bob. "Fine. You may leave. But call in here tomorrow for a coffee before you head back down so I can catch up with you properly. And tip your waiter." He hurried over to Jay. "Redirect the last of their desserts to that old couple celebrating their anniversary. Compliments of the chef."

Alice's heart skipped a beat when she heard Bob close the hotel room door behind them. She made her way over to the coffee table to set down her clutch bag. As she shrugged off her wrap, a shiver ran down her spine. It was a mixture of nerves and excitement. She really liked Bob, and the kisses and cuddles they'd shared had been intimate and tender. Their chemistry was undeniable. But it had been nearly a year since she'd last had sex, so she was feeling nervous. She took a deep breath and turned to face him. He was standing by the bed, admiring her. Without a word he approached and drew her against him. He gazed into her eyes. Just as he was about to kiss her, she pulled away.

Bob sat down on the side of the bed and gestured for her to join him. She avoided his eye as she perched beside him.

"You seem nervous, but there's no need. We don't have to do anything you're not comfortable with. You didn't want separate rooms, so we're sharing a bed. But I promise I won't touch you if you don't want me to."

But she wanted him to touch her: the thought of it had already given her sleepless nights. She locked eyes with him. "It's just that Dylan was my first. We were together for a long time. I—"

"Oh! So I'll be your number two?"

She let out a nervous laugh and clipped him on the shoulder. "Get over yourself. Stick a zero on the end of that and you might be a bit closer."

His jaw dropped.

"Let's just say, when I was drinking I was a little promiscuous, for want of a better word." She gazed at the floor. "I used to go out, get drunk and find a good-looking guy – or any guy – to take home for meaningless sex."

"Like the night we met?"

"Exactly. But none of the other men seemed to mind the fact that I was blind drunk. I'm not saying that any of them made me do anything I didn't want to. I always felt in control. But really, it was the alcohol that was in control. I was barely there. Tonight, with you, will be the first sober sex I've had that's not with the man I married. I'm feeling a little self-conscious."

He slipped his arm around her waist and drew her closer. "You have nothing to feel self-conscious about.

I'm very attracted to you. I haven't been with anyone since Christine. She wasn't my first, but we were together for a long time. I'm not nervous – the opposite, actually. I've spent all night looking at you, thinking that I must be someone special for such a beautiful woman to want to be with me. But now my ego is bruised because you've told me that you weren't exactly selective when you were picking up guys. Now I'm wondering which of your categories I fell into that night: good-looking, or just any guy."

She placed her hand on his knee and squeezed. "I did fancy you. And you must know by now that I don't think you're just any guy. I really like you." She nudged him. "Sorry if that sounded corny."

"Not corny." He nudged her back. "I like you too. And let's get any other potential awkwardness out of the way so we can enjoy ourselves…" He got up and went over to his overnight bag. He opened the side zip and took something out and brought it back. He set a packet of condoms on the bed beside her. "These can be optional, as long as you're … otherwise covered."

She smirked, then picked up the box and handed it to him. "These are compulsory."

"It's been years since I used one of those things. But you're the boss."

"And don't you forget it." She kissed him hard on the lips, then jumped up from the bed. "I'll be right back." She grabbed her bag and hurried to the bathroom.

There she slipped out of her dress and into the plum satin chemise she had bought the night before. She posed in the full-length mirror on the back of the door. *Not bad,* she thought. The heels certainly enhanced her posture and made her bum look firmer, but she had to adjust the chemise's plunging neckline to make her boobs look fuller. Next, she examined her face. Her make-up was OK, but she reapplied her cherry-red lipstick and fluffed up her hair, then made sure it was draped down over her left shoulder. A mist of perfume and she was ready. She placed her hand on the doorknob, then hesitated. She took a deep breath. *No need to be nervous,* she told herself. *It's just sex.*

While she'd been in the bathroom, Bob had dimmed the lights and closed the curtains. His suit jacket and tie were draped over the chair at the dressing table, and his shoes tucked neatly underneath. He was sitting in an armchair at the coffee table. When he saw her, he gasped. "When I saw you in that dress earlier, even though I thought it was the most amazing thing I'd ever seen, I was looking forward to peeling it off you. But that little number is... Holy fuck, you look great. Come here." He beckoned to her.

She sashayed over and stopped in front of him, keeping her legs slightly open, knowing that the short hemline and salacious thigh slit of the chemise would barely cover her modesty. He took a moment to admire her before pulling her onto his knee. Then she noticed the two glasses of what she assumed was sparkling water on the coffee table beside the chair. "Planning to work up a thirst?" she asked.

"I thought you might like some fizz to celebrate a special occasion."

She snaked her hand around the back of his neck and pulled him towards her. She kissed him while running her fingers through his hair, raking his scalp each time his tongue claimed her mouth. She felt his hands on the small of her back, then he moved them down, slowly.

When he got to her backside, he scooped her up and carried her to the bed. He laid her down and planted his hand on the pillow beside her, then climbed on top of her, coaxing her legs apart and wriggling in between them.

"Tell me what you like," he said between kisses.

"What?"

One hand had already made it under the hem of the chemise. He was caressing her inner thigh and teasing her with his thumb. "What do you want me to do to you..."

"No one's ever..." She gasped as she felt the pressure of his finger inside her. "Asked me what I like before."

He pulled away and tutted. "All those guys, but no gentlemen." He lowered himself off the bed and sank to his knees, then tugged her to the edge of the bed. "How about I do what I like, and if you're not enjoying it, just tell me to stop." Kneeling before her, he traced his tongue up the inside of her thigh, licking and kissing her gently. When he buried his head between her legs, she gripped the sheets and arched her hips against his mouth, giving in to him completely. She moaned and writhed around on the bed as he worked her into a frenzy. When he brought her to climax, curses escaped her lips and she lay, panting, desperately trying to catch her breath. When she had composed herself, she looked over at him. He was undressing. Her eyes widened when she saw him reach for the box on the bedside table. She bit down hard on her bottom lip, suspecting she was about to get the sleepless night she'd been longing for.

Chapter Seven

Alice stirred. The bed was warm and cosy. She rolled over to cuddle Bob, but found his side of the bed cold. She lifted her head and gazed around the room. He was sitting at the coffee table by the window, working at his laptop. She couldn't see his bottom half, but his top half was bare. Is he sitting there naked? she wondered.

She snuggled under the sheet and thought about the night before. It had been incredible; she'd never experienced anything like it. It had been intense, relentless and unbelievably satisfying. She combed her fingers through her hair and adjusted the sheets to flatter her chest. "Good morning," she cooed.

Bob looked up from his laptop, and a huge grin spread over his face. "Good morning, beautiful. I hope I didn't wake you. Did you sleep OK?"

"I slept great. You?"

"I tossed and turned. I don't really like staying in hotels."

"Then why did you suggest we spend the night?"

"I thought you might enjoy it."

"I did." She blushed. "Thank you."

Although she was quite content, she couldn't help wondering why he hadn't come back to bed. *Isn't he feeling as good as me? Doesn't he want to have sex again?* She certainly did. Her body was aching for his touch, but he was just sitting there, typing on his computer! Was something wrong? Hadn't he enjoyed it too? She didn't want to sound needy or desperate, so she tried to play it cool.

"I like your outfit," she teased.

"Thanks." He puffed out his bare chest. "I thought I'd look pretty silly sitting here in your nightie." He focused back on his screen.

She rolled her eyes. "Um, what are you doing?"

"Making a start on that quote from yesterday. The guy wants it on Monday. I thought if I started early, I could spend all afternoon with my girlfriend."

The word 'girlfriend' caught her off guard. She hadn't been someone's girlfriend in a long time, and never thought she would be again. Hearing it made her feel good, and it was a nice way for him to declare where he thought the relationship was.

"So, I'm your girlfriend now?" She giggled.

"I thought last night sealed the deal."

It certainly had. Maybe it was because it had been her first sober sex in a long time, but the whole experience seemed heightened and more pleasurable. As she looked at him working at his laptop, naked, without a care in the world, she felt a quiver inside. The sex had been so good because it was with Bob. She was aroused, and she wanted him back in bed ASAP.

"Hmm, I'm not sure. I might need more persuading..." She let the sheet slip to reveal her breasts.

He admired her for a few seconds, then pointed to the screen. "Can I ask you to hold that thought for two minutes?"

"Take your time." She turned and cuddled into the pillows, knowing that the sheet had fallen to reveal her bare back, and what she hoped was a flattering view of her backside.

That second, she heard the laptop close, then footsteps. Butterflies started in her tummy. He climbed into bed and cuddled up behind her. His naked skin felt cool against hers, and when he draped his cold arm around her waist, pulling her closer, excitement ran in waves through her. He caressed her stomach, then ran his hand down and in between her thighs, teasing her. He pulled her hair to the side and nuzzled her neck.

She moaned at the feel of his warm breath and soft kisses, until he stopped suddenly.

"What's this?" He touched a scar under her ear. "I didn't notice this last night."

She pulled away from him and sat up in the bed. She didn't even know where to start.

"Please tell me that this is nothing to do with your ex-husband."

"No." She pulled the sheet up to her chin. "It was an accident. I ... I did it to myself."

"How on earth?"

"I don't think you understand how far gone I was. When Dylan left, I let my life fall apart. I didn't even try to stop it. I was so depressed – the self-loathing was unbelievable. I got stuck in a cycle of drinking and regret. Every morning when I woke up, that was going to be the day I would stop. It would be simple. I just wouldn't have a drink. And I usually felt so awful that the thought of not drinking was a welcome one. I'd go to work and struggle through my hangover, but as the day wore on, I had the urge to drink. I told myself I could always stop the next day. Some days I managed not to have a drink, and I convinced myself that I didn't have a problem. I could stop if I wanted to. I just didn't want to. No problem, right?" She looked at Bob for approval.

His face was expressionless.

She ran her finger over the scar. "This was the kick in the butt that I needed. One night – I'd already hit rock bottom – I was drowning my sorrows while watching one of those godawful made-for-TV movies. Turned out to be really inspiring. It felt as if it was speaking to me directly, telling me that I didn't have to settle for what I had, and I could turn my life around. I was drunk, but I thought it sounded like a fantastic idea. And what better way to reinvent myself than to have a new haircut? I went to the kitchen but I couldn't find any scissors. So I found a kitchen knife and took it to the bathroom."

Bob drew in a sharp breath.

"I was standing in front of the mirror, hacking away at my hair, when I felt a burning, searing pain. A warm trickle. Then everything went dark. The next thing I remember was waking up in the hospital. It was a day later. My mum and brother were on one side of the bed, my sister on the other. My dad was sitting at the back of the room. They'd all been crying. I was so weak, but I moved my hand to show them I was awake. My mum came up close to my face and just stared at me. I can't even describe her expression. It was fear, relief, anger – all at the same time. She stared at me for a few seconds then slapped me across the face. Not a real slap. A pathetic one. Then she laid her head on my chest and she wept." Alice wiped a tear from the corner of her eye. "They all thought I had tried to kill myself."

"Fuck. Did you?"

"I'd be lying if I said I'd never thought about it. On some of my darkest days, I thought about how easy it would be to swallow a bottle of pills with my gin. But that night, I swear I just wanted to cut my hair. Luckily the girl I was sharing a flat with was at home when it happened. She heard me hitting the bathroom floor. She found me in a pool of my own blood, tied a towel around my neck to stop the bleeding, and called an ambulance. The poor girl was so traumatised, she needed counselling."

She glanced at Bob, who looked sympathetic. He lay down and gestured for her to lay her head on his chest. He stroked her hair tenderly. "What happened after that?"

"Everything came out. The extent of my drinking. That I'd lost my job. My brother told everyone about my driving conviction. My mum went berserk. She tried to have me sectioned under the Mental Health Act. She claimed I was a danger to myself and to others. But in the end, I agreed to seek help. After a few days in hospital I was transferred to a drug and alcohol rehabilitation centre. I was there for a few weeks."

"It must have been awful."

"No. I loved it."

"You're kidding."

"No, I did. It was such a relaxing place. Away from all the pressures of life. No alcohol, no stress, no judgement. There was a gym, reading groups, arts and crafts. I had lots of counselling – and not just about my drinking. I talked about the break-up of my marriage, my depression, infertility, and my torpedoed career."

"Infertility?" he asked quietly.

She could already feel tears welling. She tried desperately to stay strong. "Yes." Her lip quivered. "I didn't know when to tell you, or even how. It's…"

He ran his hand across her cheek. "It's OK — you don't have to talk about it."

"But it seems like we're moving forward, so I do have to tell you. If you see children in your future, then that's something I can't give you." A tear fell down her cheek and she wiped it away with the back of her hand. "I'm sorry."

His hold on her tightened. "There's nothing to be sorry for. And it doesn't change how I feel about you. But how do I..." He trailed off.

"How do you what?"

He scratched his head and sighed. It was a few seconds before he spoke. "Nothing. Fuck. It's a lot to process, Alice. You're right – I had no idea what you've been through. But I can tell you honestly that children have never been on my agenda. Christine and I were certain from the get-go that we didn't want kids. Some of our friends had kids, and we saw how difficult and expensive it was, and how selfless they had to be. It wasn't for us. But you really wanted one, didn't you?"

"For as long as I can remember. Dylan did too. We met when we were eighteen, during our first week at university. We were sitting next to each other in Abstract Mathematics and we hit it off immediately. We both wanted the same things and we knew what we had to do to get them. After our degrees, we both did a master's, and he proposed to me on our graduation day. We were only twenty-three – we had our whole lives ahead of us. So we spent the next few years taking our first steps on the career ladder, then we bought a house, planned the wedding and got married at twenty-six. But we didn't want to settle down yet, so we spent the next few years working – but playing as well. We were really good to ourselves: fancy meals out, holidays, spas, whatever we wanted. The plan was to start trying for a family when we were thirty. After about six months, nothing was happening, so I went to my GP. She said it was completely normal. I'd been taking the pill for over ten years. She said it could take a while for my fertility to return and just to relax and enjoy all the sex."

Bob blushed.

"But that wasn't part of our plan. We didn't want to relax; we wanted a baby. We were both making good money, so we decided to go to a private clinic and have some tests done. It didn't take long to find out that it was my problem – a congenital uterine malformation. I asked the consultant if there was a possibility, like in a movie, that one day I'd suddenly find out I was pregnant and we'd have a happily-ever-after. The look on her face said it all. She said it *could* happen, but even with IVF my chances were about the same as of winning the lottery. All of a sudden, the future we had planned for twelve years was gone. And then, almost immediately, Dylan started looking at me differently. We talked and talked – he swore he loved me and that it was all going to be OK. But we'd already lost something. I started drinking, just a bit more than usual. We both did. After a few weeks, when the shock began to wear off, I started looking into other options. We loved children and there were loads of them out there who needed good stable homes. We had that to give. I researched fostering, adoption, even surrogacy. I got a whole load of information together and one night after dinner I presented the options to Dylan."

She took a deep breath. "But as it turns out, while I was looking for a solution, a way to get our plan back on track, he was forming a new plan. His own plan.

Without me. He told me that he loved me, but I couldn't give him the family he'd always wanted. He was still young – he had time to meet someone else. Have *his own* family. He'd already been to a solicitor to talk about divorce, had begun to separate himself from me financially. He had even rented a flat. My world just fell apart. I thought I had everything, and suddenly I had nothing."

"And that's when your drinking got out of control?"

She nodded.

"Forgive me for saying this, but it's no fucking wonder. Your ex-husband is a complete and utter bastard."

"Thank you." She wiped her eyes. "And things got worse after that. We put the house up for sale, and I took a room in a shared flat. The girl I lived with was a student and out drinking a lot, so I went with her. My work started to suffer. I couldn't concentrate – my head was all over the place. I was showing up to work late, hungover, or sometimes not at all. After a few weeks my boss got concerned and called me into his office to ask what was happening. I broke down, told him everything that had happened with Dylan, and I even told him I had depression and that I knew I was drinking too much and I needed help. I was so ashamed, I could barely look him in the eye. But when I finally looked at him, he was also crying. He was so sympathetic. He took me straight round to human resources, and they were amazing. They offered me paid sick leave – even arranged for me to see a therapist on the company insurance. I agreed initially, then I backed out. I threw everything they tried to do for me back in their faces. When they eventually let me go, I couldn't blame them.

And that's when things got really bad. That night I drank so much I fell asleep with the bottle in my hand. When I woke up the next morning, I didn't have to pretend to be sober for work, so I just drank the dregs."

"Oh, Alice." He sighed.

"I was rarely sober after that. Every time I felt the hint of a hangover, I drank to make it go away. Every time I felt depressed or thought about Dylan and the kids we'd never have, I drank to stop myself thinking. To pass out, so I didn't have to think about it. I don't know how, but I hid it quite successfully from my family. But Tam started commenting, 'Every time I see you, you're drinking or hungover. Maybe you should take it easy for a while.' I'm ashamed to say it, but after that I tried to shut her out of my life. I cancelled plans to see her, stopped texting her or answering the phone. I even pretended I was out when she called round to see me. I was such a mess, even my flatmate stopped talking to me. That was about the time I had the accidental haircut and ended up in rehab. And it was awesome. OK, the recovery from my accident and the withdrawal symptoms were horrendous, but once I got my head straight, I didn't want to drink. I embraced a new way of thinking: I was going to set the world on fire. When I had been sober for a few months, I even wondered if I had been a real alcoholic. I'd just been going through a hard time and I drank too much. I've moved on from that phase now, I thought, so maybe I could have a few then stop, right?"

"I don't think that's how it works, Alice. You didn't want to stop the night we met. What happened? What went so wrong that day that you felt you needed to drink?"

"I bumped into Dylan on the street. He was with his girlfriend. She was pregnant. I turned and I ran – straight into that bar, and straight into you."

"And I didn't help. I enabled you when I should have stopped you. I didn't know how."

"If you had tried to stop me, I would probably have drunk even more, just to spite you – a total stranger – and to spite myself. If I hadn't met you, God knows where I would have ended up, and in whose bed." She shrugged. "I'm sorry. It's in the past; I shouldn't be dwelling on it. After all that I've just told you, are you sure you still want me to be your girlfriend?"

"I'm sure. And I hope that when I tell you my own depressing story, you still want to be with me. It's like you just said – when is the best time to open up? To tell you all, and hope that you can take it?"

"That sounds ominous."

"It's just complicated. When my sister died, I..." He groaned and looked away.

"It's OK. Tell me some other time. I can't cope with any more sad stories today. We're meant to be enjoying ourselves, after all."

"Then how about breakfast? I'll grab the menu and you can see what you'd like to have sent up."

"We're not going down? Breakfast is the best part about staying in a hotel."

"I got us a late checkout. I thought we could spend the morning in bed."

"But what about the fruit and cereal? The cheeses, hams, pastries – and then there's the cooked food. I'm ravenous after last night." She tilted her head up and kissed him. "Let's get cleaned up and go downstairs and regroup over breakfast and lots of coffee. Then we can come back up here and get dirty again." She climbed out of bed and headed for the bathroom. She turned back to smile at him. He was lying on his side, watching her intently. God, she was really falling for him. Just over two months ago she hadn't even wanted to date – and now this. She couldn't get enough of him, and there was no way she could wait until after breakfast to feel his touch again.

"You know, I think there might be room in the shower for two," she cooed.

He leapt out of bed and followed her into the bathroom.

After a leisurely breakfast, a morning of steamy sex, and a late lunch at Jack's restaurant, it was after eight o'clock when Alice and Bob arrived home at her flat. Tamzin was in Edinburgh seeing her fiancé, so they had the place to themselves. Alice pointed to her overnight bag in Bob's hand and gestured to her bedroom. "You can put that in there." She followed him down the hall, but he stopped at the door.

"Is it safe? The last time I was in there, I barely escaped with my life."

"I thought we weren't going to mention that night any more?" She ushered him into the room. "Don't worry, you're free to go, but I thought you might like to stay."

"I'd love to, but I've still got to finish off this quote. There's some specialist machinery prices I have to check in the catalogue at the office. And I haven't even calculated the man-hours yet. It's probably going to be another late night for me. And unlike some people" – he grabbed her and pulled her to him – "I didn't get to sleep the whole journey home."

"What can I say? I'm exhausted."

"Me too. It was quite a night." He kissed her softly. She wrapped her arms around his waist and took a few steps backwards towards her bed, pulling him with her. He resisted. "I'm sorry. If I get into that bed with you, I'll never want to get out."

"Then don't." She held his gaze while she crossed her hands and ran them down her torso to grip the seam of her tight T-shirt. In one fluid motion she pulled it over her head and tossed it onto the floor. She kept eye contact as she slid down the zip of her jeans, then bent over and shimmied them down her thighs to the floor, pulling them off along with her socks. She straightened up and stood before him in her underwear, then wrapped her arms around him and pulled him towards the bed again. This time he didn't resist. Alice fell backwards onto the bed, pulling Bob on top of her.

"Close your eyes," he whispered before his mouth covered hers. Alice closed her eyes and let herself melt into his hungry kiss. She was expecting to feel his hands on her, but none came. Just his mouth, his tongue, kissing and licking, moving to her neck, her breasts, then back to her mouth.

Her body arched when she felt his fingers, warm against her bare skin. He traced right down her chest, skimming her belly button, before brushing the inside of her thigh. He slid his hands around her backside and coaxed her to lift her hips, just enough for him to remove her underwear. He wriggled between her legs and kissed her hard on the mouth. She pressed her head back into the pillow, moaning in pleasure as he took his time devouring her.

Afterwards, they lay entwined in each other's arms, breathless and content. Alice was exhausted, but truly happy for the first time in ages. She was crazy about Bob and was excited about where their relationship was going. It was still early days, though, and she knew she had to be careful. If she got hurt again, she wasn't sure if she had enough left in her to put herself back together again.

"What are you thinking?" he whispered.

"Nothing," she lied. "Just enjoying being here with you."

"Me too. To think I nearly passed this up to go and do a quote. But it still needs to be done. Are you going to hate me if I take off first thing tomorrow?"

"You mean today." She pointed to her alarm clock. It was nearly 2 a.m.

He groaned. "Time to get some sleep."

Alice gave him one last, lustful kiss then rolled over onto her side. Bob snaked his arm around her waist and snuggled in behind her. She fell asleep, content and safe in his arms.

The next morning Alice was wakened by the most delicious kiss. It was so soft and tender, she wondered if it was a dream until Bob ran his hand across her cheek.

"Morning, beautiful."

She squinted at him. He was already dressed. She looked over his shoulder at the alarm clock, which showed that it was seven thirty. "Why so early?"

"It's late for me – I'm an early riser. I've been lying next to you for the last hour, just watching you sleep. Snuggle back down, I can see myself out." He tucked the duvet round her.

"Do you want to do something this afternoon? I mean, if you get the quote finished."

"Sorry. I'm going to my parents' for Sunday dinner."

She stuck out her bottom lip.

"You can come with me if you want. I haven't told them I'm seeing anyone yet, so it might be a shock for them. And for you. And there are still some things I need to tell you..."

Is he serious? It's far too soon to meet his parents. Unless it's an empty offer and he's counting on me to say no. Then she considered that he might be joking, and she was overthinking it. She stuck her tongue out at him. "No, thank you. Monday?"

He grimaced. "Nope. And I probably can't do Tuesday either. How about Wednesday? Dinner."

She groaned. Sometimes arranging to meet him was a real effort. He seemed so busy, and she didn't want to play games, but she didn't want to get into the habit of being at his beck and call. She shook her head at him. "I usually go to the gym on a Wednesday night. There's a legs, bums and tums class I don't want to miss."

"Then I'll see what I can do. I'll call you later." He kissed her on the cheek then left, closing the bedroom door behind him.

She snuggled into the pillow and thought about the weekend. It had been amazing. Bob was amazing, and the sex... *I didn't know it could last that long. And multiple orgasms? Holy shit! I had sex with Dylan for about eleven years, and I came about eleven times. Total. I've been with Bob for just a weekend and it's already nine, or ten. I've lost count. Was it ever that good with Dylan? When we were trying for a baby, it did get a bit monotonous, but all I can remember is it being pretty vanilla compared to sex with Bob.*

Her mobile beeped. She picked it up from the bedside table and saw a text from Bob.

Missing you already x

She replied to say she missed him too, and waited for a minute in case there was another message. When none came, she tossed the phone aside and snuggled back under the covers. The last few Sundays she'd attended the AA meeting at the church hall, but that would put a real dampener on the weekend. How could she go from mind-blowing orgasms to mind-numbing confessions? Skipping one week won't hurt, she thought. *I'll lounge in bed for a while, have a late breakfast/early lunch, then head to the gym for a few hours. Then I'll have a long soak in the bath. After that, Tam should be back and I can tell her all about my fantastic weekend.*

Chapter Eight

On Monday morning, Alice waved Tamzin off to work, then relaxed on the sofa with her second cup of coffee. Expecting an early call from the agency, she'd already showered and was dressed in her go-to temping outfit of a crisp white blouse and short black skirt. She sipped her coffee and slipped into a daydream about Bob. She closed her eyes and tried to remember the taste of his lips and the feel of his hands as he ran them over her body. She was just getting aroused when her mobile rang. It was the agency, but she wished it had been Bob.

A short while later, Alice arrived at the Exchange – a telesales company – for an emergency placement. The reception area was busy and there was no one behind the desk, which was where she had been told she would sit. But there were at least a dozen other people waiting, who all looked like temps too. She wondered if there had been a mistake. Then a woman rushed out from the main office and gasped at the crowd. Alice made her way towards her.

"Hi, I'm Alice Patterson. Your temp."

The woman looked at her as if she was a long-lost friend. "I'm Tina, and I'm so glad you're here. Our receptionist phoned in sick – heatstroke. Don't get me started. Usually we could struggle through without her for a day, but we're holding open interviews and there will be people in and out all week. I need someone to meet and greet, take names, hand out forms, do photocopying and general admin duties. You're OK with that, right?" The desperation in her voice suggested it was a command rather than a question.

"Sounds totally doable. Am I here?" Alice pointed to the reception desk.

"Yes. I'll show you where everything is and how to work the switchboard. There should be a manual around somewhere." She pointed to the messy reception desk. "But you'll be fine. Please say you'll be fine. Who gets heatstroke from a sunbed, anyway? I can't handle this today."

"It'll be fine. Can I get you a coffee?"

Tina patted her chest and sighed in relief. "Alice, you're an angel."

Alice spent the morning organising the interviewees. It was busy, but enjoyable. Most were friendly and the morning passed quickly. At lunchtime, an older lady emerged from the main office.

"I'm your lunch cover. You can take forty-five minutes."

"Great. I'm starving. But I don't know this part of town well. Can you recommend anywhere nearby for a sandwich?"

"Yes. Krust. Go out of the door, turn left and it's just around the corner. Their signature panini is to die for."

"Krust it is, then. Can I bring anything back for you?"

"No, thanks."

Alice picked up her bag and jacket and made her way outside. The bright April sunshine felt heavenly on her skin. She skipped down the street, feeling wonderful. She'd had a great morning at work, and she was still on a high from her weekend with Bob. When she arrived at Krust, it was really busy. There didn't seem to be any free tables, so she decided to take her lunch back to the office. Just as she was making her way to the counter, she spotted Bob, sitting at a table alone. *What are the odds?* She hurried over to him.

"Hey, handsome," she cooed.

He looked up at her and a smile spread across his face. "Alice, what are you doing here?"

"I'm working at a place down the street."

"If I'd known, I could have called for you."

"May I join you now?"

"Um…" He pointed to his empty plate. "I've just finished. I have a meeting in fifteen minutes, but I could keep you company until then. It's not table service, so you need to go and order." When he pointed to the counter, a glimmer of something shiny caught her eye. *What was that?* She looked at his left hand. He was wearing a gold wedding band. He saw her staring at it, and his face fell. He held up his hand and pointed to the ring. "This isn't what it looks like."

"Good," she spluttered, "because it looks like a wedding ring."

"It is. But I can explain…"

Her head was spinning. She wasn't sure if it was due to shock and anger at Bob, or disappointment in herself for letting her guard down. She fought to hold back her tears. "I don't want to know." She turned and hurried out of the door.

He wasn't far behind her. "Alice! Alice, wait!"

She stormed down the street towards the Exchange, but he caught up with her and put his hand on her arm to stop her.

She shrugged him off. "Leave me alone. I don't date married men."

"It's complicated."

Complicated? How could it be? Either he's married or

he's not. I've never seen that ring before, which means he takes it off every time he sees me. He must have taken it off at the bar the night we met. He was intending to hook up with someone. It probably wasn't even a male friend that stood him up, it was probably a woman, and I was the next best thing. How can this be happening? I should have known better than to trust another man. She scowled at him, but the look on his face was one she had never seen before. He was usually confident and charming, but today there was something different about his eyes. They'd lost their sparkle. He really didn't seem like a cheat, but which man did? Alice wanted to know the truth – how badly she had been duped. She took a deep breath. "All right, explain it to me."

He checked his watch. "Can we meet tonight? I have a meeting in fifteen minutes. It's a quote for a job."

"There's always a quote!" she yelled. "Is that your get-out-of-jail-free card?"

"No. It's my livelihood. My car is just over there. Sit with me for ten minutes. I can explain everything."

She stood firm.

"Please, Alice. Don't you want to know what I have to say?"

God, yes. "You have five minutes." She stormed towards his car.

He opened the door for her, and she immediately spotted a child seat in the back. Her stomach churned. Had she eaten already, she was sure she would have vomited at the sight of it. *He's married with a child. How did I get him so wrong?* She wanted to run, but had to climb into the car before her legs gave way beneath her.

He got into the driver's seat and turned to face her.

He held up his hand and pointed to the ring. "I wear this to work, just like I wear a suit. And just like the suit, it comes off as soon as I get home. I wear it to save face when I'm working. My employees don't know that Christine has left. And clients want the family business, Christine Cleans. What is the business without Christine?" He sighed. "It's not all about work, though. It's pride. I don't want people to know that my wife has left me."

"And why exactly did she leave you? You've danced around it, but you've never actually told me." Her gaze darted to the child seat in the back.

"I told you about my sister, right? She passed away a few months ago."

"What's she got to do with this?"

"Rebecca was … a free spirit. Totally irresponsible. She lived her life like her actions had no consequences. She lived in Germany for a couple of years, but she came back to London when my dad had a heart attack. She was six months pregnant, and that was the first we knew about it. She never told us who the father was. She said he was abusive, and she'd broken up with him before she even found out she was pregnant. She didn't tell him about the baby, and she didn't name him on the birth certificate. She was so blasé, said she didn't need a man and she could do it on her own. But she didn't even have a job or a place to live. My parents ended up paying her rent. Once the baby was born, she swanned around doing little gigs here and there, always landing on her feet. Until … well, until she was killed in a car crash. She wasn't wearing a seat belt. The police said if she had been, things might have been different. But they weren't, and she left behind her son."

Tears stung Alice's eyes at the thought of the poor child.

"His name is Sam and he's five years old."

"What happened to him?"

"My parents took him in. But they're both in their seventies and my dad's health hasn't been great since his heart attack. It became obvious pretty quickly that they wouldn't be able to cope. So the next logical choice was me and Christine. The social workers said we didn't have to take him. He could be fostered, or he could have an open adoption so we could still keep in contact with him. But that would have broken my mother's heart. And how would Sam have felt? He loses his mum and then the only family he has left kicks him out? I couldn't do that to him. He belongs with his family. So I said we'd take him. I was telling the truth when I told you that Christine and I didn't want kids. But under the circumstances, what else could we do? But Christine was adamant: she didn't want children of her own and she sure as hell wasn't going to raise someone else's. We fought and fought about it. And in the end she made me choose – him or her."

Alice shook her head in disbelief.

"Honestly, I thought she'd relent. That she would decide she loved me enough to stay. But she packed her bags and left. That was nearly nine months ago, and I haven't seen or spoken to her since."

"What?"

"We've had no contact. Nothing. There's no divorce. But only because I don't know where the hell she is."

Alice was dumbstruck. She had no idea what to say. Her head was spinning.

"I'm so sorry I didn't tell you. But it's like you said at

the hotel. When you're in a new relationship, at what point do you admit you have baggage? And it's not even my own baggage. I tried to tell you, twice. On our first date, but I chickened out because I wasn't sure if you liked kids or even if you wanted them. And I didn't want to scare you away or for you to think that I was grooming you as some sort of surrogate mother for Sam. Then I had planned to tell you after we … you know, decided that we were in a proper relationship. But then you told me about your infertility. How could I have told you then? How could I tell a woman who was desperate for a child that I had one I hadn't wanted? I've been trying to work out how to tell you."

She was looking everywhere but at him.

"Say something. Please."

What on earth am I supposed to say? Our whole relationship has been a lie. It's only been two months, but two months of lies. "You lied to me."

He took her hand. "I know. I'm sorry. But I swear that Christine is out of my life, and I've made my peace with it. I've been focusing on building a relationship with my nephew. I hadn't even considered dating until I met you. Obviously, there was an instant physical attraction. Then I talked to you and I found out you were kind, funny and incredibly smart. When we kissed at your flat, I felt a chemistry between us. And when you threw your shoe at me, I fell a little bit in love with you. And I fall a bit more in love every time I see you."

She looked at him. He was waiting for her to speak, but what could she say? Her first mistake had been to date him in the first place. She hadn't been ready. Her second mistake was to get hopeful about the relationship when she knew she shouldn't be in one;

she wasn't strong enough. She wasn't going to make a third mistake by forgiving his lies.

"I've been brutally honest with you. Do you think any of that was easy? Telling you the most shameful and embarrassing things about myself? All you had to do was tell me about your nephew. And that..." She pointed to his wedding ring. "That must still mean something to you, or you wouldn't be wearing it. We're done." She reached for the door handle and got out of the car.

He jumped out after her. "Alice, please!"

She looked across the roof of the car at him. His hazel eyes were glazed with pain, and there was desperation on his face. Everything inside her wanted to rush over and throw her arms around him. But it was a mistake – for both of them.

"I'm sorry for your troubles. I've got my own to deal with. Take care, Bob. Make sure you look after that little boy."

"But—"

"Goodbye, Bob."

She hurried off down the street and didn't look back.

Alice felt drained when she got back to the office. Her anger at Bob had turned to regret, and disappointment in herself. She slumped down behind the reception desk. *How could I have been so stupid? I should have known better than to let my guard down. I'm done with men. For real this time. They're responsible for the worst times in my life. Why the hell is life always so hard?* Usually a drink helped when she felt like this. It gave her something else to focus on, something to take her out of her shitty life, if only for a while. And she really wanted a drink. She wanted to drink to spite Bob, to spite Dylan, and to spite the last interview candidate who couldn't remember his National Insurance number. She'd memorised her own the day she got it. Didn't everyone do that?

She was considering gathering her stuff, walking out of the office and heading to the nearest pub. She'd only have one drink, or two, and she would stop again tomorrow. She'd done it before. It wasn't that hard. It was no big deal. Well, as long as Tamzin didn't find out...

Just then, Tina popped her head around the door and winked. "I hate to jinx it, but this is going really well. Can you send in the next one?"

Alice forced all her thoughts of drinking to the back of her mind and resolved to keep busy until the urge to drink had passed. She smiled back at Tina, then called the next name on the list.

Alice threw herself into work that afternoon. She made sure that each candidate dotted every 'i' and crossed every 't'. The woman who filled in her mobile number but put ditto marks in place of her home telephone number got branded an underachiever for not filling out the form in full. And Alice could barely stand to look at the guy who was wearing a Star Wars T-shirt to a job interview. What was wrong with these people?

By the end of the day, Alice was hyper. Tina came into reception and was astonished to see that Alice had tidied up, emptied the bins, refilled the paper cups at the water machine, straightened the chairs and put the old newspapers in the recycling. The once messy reception desk was tidy and organised, and the plants on the windowsill looked like they'd been dusted.

"Alice, my love. You saved my life today. Can you come back tomorrow? Even if Scorched Sally makes it in, she'll get her knickers in a twist about something. It was manic today. I couldn't have done it without you." Tina checked her watch. "I'm not being picked up for another thirty-five minutes. Let me take you across the street and buy you a glass of wine as a thank you for all your hard work."

Did she say wine? Alice drew a long deep breath in through her nose and breathed out through her mouth. *No.* She had had the urge to drink earlier, but that was gone now. She had worked through it. But it was always so embarrassing telling people about her little problem. She really couldn't face it today.

"Aw, thanks, Tina. But I don't really drink."

"No, me neither," she said sarcastically, then mimed putting a glass to her lips and chugging it. "One glass — it's all I have time for. Please, it's been a day. And I'm not being rude, but you didn't seem as chirpy this afternoon. Is everything all right?"

"I broke up with my boyfriend at lunchtime."

"Oh no! Were you together long?"

"No. Just a couple of months. But it was starting to get serious, then poof – gone!"

"Then you definitely need a drink. I'm not taking no for an answer." She linked arms with Alice and led her to the pub.

Alice held her breath as the large frosted glass of white wine was set in front of her. It looked so inviting. She thought back to her first night with Bob. That night, she had drunk like it was going out of fashion, yet she hadn't wanted a drink in the morning. She must be cured. She could have this drink, then stop. She didn't even have to drink it all. A few sips would prove that alcohol didn't control her any more; *she* was in charge. She lifted the glass and took a sip. The cold, crisp chardonnay slid effortlessly down her throat, and she immediately wanted another sip. *Pace yourself. Pace. Pace. Pace.* She watched Tina; she'd had one sip too. Alice waited with bated breath until Tina took her second sip, meaning she was free to do the same. Tina then mumbled something about her son's football match, which she was going to that night, but Alice wasn't listening. She was willing Tina to take a third sip. Then a fourth.

She matched Tina sip for sip. When their glasses were empty, the women left the bar. Tina went off to her lift and Alice to catch her bus. She was still upset about Bob, but she was a little high from the wine. Kudos to Tina for springing for the large glass. Alice congratulated herself on her ability to stop after one drink. It was a huge step forward. And she could quite easily arrive home and Tamzin would be none the wiser. But just to be on the safe side, she popped into a newsagent for some chewing gum before she headed to the bus stop.

"But I don't understand." Tamzin threw her hands in the air. "Isn't that exactly what you wanted to do with Dylan? Adopt a child and give the poor thing a good home?"

"Yes. But Dylan was my husband. We were together for twelve years. We talked about having kids all the time. I just met Bob two months ago."

"The fact that he's caring for his nephew shouldn't

change how you feel about him. And it's not like you're stuck with him; you can break up with him if it's not working out."

"No. I can't do that to a child. It's not fair to go in and out of their lives. Poor kid has been through so much already – the last thing he needs is me messing him up. I can't be around kids. I'm an alcoholic. I am no role model for a child."

"You have that under control, Alice."

She thought back to her glass of wine earlier. Tamzin was right – she did have it under control. That was two occasions now where she'd stopped after one. Well, one drink and one binge. But she wouldn't tell Tamzin about her trip to the pub yet; it was too soon. She just nodded.

"That asshole Dylan has robbed you of all your self-worth. You're an amazing person. I'd trust you with my child's life. You know you're going to be godmother when Cameron and I have kids. They're going to love their Auntie Alice."

Alice gave Tamzin a firm hug. "And I'm going to spoil them rotten. But what about the fact that Bob's still married?"

"You already knew that! But you didn't get your moral compass in a twist when you were in Manchester engaging in your sexual smorgasbord. I think you're being too hard on him."

"I'm not."

"You are. I love you. And I don't mean to upset or offend you. But you've been worried about how men would react to your 'condition'. And Bob – well, he's been pretty amazing about it, by all accounts. You've been happy these past few weeks, and you seem to really like him. He's accepted you for what you are. Can't you do the same for him?"

"But he's lied about getting a divorce this whole time."

"I'm not married yet, so I don't know how it feels. Everyone tells me that it feels like more than a piece of paper. But how did it feel when Dylan told you he picked having children over you? How did it feel when he walked out of your marital home? Did you feel married?"

She looked down at the floor. "No. I felt betrayed and totally alone."

"That's probably how Bob feels about his wife. Please tell me you'll talk to him."

"Why do you care so much about me dating Bob?"

"Because if you're out with him, it means you're not at the gym. You look fucking great. You're going to show me up on my wedding day."

"Don't worry, I won't upstage the bride. I promise I'll binge-eat carbs the whole week before."

"You'd better!"

Alice went to her room and threw herself onto the bed. She hated to admit it, but Tamzin was right. Like her own, Bob's marriage was over the minute his wife walked out on him. There's no way they could come back from that. And she was really falling for him, because he was easy to talk to, kind and generous. She felt safe and content in his company. The sex was amazing, but it was more than just physical; they had an emotional attachment too. She reasoned that he had tried to tell her about his life, and she remembered wanting to avoid having another awkward conversation.

Even though she was still angry with him, she was missing him already, and the thought of never seeing him again was too difficult to entertain. Deep down she knew she had to see him, or she'd go crazy thinking about him. She reached into her handbag for her phone, which she had put on silent before she went back to the office and hadn't looked at since. Would there be lots of texts and missed calls from Bob, begging for another chance?

There were only three new notifications. One text, one missed call, and one voicemail message. She cleared the missed call, which was from Bob, then read the text, which was also from Bob. It was his address in Blackheath. She berated herself for never questioning why he hadn't invited her over; she'd assumed it was because they were keeping things causal before their trip to Manchester. She had never suspected it was because he had something to hide. She took a deep breath and called her voicemail.

Hi, Alice. I hope you're OK. I, um, wanted to chase you down the street. I wanted to go to your flat and sit outside until you got home. Or stop by the gym in case you went there. But I knew you wouldn't want that. So I'm going to give you the time you need to process this. I'm not making excuses, but my life has changed so much in the past few months. It was too tough to deal with, so I buried my head in the sand as much as I could. Some people know that Christine is gone. My parents, Jack, a few other close friends. But I thought if I didn't tell people she was gone, I wouldn't have to admit it to myself. And it was wrong of me not to tell you about Sam. The truth is, I didn't know how to approach it. It was easier not to talk about him. I lied, and I'm sorry. I hope you will forgive me. I really want to talk to you, in person. I'll text you my address. Come to my house when you're ready. I'll show you I have nothing else to hide. Or just call me, text me... I need to hear from you.

Alice listened to the message again. He sounded broken, but sincere. She wanted to give the relationship another chance, but was it a good idea? They'd both been through so much heartbreak and upheaval, maybe they should take time to cool off and let things settle for a while before making any decisions about how to move forward. But before she knew what she was doing, she had burst into Tamzin's bedroom. "Will you drive me over to Bob's?"

Tamzin jumped up and pulled on her shoes.

Alice stared at the doorbell. Maybe she should have called or texted to say she was on her way over, but she had wanted to catch him off guard, make sure that he really didn't have anything to hide. Just as she was about to ring the bell, she thought about Sam. Was he going to be there? The last thing she needed was a five-year-old audience. She checked her watch. It was nine thirty – surely Sam should be in bed by now.

She knocked on the door gently. After a few seconds, it opened. A smile spread across Bob's face when he saw her. He stepped back and beckoned her to come inside. Alice turned and signalled to Tamzin, who was waiting in the car, that it was OK to leave.

The first thing Alice noticed when she stepped into the living room was the crystal tumbler on the coffee table. The liquid inside was golden, like whisky. Bob noticed her staring at it and rushed over and picked it up.

"I'm so sorry, Alice. I poured this ten minutes ago, after Sam went to bed. I've had one sip. If I'd known you were coming, there's no way I would have poured it."

She wasn't surprised that he wanted a drink; the first thing she had wanted to do after she left him at lunchtime was to have a drink too. At least Bob had enough restraint to wait until nine thirty. Although she wondered, did he need it? Really need it? Like she did? And would he stop at one, or two? Or would he drink until he passed out, like she did? Then she thought back to her glass of wine with Tina. That was just one drink. Then she had stopped. Perhaps she could have another. She smiled at Bob. He would know how much she wanted a drink. He'd let her drink freely the night they met. Maybe after the shock she'd had at lunchtime, he might be agreeable to her having one … or two. Just to take the edge off.

"It's OK if you have a drink. You've had a hard day. We both have. Why don't you pour me one too?"

He narrowed his eyes at her. "Over my dead body. Take a seat and I'll make us some coffee." He picked up the glass and took it out of the room.

"I was kidding," she called after him, and prayed that he believed her. She sat down on the sofa and looked around the large living room. The toys scattered on the floor and the pair of tiny shoes by the side of the sofa looked totally out of place among the expensive furniture. There was art on the walls and no sign of any family photos or portraits – the kind that lined the walls of her family home.

Bob arrived back with the coffee. He handed her a cup and sat down beside her. "I'm so glad you're here. I—"

"Can I speak first?"

He nodded.

"I've been going back and forth over what's happening between us. I was right when I said I wasn't ready to date. I wasn't ready to feel this way about anyone, or risk getting hurt again. But I enjoy your company and I miss you when I'm not with you. The sex … it's out of this world. But mostly, I like how you just accept me for who I am. I feel like I can tell you anything, and that you're never going to judge me. That's when it hit me – I've been the one doing all the talking. I never really gave you a chance to tell me anything important about you. So that's why I'm here. To listen."

"Where do you want me to start?"

"I don't know."

"I haven't told you much about Christine. I met her when I was twenty-one and she was eighteen. She was one of my first employees."

Alice frowned at him.

"I know, I know." He held up his hands. "A mate and I had just started up the business – domestic cleaning, nothing too exciting. Peter did the books, admin and purchasing, and I drummed up the business. At the Christmas party – a few boxes of wine and some pizzas at the office – Christine and I ended up getting together, and that was that. We dated for a couple of months and then she told me she didn't like cleaning and asked if she could work in the office instead. But there wasn't enough work for two. After a week or so of Christine sulking, I had an idea: we could expand, do more varied types of work, commercial and industrial, to see if we could increase the business – and create more office work. Peter said he wanted to stay small with domestic cleaning. Really, he was just jealous of me and Christine. He'd fancied her too. But he wouldn't budge, so I bowed out of the business and set up on my own. I got the jobs and Christine cleaned. The business grew, we got regular contracts and one or two more staff, and Christine began to work in the office full-time. I landed a big job every now and then, for which I hired temps. We muddled through for a few years. Then we got our big break. I won a contract to clean one of the movie studios just outside London. It was specialist, high-paid work. We started getting invited to parties. There were celebrities and TV people – Christine was in her element. We started eating in expensive restaurants, going on fancy holidays and mini-breaks. Before I knew it, I was wearing expensive suits, driving a nicer car. She gradually reduced her hours until she was no longer working. It didn't even occur to me to take her off the payroll. Some people would call me a pushover, but I don't think that's what I was. I enjoyed working; she didn't. I wasn't unhappy. I had a beautiful wife, nice house, nice car. Life was good. Then my sister died."

She put her hand on his knee. "That must have been awful."

"It was and it wasn't. We hadn't been close since we were kids. She played acoustic guitar in an indie folk band and she travelled a lot. And she and Christine hated each other, which didn't help. I was upset; I had regrets about not being a better big brother. But I could handle that. Mum and Dad were devastated. Seeing that was awful, and we were all so worried that Dad would have another heart attack because of the stress. Sam was…" He trailed off.

She put her arm around him.

He took a deep breath before he continued. "I'd never really bothered with him before that. Mum always reminded me to send a present on his birthday or at Christmas. We saw him at family gatherings, when Christine and I could be bothered showing up. But that was it. We had no real relationship. I didn't know him – not properly. But I do know that he was happy, outgoing, really talkative. But when Rebecca died, he stopped being all those things. My parents took him in initially – they were so grateful to have a part of Rebecca still with them. But Sam was distraught, angry, disruptive. There were social workers, counsellors, doctors, solicitors. My dad was getting confused, upset by it all, and my mum couldn't cope with both of them. She didn't want to entertain the thought of foster or respite care, so she begged us to take him. I agreed straight away, because I knew it was the right thing to do. But Christine was adamant that she didn't want him. She didn't want to give up her lifestyle. And she was so used to getting her own way about everything, she was gobsmacked when I told her I'd made the decision and we were going to take him. I told her I'd get a childminder and babysitters so we could still go out. And my folks would help as much as they could. She would have to do very little, and it wouldn't be that bad. Sam would settle down, he'd soon grow up and be less of a hindrance. I suggested that we might even grow to like having him around. Then came her ultimatum. What could I do?" He wiped a tear from his eye.

"Honestly, I think you did an amazing thing."

"It didn't feel amazing. Christine packed a few things, and she didn't even look back. That was the last time I saw her. I spent the next few weeks expecting her to be there every night when I got home from work or wherever. I'd sit on the stairs, watching the door, trying to process how on earth she could do that to me. She said she loved me..." He placed his hand on Alice's knee. "I know you know how that feels."

She nodded.

"Well, I don't feel that way any more. I pulled myself out of it. I focused on Sam. He calmed down a lot when he came to live here. I think he was afraid I'd get rid of him if he put a foot out of line. But he's settling a bit. Doing OK at school. He still gets counselling. It's been tough, but we're getting used to each other. And I got a childminder, Pauline. I'd be lost without her. I drop Sam at her house every morning. She gives him breakfast and takes him to school, then she picks him up, helps him with his homework and gives him dinner. I pick him up after work, give him a bath – but most nights that's optional – then put him to bed. Weekends are hard. Sometimes I have to take him to work with me. Or we go to my parents and stay over. They're always so happy to see him and it's just a bit easier when we're all together. They had him last weekend when we were in Manchester. But weekends are about as long as they can cope with him. He's really hard work. Just on the go the whole time."

"I know – I have two nieces and a nephew. I adore them and I enjoy spending time with them, but I'm always glad to hand them back after a day of babysitting."

"So that's it. Now you know everything."

She was silent. "Not everything. You've told me why you still wear your ring, but I still don't know why you haven't started off your divorce. Are you hoping for a reconciliation?"

"Absolutely not. I can't lie; for the first few weeks I'd have rolled out the red carpet for her. I was so desperate to have her back that I kept paying her salary. When her credit card bills arrived with hotel charges, I paid them, hoping she just needed some time and would reconsider and come back. But then the hotel charges stopped. I figured she'd made her decision or, worse, met someone new. I was angry, and I thought about withdrawing financial support. Then I realised that while she was gone, she wasn't causing any trouble. I got to keep my house, which Sam has settled into, and full control of my business. Once we started talking about divorce, she'd want her share of our money. I don't know if I can afford to buy her out."

"Yeah, that's tricky."

"And now there's you. I wasn't expecting you. And I'm sorry I lied, and I've told you the reasons why I did. I need you to forgive me and give me another chance." He took her hands and gazed into her eyes. "It's really important that you fall in love with me."

"Why?"

"Because I'm falling in love with you."

She broke eye contact and looked down at the floor. She *was* falling in love with him, but it was happening too fast. And now there was Sam to consider. She'd longed for a child, and she knew Sam would never be her own, but she could be like a mother to him. If things worked out, she would have everything she ever wanted. But if they didn't... She had to bite her lip to stop herself from crying. Suddenly Bob's hand was on her cheek. He cupped her chin and lifted her face upwards. When her eyes met his, all her insecurities melted away. She placed a gentle kiss on his lips, but when he tried to kiss her back, she pulled away.

"I have feelings for you too. But I can't be with you if you're married to another woman. You need to initiate the divorce."

"But I don't know where she is since she left the hotel. She's blocked my number..."

"Then cancel her credit card. She'll be through that door before you can say 'transaction declined'."

"No! I don't want to make her angry. God knows what she'd do out of spite. She thinks I betrayed her."

"OK, then. There are things called enquiry agents – google one. They'll find her in no time. You just have to make the call."

"The call that's going to cost me half of everything I own."

"Then it's just as well I don't want you for your money."

"You still fancy me? Does that mean you're not cross with me any more?" He placed his hand on her knee and made circles with his finger.

"I'm seething." She pushed his hand off her knee. "And it's late. I should go."

"Stay here tonight."

She shook her head.

"Please. I don't want you to go. Not because I want sex. But because I want you. And tomorrow, everything's going to change. My cousin is a family solicitor. I'll talk to him about getting a divorce. I'll tell everyone at work, and I'm going to get rid of all the alcohol in this house. That drink I had tonight will be my last."

"You don't have to do that."

"Of course I do. I enjoy the odd drink, but I don't need it. It's not an issue."

Alice remembered her glass of wine with Tina, and shifted in her seat.

Bob winced. "Shit. I'm so sorry. I didn't mean to imply that it should be easy for you too. I'm impressed by how well you've recovered after the night we met. You're doing great. I'm really proud of you."

The smile she forced onto her face belied the guilt she was feeling. *If he finds out about that glass of wine, he'll be disappointed in me. He might even blame himself for upsetting me and driving me to it. Telling him will do more harm than good. And there really is no need; it won't happen again.*

"Thanks," she whispered. "OK, I'll stay. But no sex. Maybe just a cuddle or two."

"Sounds perfect." They got up from the sofa. Bob took Alice's hand and led her upstairs.

Chapter Nine

The next morning Alice was still asleep when Bob crept back into the bedroom. He set a cup and a plate on the bedside table, then perched on the bed beside her. He watched her sleep for a few seconds then patted her cheek to wake her. She groaned and lifted her head slightly. "What time is it?"

"Six o'clock."

"It's the middle of the night." She snuggled back into the pillow.

"I hate to do this, but I have to sneak you out. This isn't how you and Sam should meet."

"Ugh, you're right. But I'd like to meet him soon. I'm falling for you; I can't wait to start falling for him too."

"He's going to love you."

"I hope I'm good enough for him."

"What are you talking about? You're amazing."

She rolled her eyes. As much as she would love to believe him, something inside wouldn't let her. She often wondered what he saw in her, and why he would want to be with someone whose life had spiralled so out of control. "I'm talking about my drinking. Not a great role model."

"You've got that under control. And now that I've given up drinking, there will never be any temptation coming from me. You're still going to meetings on Sunday mornings, right?"

She winced.

"*Alice?* How many have you missed?"

"Just one. I won't miss any more. I promise."

"Good." He pointed to the plate on the bedside table. "Now eat your breakfast before it gets cold."

She sat up in bed and smiled when she saw the coffee, toast and sliced banana. Not exactly the cooked and continental fare she'd had at the hotel, but the gesture was so appreciated that she didn't have the heart to tell him she hated bananas. She popped a slice in her mouth.

"Are you working today?"

She nodded as she forced down the banana. "Same place as yesterday."

"I'll be in the area too. Do you want to try lunch again? That place, Krust, is really nice."

"That depends. Will you be wearing your wedding ring?"

He held up his left hand and wiggled his bare ring finger at her. "Nope. But I wasn't sure what to do with it. What did you do with yours?"

"I put them in the bin, then I took them straight back out again. They were a diamond-encrusted platinum two-set and they cost a fortune. They're in my jewellery box."

"Any room in there for mine?"

She screwed up her face. "Absolutely not. Just chuck it. It'll be cathartic."

"Yeah, I might. So, when I get to work I'm going to tell everyone that Christine is gone. Then I'll call my cousin and get the divorce in motion. Tonight, I'm going to tell Sam all about you. I should probably tell Pauline too – although she's been over the moon with all the extra babysitting since you and I met. She thinks I've been working way too hard."

"You mean every time you've seen me you've packed

Sam off to the childminder?"

He shrugged. "Or my parents, or the neighbour's seventeen-year-old daughter, who's saving for her first trip to Ibiza."

"Well, that stops now. I feel terrible stealing you away from him. He needs his Uncle Bob."

"Uncle Robert. Everyone has always called me Robert." He shrugged again. "I don't know why, but when I met you I wanted to be Bob."

"I like Bob." She grinned.

"Bob likes you." He lifted the duvet and slipped into bed beside her.

"What happened to sneaking me out?"

"Sam usually doesn't wake until seven. I can keep you for a few more minutes..."

Alice arrived for work at the Exchange with a spring in her step and a huge smile on her face. She hummed to herself while she arranged the newspapers on the coffee table, and couldn't help thinking about the night before. Even though they had agreed not to have sex, once they were in bed together, they couldn't keep their hands to themselves. It was incredible. It seemed like every time they had sex, it was better than the last time. And that morning, when he touched her... She fanned her face.

That day, there were just under forty job applicants. It was a busy but enjoyable day. Tina said that Scorched Sally would be off for a few more days, and had called Alice's agency to book her for the rest of the week. Alice met Bob for lunch as planned. They canoodled over their paninis and when he walked her back to the office, he kissed her passionately on the doorstep to say goodbye. She floated back to her desk, feeling normal for the first time in ages. She had a good man in her life, and she was also about to meet his nephew. Work was good, and she looked and felt great. So, when Tina suggested a glass of wine after work again, Alice thought there would be no harm in it. It's what normal people did. But she didn't mention the wine when she spoke to Bob that evening; she didn't think he'd understand what she was trying to prove. It would be better to wait until she was *sure* she could always stop after a single drink; it might take a bit more practice.

For the rest of the week, things were much the same. Alice continued to enjoy working at the Exchange and was building a rapport with a few of the other people in the office. On Wednesday, she was disappointed when Tina didn't suggest a glass of wine after work. She briefly considered going by herself, but resisted, vowing to keep her one drink strictly sociable. She would never drink alone. She didn't see Bob again that week, but they had texted on and off, and every evening they talked on the phone. Alice was enjoying hearing more about Sam, and they had agreed a play date at the park on Saturday so that the pair could meet.

On Friday afternoon Alice was a bit more sombre. It was her last day at the Exchange. She was packing up her stuff to leave when Tina burst into the reception area waving a piece of paper in the air. "I just had a brilliant idea. Fill this in and you can start on Monday." She slapped an application form down on the desk in front of Alice. "I know it's telesales, but I think you can handle it. I don't want you to go."

"I'm not sure. I'm supposed to be finding my way

back to being an actuary again. This really is a step in the wrong direction."

"Oh, please..." Tina joined her hands in prayer. "We love having you here."

Alice laughed. She'd never felt so appreciated at work before. She did enjoy it and it would be a steady job until she found something more suitable. "Oh, all right, as long as you don't take it personally when I move on."

"Absolutely not. Get that form filled in pronto. Your interview is in the pub at ten past five. Vino's on me." She clapped her hands and skipped off into the main office.

Alice felt like skipping too. A new job and a glass of wine would finish off the week nicely. But when they got to the bar, instead of buying two glasses of wine, Tina bought a bottle. Alice helped her drink it, without one word of protest.

On Saturday afternoon Alice stood at the gates of the play park, waiting for Bob and Sam to arrive. She wasn't sure if it was the heat of the sun that was making her sweat, or if it was nerves. She hadn't a clue why she was so nervous. Sam was only five – nowhere near old enough to judge her or make adult assumptions about her. All she had to do was relax and be herself. She spotted Bob walking towards her. Sam was beside him, pushing himself along on a scooter. He was cute, with messy brown hair.

Bob had to grapple with him to get him to stop beside Alice. "This is my friend, Alice," he said cheerfully. "The one I've been telling you about."

Alice gave him a little wave. "Hi, Sam."

Sam examined her from top to toe before he returned a shy smile.

"I have a nephew who's five too. He loves Pokémon. Do you?"

He nodded.

"Good, 'cause I got you these." She offered him two packets of Pokémon cards. He looked at Bob for permission to take them.

"Go ahead. Just remember to say thank you."

Sam grinned and held out his hand but, just as he was about to take the cards, another boy came running over to them. "Sam! Come play with me."

Sam looked at Bob with excitement. "Can I, Uncle Robert?"

"Of course you can. But stay where I can see you."

Sam ran off and didn't look back. Alice put the cards back into her handbag. "He'll be back for them at some stage."

"You can count on it. Let's get a coffee." Bob slid his arm around her waist and directed her towards the coffee hut. The queue moved quickly, and it wasn't long before they were sitting down to enjoy their Americanos on a bench at the side of the park. While they watched Sam, Alice told Bob about what had happened with Tina the day before – although she left out their trip to the pub, and drinking half a bottle of wine.

They watched Sam scale the climbing frame. When he got to the highest point he shouted down, encouraging his friend to follow him. Alice sat up straight when she noticed Sam's foot slip off the frame, but she relaxed again when he regained his balance. "Is he OK up there? Seems pretty high."

"Yeah, he's up there all the time. He loves this place. We come when we can. Usually I bring a newspaper." He grabbed her hand and squeezed it. She squeezed back, but didn't take her eyes off Sam.

"I can't believe how much he looks like you. If I didn't know better, I'd say he was your son."

"Most people assume he is – it's probably the nose. Unfortunately for Rebecca, Dad gave it to both of us."

"And excuse me for saying, but I wasn't expecting him to look so happy."

"He is, generally. But he still wakes in the night asking for her. Then there's the nightmares, bed-wetting, and tantrums. But either they're getting less frequent and intense, or I'm getting better at dealing with them. His teacher says he's doing a bit better in school too. Coming out of his shell." He pointed up at him. "Look at him up there, laughing and carrying on. That's not the same child who came to live with me all those months ago. And like I said to Christine, I've got used to having him around. Don't get me wrong, we've had tough times. Times when I thought I'd made the worst mistake of my life. But when I think about the alternative … scheduled visits to the strangers who were fostering or adopting him, not having a say in how he was raised, then I know I did the right thing."

Alice snuggled against his shoulder. "You did. And you seem to be doing great."

"Thank you." He kissed the top of her head. "Oh, I have news on the divorce. My cousin is preparing the paperwork. And you were right – he said Christine won't be too hard to find. He gave me a real lecture for not contacting him sooner. If I had, I'd be much further on."

"Well, you've started the process, and that's the main thing. It's not like you're in any rush to get married again."

"I wouldn't be too sure about that." He winked.

Alice turned her head away so that he wouldn't see her cheeks turning red. *Oh my God. Why did I mention marriage? I've never even thought about it, but is that what he wants? Does he want to marry me?* She composed herself and glanced at him out of the corner of her eye. He was taking a sip of coffee. Perhaps she was overthinking it, but she was delighted that his divorce was finally in motion, and was quietly optimistic about a normal-ish future which could very well include him and Sam, now that she had her drinking under control.

After an hour or so, Sam's friend left the park. Sam played by himself for a while longer then returned to the bench. He glanced at Alice's handbag, then whispered something in Bob's ear.

"Ask her yourself," Bob said.

Sam shook his head.

"Alice, Sam would like the cards, please. If that's OK?"

"Of course it is." She rummaged in her bag for the cards and offered them to him. "Here you go."

"Thank you," he mumbled. He tore off the wrapper and ran off to put it in the rubbish bin.

"He seems like a great kid."

"He can be, but don't let him fool you. He can be a little rascal sometimes too. He's on his best behaviour because he's been promised that we'll go to his favourite pizza place for dinner."

Sam arrived back at Bob's side just in time to hear the word 'pizza'. "Is Alice coming too?"

"I'm not sure. Would you like her to?"

Sam nodded.

"Would *she* like to?" Bob asked Alice.

She nodded too.

"Then let's go."

Alice and Bob walked hand in hand to his car while Sam scooted beside them. She laughed as Sam did his best to dodge the trees, and the other pedestrians, and sighed in happiness when Bob let go of her hand and slid his arm around her waist. Tamzin was right: this is what Saturday afternoons were all about, not hiding away in the gym.

When they got to the car, Bob put the scooter in the boot and strapped Sam into his seat. Before he opened the passenger door for Alice, he took her by the hand. "I hope you don't mind if we drop you home after pizza. I think you two should meet a few times before you become a regular visitor at the house."

"That's fine. I don't want to rush him."

"Although, if you wanted to come over about half nine, he should be fast asleep."

Alice winced. She hadn't particularly enjoyed sneaking out of his house the other morning; it brought back bad memories of the mornings after the nights before when she had gone home drunk with a total stranger. Although those mornings had been preferable to the ones where she had to pretend to be asleep in her own bed and wait for the guy to leave. Suddenly Saturday nights at the gym had regained their appeal.

"No, thank you. I had plans tonight anyway."

"The gym?"

"Maybe."

Chapter Ten

The weekend had been fantastic. Alice had great fun at the park, and Saturday evening at the pizza place went so well that Bob insisted they all do something on Sunday too. They went for a drive in the countryside and happened to find an open farm that was having a fun day. They fed and petted the animals, had lunch, and Alice and Sam got their faces painted while Bob watched in amusement. Alice felt a pang of sadness when they dropped her back to her flat and headed home without her, but she arrived home just as Cameron was leaving for Edinburgh, so she and Tamzin curled up on the sofa together and binge-watched the last few episodes of *Grey's Anatomy*.

Alice's first day of telesales at the Exchange was a complete disaster. She was provided with a script and a list of telephone numbers, and her job was to cold-call the people on the list and sell them insurance. It wasn't easy. It took eight calls before she even got past the first paragraph in her script. She'd had no idea, up until then, how rude some people could be.

By the end of the day she was nowhere near her sales target, but she didn't care. She wouldn't be back. At five o'clock she gathered her things and said goodbye to the few people she'd liked. They exchanged phone numbers, but Alice knew she'd soon be a distant memory. She stopped at Tina's office and popped her head through the door. "Hey, Tina. I don't think this is the job for me."

Tina nodded and gestured for Alice to take a seat.

"Tucker told me your tally. It's not unusual not to make a sale on your first day. Maybe you'll do better tomorrow."

"No, I won't. I quit. I'm sorry."

"Oh Alice, I don't want to lose you. Maybe insurance isn't your thing. How about tomorrow we move you over to the warranty team?"

Alice screwed up her face.

"No-fault accident claims?" Tina offered.

"I'm sorry. I'm disappointed too. But if you ever need a receptionist, or some accounting work comes up, give me a call."

"Of course."

"I don't have any plans this evening. Do you want to grab a quick glass of wine before we head home?"

"Sorry. I have a few things left to do here," Tina replied. "I'll give you a call in a week or so. We'll have a proper night out."

Alice left the Exchange feeling low. Her gaze darted across the road to the pub and she considered having one final drink there. But she decided against it when she remembered her promise to herself not to drink alone – and definitely not to drink when she was feeling low. But what to do? She didn't fancy going to the gym. Tamzin was at work and Bob was busy with Sam. OK, just one drink before I head home, she thought. At that very moment Bob's car pulled up beside her. He honked the horn to get her attention.

She climbed into the passenger seat. "What are you doing here?"

"I was wondering how your first day was going, then I realised I hadn't had you to myself in nearly a week. I asked Pauline to keep Sam a bit longer and I thought I would take you out for an early dinner. If you don't have plans, that is."

Suddenly she felt sick to her stomach. If he'd arrived thirty seconds later, he'd have seen her going into the bar, alone. *That was a close call.*

"Are you OK? You look pale all of a sudden. If you have plans, it's OK."

"I don't have plans and I'd love dinner. It's just that today didn't go too well. I quit."

"After one day?"

"I'd rather scrub toilets than sell anything over the phone."

He cocked his head at her. "Is that so? You know, I'm currently doing a handover clean of a new office building. I'm ordering temps by the dozen. First thing tomorrow, sign up with the agency I use and I'll put you on my preferred list."

She wanted to say no, but after her glib remark she didn't dare. "OK, but do I have to call you Mr McKendry while I'm at work?"

"No. Kristof is supervising the site; I won't even be there. Although I'd appreciate it if you didn't tell anyone we're dating. Not yet. I've only just told them about Christine."

She narrowed her eyes at him. "Are you sure you've told them?"

"I'm sure. And on second thoughts, I'll tell Kristof about us."

"Really?"

"Really. New me. No secrets." He started the car.

Alice winced as they passed the bar. *No secrets. I forgot about that.*

On Friday just before 5 p.m. Bob stopped off at the office handover clean under the pretence of assessing the progress of the job. But really it was so he could give Alice a lift home.

"I'm impressed that you've stuck at cleaning longer than you did at telesales."

"It wasn't too bad. You see dirt, you clean it. It's really therapeutic."

"Then maybe you should pay me. Want to come back again next week?"

She sighed. "No. I'm exhausted. And my nails are shot." She held up her hands to show him the chips in the polish.

"Ugh – put those away or you'll make me crash the car."

Bob pulled up outside her flat. He leant in to kiss her goodbye, but it got steamy and very handsy quite quickly. Alice pulled away and flashed him a sexy smile. "Do you want to come inside for a bit?"

"I'm sorry. I'm already going to be late to pick up Sam. He has to be at Burrito Burger by six for a friend's birthday party. But we do need some alone time together. Perhaps I could ask my mum to take him tomorrow night. I'm sure she wouldn't mind if I dropped him off at lunch and picked him up on Sunday evening. We could go away. Down to the coast, if you wanted."

"I thought you hated hotels."

"I do, but I need a change of scenery. I've never spent so much time at home – the walls feel like they're coming in on me. And I'm still a bit on edge that Christine's going to show up out of the blue."

"It's not really worth the bother, going away for just

126

one night. Tam left for Edinburgh this morning so I have the flat to myself. Why don't you come here?"

"That's a great idea. Can I ring my mum tonight and let you know?"

"Absolutely. Tell Sam I said hello, and hopefully I'll see you tomorrow." She jumped out of the car and waved him off.

The flat seemed empty without Tamzin, and it made her pine for Bob and Sam even more. There was nothing tasty in the fridge for dinner, so she strolled down to the Tesco Express on the corner. She was tired after all the cleaning, but she'd had a great couple of days. Kristof and the others were good fun to work with, and once they'd found out she was seeing Bob, they didn't hold back on sharing some funny stories about working with him over the years. The only downside was that there was no one to have a glass of wine with to unwind after work. She bypassed the frozen pizza and headed straight for the drinks aisle. One glass of wine wouldn't do any harm. She lifted the single-serve bottle. *What am I thinking?* She put it straight back down again. *Look at the price! It would be much better value to buy the full bottle. A full bottle? I couldn't. Could I? I'm in a good place emotionally. I wouldn't be drinking to drown my sorrows. I won't even drink it all.*

Innocently, she popped the bottle into her basket and went back for a pizza. She also threw in some chocolate and crisps. Movie night, she thought. She hadn't seen *Dirty Dancing* in ages, because Tamzin hated it. *I'll put the wine in the fridge to chill, then after dinner I'll pamper myself – a face mask and a soak in the bath with a cold glass of wine. I'll have one more while watching the film, and pour the rest down the sink. I'll hide the bottle at the bottom of the bin. Tam wouldn't understand.*

But after Alice had had one generous glass with her pizza, one in her bath, and another two while binge-eating treats during the film, there was nothing left to pour down the sink.

The next morning, Alice woke up with a headache. She trudged to the bathroom and examined herself in the mirror. *What was I thinking, drinking the whole bottle? It was silly to overdo it like that. I won't do it again.* Her hangover was tame compared to the ones she used to get; it was nothing that two paracetamol and a glass of water wouldn't cure. And she had plenty of time to recover before Bob was due. She busied herself with tidying the flat, changing her bedsheets, and making herself look stunning.

She was admiring herself in the mirror when she heard the front door open, and popped her head out into the hall to see Tamzin walk in through the door.

"What are you doing back?"

"I'd just walked into King's Cross when Cameron called to say he'd been summoned into work. Some disaster only he could fix. I wasn't going all the way up there to spend the weekend in his flat by myself, so I jumped on a different train and went to see Natalie." She braced herself.

"And how is *Natalie*?" Alice grumbled.

Natalie was Tamzin's second-best friend. They had met in sixth-form college and remained close. Alice and Natalie didn't get along, and could never understand what Tamzin liked about the other.

"She's good. She, Lionel and I went out and had a few drinks. I didn't think it was fair to come back here, so I slept on their sofa."

That was close! If Tamzin had come home, she would have found out about the wine. Alice promised herself she would never do it again – not in the flat, anyway.

Tamzin seemed to notice her unease. "I'm sorry. I haven't had a drink in ages. I just wanted to let my hair down."

I know exactly how you feel. "Never apologise to me for having a drink. And thank you for not coming home and rubbing it in my face."

The doorbell rang.

"That'll be Bob."

"Where are you going today?"

"We were going to stay in. I hope you don't mind." Alice opened the door. "Hey, handsome."

Bob stepped into the hall and looked startled to see Tamzin.

"I don't think you two have been properly introduced. Bob, this is Tamzin, and Tam, this is Bob."

"Nice to meet you." Bob nodded.

"You too. I've heard a lot about you..." Her gaze dropped to his crotch and didn't move. Alice whacked her on the arm.

Tamzin gave a wicked smile. "Don't worry, I'll confine myself to my room and put my earbuds in. Just act like I'm not here." She scurried off to her room and shut the door behind her.

"Sorry. She came home early."

"That's OK. Let's go to my house."

"But we're already here."

"I know, but I wanted us to be naked for most of the

day. And noisy…"

Her cheeks reddened. "You heard her; she's putting her earbuds in."

"Then she'd better have that music turned up really loud." He grabbed Alice's hand and dragged her to her bedroom. He set his bag onto the bed, took an envelope from it and offered it to her. "I hope we can settle out of court?"

Assuming it was something about his divorce, Alice took it cautiously. "What is this?"

"Compensation for the industrial injury you suffered on my building site."

She raised an eyebrow and opened the envelope, to reveal a voucher from a fancy nail bar for a deluxe manicure and gel polish. "I haven't had my nails done properly in ages. This is so sweet, thank you." She threw her arms around him.

"I'm a sweet guy."

"Hopefully not too sweet to let me do the things I like…" She licked her lips and dragged him to the bed.

Later that evening, Alice knocked on Tamzin's door. She waited but there was no answer. She inched the door open and popped her head in. Tamzin was sitting on the edge of her bed, painting her toenails. She still had her earbuds in. Alice crept over to her and plonked down beside her. She plucked the earbud from Tamzin's ear and whispered, "We're ordering dinner. Chinese. What do you want?"

"Um, that noodle thing I like. But with beef this time, not chicken. And a fat Coke. Just bring it in to me when it comes."

"No. You'll eat in the kitchen with us. We're going to

watch a film after and you're more than welcome to join us."

"Third wheel? No, thanks!"

"Come on. You make me be the third wheel with you and Cameron all the time. Please, I want you and Bob to get to know each other."

"Ugh, but I hate meeting new people."

Alice rolled her eyes. Tamzin was one of those people who made friends with everyone she met, and was always the life and soul of the party. Alice usually felt like her lady-in-waiting, just there to hold her coat. "Bob's OK."

"More than OK, from what I heard between songs. What the hell was he doing to you in there?"

Alice bit her lip and whispered, "Everything. He went down on me and I had my first orgasm before he'd even taken his trousers off. I never came like that with Dylan. His idea of foreplay was mumbling, 'Hey baby, look what I've got for you' before he mounted me." She giggled. "I had no idea sex could be this satisfying. Or adventurous. Bob's had me in positions I've never even dreamed of. Even though it might sound dirty, it's really intimate and tender. It feels like more than just sex. Does that mean I'm in love with him? I think I might be."

Tamzin sighed. "Sex isn't love, girl."

"I know that! And believe me, this is the last thing I expected to happen. I never imagined I'd ever feel this way about anyone again. It's terrifying."

"Please tell me you haven't told him."

"Eh, no. It's far too soon."

"Good girl. Just play it cool. And be careful — I couldn't bear to see you get hurt again."

"Fuck. Neither could I. That's why I wasn't keen to date, but what's the alternative? Spending the rest of my life on my own is pretty terrifying too. I loved being married, having someone special. Being someone's someone special. I don't know if Bob and I will go the distance, but things are going really well with him and Sam. I think this is the happiest I've ever been."

"What happened to playing it cool, bunny boiler?"

"Hey!"

"I'm kidding. I'm glad you're happy. And as long as you don't drink again, everything will fall into place for you."

Alice gave Tamzin a hug. She felt guilty keeping her recent drinking a secret, but it was for a good cause. Everyone was going to be so happy when she told them she wasn't an alcoholic any more.

Alice laid all the food out on the kitchen table and called to Tamzin, who hurried into the kitchen and took the seat next to Bob. She nudged him. "I like your car. Most men buy flash motors like that because they're compensating for something, but Alice tells me that's not the case. Good for you. Any chance I could get a test drive? Of the car, not your cock."

Bob's eyes widened.

Alice put her hands over her eyes. "I apologise for my friend, Bob. She has no filter. At all."

Bob laughed and spooned some food onto his plate.

Tamzin nudged him again. "What's that, kung po? Do you mind if I try some?" Without waiting for an answer, she helped herself to a forkful from his plate. "Ugh, that is delish." She took a second forkful.

Alice giggled. "Sorry. We don't stand on ceremony in this house."

"And food isn't the only thing we share..." Tamzin made eyes at Bob, making him drop his fork.

"She's kidding."

"Of course I am. I'd never let Alice sleep with Cameron. She's so smoking hot, I'd never get him back."

"She certainly is." Bob smiled and held Alice's eye as he reached over the table for her hand. He drew her palm up to cup his cheek, then kissed her exposed wrist.

Tamzin clapped her hands. "Public displays of affection. Love it! I'll stop messing with you, Bob. You now have my official approval. Just don't hurt my best friend; you wouldn't like what I'd do to that *car* of yours."

Bob winced. "So, Alice tells me you're getting married soon. You must be excited."

"I can't wait. Six months and counting. And I don't mean to put any pressure on you two, but Alice, if you want a plus one, you'd better tell me before we start on the table plans. You'll be at the top table with me, but I suppose I could put Bob at a table with Natalie, Lionel and the best man's wife."

Alice glanced sidelong at Bob to judge his reaction to making plans so far into the future. He didn't seem to react. *That's a good sign.* She tried not to blush. "Plus one? Don't forget I've got *two* men in my life now."

"Of course! Sam is welcome too. Oh..." Tamzin clapped her hands again. "I could get him a little tux. He could walk down the aisle with Cameron's nieces. It'll be so cute."

"Sorry, Tamzin," Bob interrupted.

Alice braced herself, thinking that Bob was about to decline the invitation altogether.

"While I'd love to come to your wedding, I think I'll

leave Sam with my mum. He wouldn't know anybody – he'd be bored."

"Aw!" Tamzin pouted.

Alice tried to subdue her grin.

"And what are the plans for the big hen night?" Bob asked.

Alice's grin faded when Tamzin glared at her.

"What?" He frowned. "They're still a thing, right?"

"It's a bit of a sore point, Bob," Tamzin snapped. "We're going to a fancy hotel for spa treatments and dinner, then heading out clubbing and finishing off with breakfast the next morning. But Alice is refusing to come. Can you believe that? My maid of honour won't come to my hen night?"

"We talked about this. I'm upset too, but I really don't think I could handle it. All those girls partying, drinking – temptation would be everywhere. And I don't want the other girls feeling awkward around me, afraid to enjoy themselves. You know I'll do anything for you on your wedding day. But the hen night, I'm sorry. You'll have much more fun without me."

"Lucie won't be drinking either. You can chum around with her."

"Are you insane? You think I want to spend all night talking babies with a pregnant woman? That would drive me to drink."

Tamzin's Coke fizzed in the sudden silence. Bob looked between the friends, who were both pushing food around their plates.

"Um, maybe I could come?"

They glared at him.

"Usually where there's a spa, there's a golf course."

Tamzin cocked her eyebrow. "There is..."

"I'm well overdue a bit of 'me time'. I haven't set foot on a golf course since Sam came to live with me. I'll play some golf while you girls do your spa thing, I'll get room service while you do dinner, then when the rest of you go off clubbing, I'll keep Alice entertained. Then in the morning, I'll take breakfast in bed while Alice can join you all downstairs, totally smug while you girls nurse your hangovers. You can fill her in on what she missed."

Tamzin looked at Alice and shrugged. "It's a compromise."

"It could work," Alice said, then turned to Bob. "Would you do that for me?"

"Of course. You can't miss your best friend's hen. You can still be a part of it, while maintaining a reasonable distance from the booze."

"That's a really kind thought, Bob, thank you." Tamzin winked at him then turned to Alice. "I'm really starting to like him."

Bob blushed. "Don't get too excited just yet. It depends if my mum can take Sam."

Later that night Alice and Bob lay in bed, breathless and entwined in each other's arms.

"How do you do that to me?" She sighed.

"It's not entirely selfless. I really enjoy pleasuring you."

"And not just in the bedroom. Your idea for the hen night was amazing. There's no way I could have gone otherwise. And I haven't told Tam, but I'm dreading the wedding too. They're getting married in the church where Dylan and I got married. She's asked me to do a reading, and as if that wasn't bad enough, her dad's asked me to say a few words during the speeches too. Then there's the evening do – and you know how much people usually drink at those things. It's going to be really tough, so it will be good to have you there for moral support. But it's still a few months away – are you sure you want to commit that far into the future?"

He sat up and frowned at her. "I was. But it sounds like you're having doubts."

"No. I just..." She thought back to her earlier conversation with Tamzin. Alice had promised not to confuse the amazing sex she'd been having with actual love; she thought she was already in love with Bob. She wanted to make plans for her future, and she wanted those plans to include him – and Sam. Bob had practically just told her that he was on the same page, so it was probably the right time to have *that* conversation.

Alice looked up at him. "We haven't properly talked about where this relationship is going. I don't want to sound too forward, but—"

"I love you, Alice."

She drew a sharp breath. She'd only ever heard those words from Dylan, and imagined they might sound strange coming from someone else. But they didn't sound strange, they sounded perfect. She reached up, slid her hand around the back of his neck and pulled him closer to her. "I love you too," she whispered as their lips met for a tender kiss.

Bob lay back down and pulled Alice into an embrace. She sighed with happiness. Everything was coming together. All she needed to do now was to get back to her career and life would be normal again. She snuggled against Bob's bare chest and thought about what they should do together tomorrow. After her early AA meeting, they had the rest of the day to spend together, as Bob didn't have to collect Sam until after dinner. *But Bob hasn't mentioned the AA meeting. I'll skip it. Find one on Monday.*

Chapter Eleven

Alice didn't attend an AA meeting on Monday, or any day that week. On her way home from work on Friday she stopped at the shop to buy provisions for a picnic that she'd planned with Bob and Sam the next day. Ham, cheese, bread rolls, crisps and a large bar of chocolate for them all to share. Then she thought about drinks. Tamzin had a flask and picnic mugs she could use for coffee for her and Bob, but she'd have to buy juice for Sam. As she added a carton of juice to her basket, she thought about getting herself a bottle of wine again. Tamzin had left for Edinburgh that morning – for real this time – and Alice thought she could do the same as last time: a bottle spread out over the evening with bath and a movie. Two paracetamol and a pint of water the next morning and she'd be right as rain for the picnic. Alice went to the drinks aisle and selected a nice bottle of Chablis. But as she popped it into her basket, she remembered how disappointed she had been last time when the bottle was empty. She'd only had four drinks. She reached for a second bottle, then froze. *I can't buy and drink two bottles of wine. That's ridiculous.* She took the wine out of her basket, put it back on the shelf and went over to the spirits section. *I'll buy a half-bottle of gin, have a few generous measures, then throw the rest away.* She had her hand on a half-bottle when she remembered that Tamzin would be away for two nights. She chose a litre bottle and headed off to find the tonic.

The next day, despite Alice's hangover – which she disguised as a run of the mill headache – the picnic was a huge success and they had a great day. Alice wasn't as upset as she had been previously when Bob dropped her back to an empty flat, because she knew what was waiting for her in the fridge. And because Bob and Sam were spending Sunday at Bob's parents and Tamzin wouldn't be back until late, she'd have the luxury of sleeping off her hangover in peace.

Over the next two months, Alice continued to drink whenever she had the opportunity to do so. She accepted every invitation to lunchtime or after-work drinks with people from her various temping jobs. She only ever had one or two and kept a supply of chewing gum and paracetamol in her handbag. She even started to sneak bottles of gin and tonic into her room and would head off to bed early the odd night to enjoy a few drinks. She convinced herself there was no harm in this, as she rarely drank enough to have a proper hangover, and when she was out with Bob and Sam, she didn't miss drinking or hurry home in order to do so.

They did fun things, like visit the zoo and the cinema, and going for ice cream, and a few normal things, like grocery shopping or taking Sam to get his hair cut. Bob and Sam went to Alice's flat for dinner and Sam met Tamzin, who spoiled him rotten. In return, Alice went to Bob's for dinner and was pleasantly surprised to find out that he was quite accomplished in the kitchen. Over the years his friend Jack had furnished him with several delicious, yet relatively simple, recipes. The bond between Alice and Sam grew stronger each time they met, and Alice and Bob had soon decided that they were sufficiently comfortable with each other for Alice to begin staying overnight at Bob's house.

One Saturday, she arrived just after lunch with a brand-new packet of Uno cards. She taught the boys how to play. Sam needed help to remember the rules, so Alice joined forces with him. They wiped the floor with Bob until dinner time. Then, after a delicious dinner, which Alice and Bob enjoyed cooking together, they relaxed on the sofa to watch a movie. Alice was beside herself with joy when Sam demanded that he sit beside her so he could snuggle up against her. She sat between him and Bob, feeling more content than she'd ever been. But all too quickly the movie was over and Bob announced it was Sam's bedtime. Reluctantly Sam got up from the sofa and glanced between Bob and Alice. "Uncle Robert, can Alice put me to bed?"

Bob looked over at Alice, who winked at him then turned to Sam. "Only if I get to pick the story."

Sam's eyes lit up. "Uncle Robert never reads me a story."

Alice gasped and threw Bob a stern look. "Then thank goodness I'm here. Come on, show me what books you have." She waited while Sam gave Bob a hug, then took Sam upstairs to brush his teeth.

Alice grimaced when she saw Sam's bedroom. There were plenty of toys, teddies and books, but the room itself was far from ideal. There was a double bed, with flowery patterned sheets, and the walls were lined with designer paper. Sam had already grabbed a book and jumped into bed, and could hardly be seen amid the mass of pillows. Alice perched on the bed and started to read. She made up funny voices for the different characters, like she usually did when she put her nieces or nephew to bed. Unlike them, Sam didn't interrupt with questions, but quietly hung on her every word.

Enjoying it as much as Sam seemed to be, Alice drew out the story to make it last as long as she could. His eyelids were heavy when she finally finished. She planted a kiss on his forehead as she tucked the covers tightly around him. "Goodnight, sweetie," she whispered and crept out of the room.

When Alice returned to the living room, she gave Bob a stern look.

"What happened?" he asked.

"Nothing. He's settled down to sleep like a little angel. But you have to do something about his bedroom."

"What's wrong with his bedroom?"

"You've obviously just shoved him in the guest room. You need to decorate it appropriately. A young boy needs rocket ships or trains on his wall, not Laura Ashley wallpaper."

"It never even occurred to me. What do we need?"

"New wallpaper. New bed – or new sheets at the very least. Perhaps a desk and chair. And a proper bookshelf. Oh, and some..." She noticed Bob was smirking. "What?"

"Nothing. It's just nice to see you so excited about decorating his room. He will be too. And not just because he'll be getting new stuff. He really likes you."

She plonked herself down onto the sofa. "And I think he's amazing. Despite what he's been through, he always seems so happy. My heart melts every time I see his smiley face."

"He's not always smiling, though. You haven't seen one yet, but he still has bad days. And nights. If he wakes one night when you're here, don't worry. Just stay in bed. I'll take care of him."

Alice sighed at the thought of all Sam had been through in his short life, and hoped that one day he'd let her take care of him too.

Bob leant in and kissed her. "I love you. You're doing great. He talks about you all the time. He was so excited you were coming today. And how about we all go out tomorrow and get some paint? I don't really fancy stripping walls."

"Um, OK. I was going to take off after lunch because I have an application form to fill in, but I guess I could stick around a while longer."

"Application form?"

"For a real job. I'm ready to get back to being an actuary again, but I'm struggling with how to explain the gap in my employment last year."

"Say you took some time off to 'find yourself' – employers love that bullshit. And technically it's not lying. But why are you applying for a job? I thought you were happy temping."

"I am, but it's mostly minimum wage. In my last proper job, I was earning £49,000 and had the potential to earn much more. I need to earn that sort of money again. Tam's getting married in October, and Cameron's secondment to Edinburgh ends not long after the wedding. He'll be moving back full-time and they can't start their married life with me there."

"Why don't you move in here?"

"Are you crazy? It's far too soon."

"No, it isn't. I love you. Sam adores you. It's been great today, the three of us just hanging around the house."

"But Dylan and I were together for almost six years before we moved in together."

"And look how that turned out..."

She threw him a dirty look.

He held up his hands. "I'm sorry. I'm not familiar with the official moving-in together guidelines."

"There aren't any."

"Exactly. Because you do it when it feels right. October's ... four months away. That's plenty of time. Spend a few weekends here, then we'll progress to a few nights during the week. Move your stuff in gradually and it won't seem like such a big deal."

She shrugged. "I'll think about it."

"That'll do."

She snuggled down onto the sofa beside him. It wasn't long until his hand was on her thigh, caressing her. "Now, can I tell you what I'm thinking about?"

"Oh, I can guess." She smirked. "You'll have to hold that thought until we're sure that Sam is fast asleep. But don't worry, you know it'll be worth the wait..."

Chapter Twelve

The next morning while Bob made breakfast, Alice and Sam snuggled on the sofa watching *Paw Patrol*. Sam was explaining the roles of each of the pups when the living-room door opened and a woman walked in and stood right in front of the TV.

Alice stared at the tall, blonde, good-looking, well-dressed woman, then looked down at her fleecy unicorn pyjamas. *Why couldn't I still be wearing that black satin two-piece I slipped into last night after Sam went to bed?*

Sam snuggled against her, which prompted her to sit up straight and take charge of the situation. "You must be Christine," she said in her most polite receptionist voice.

"And you must be the babysitter." Christine sighed. "Sam, dear, where is Uncle Robert?"

Sam didn't speak, but his grip on Alice's arm tightened.

Alice ruffled his hair. "Sweetie, why don't you go upstairs and get dressed. I'll be up in a minute."

He jumped up from the sofa and headed for the door, avoiding eye contact with Christine on the way past.

"Uncle Robert is in the kitchen." Alice pointed the way.

"I know where the kitchen is, dear. This is *my* house." She turned on her heel and headed for the kitchen.

Alice leapt up off the sofa and followed her, in a futile effort to warm Bob about his visitor.

"Hello, Robert," Christine cooed, marching into the kitchen.

Alice got to the door just in time to see Bob's coffee cup slide out of his hand and smash on the floor.

"What are you doing here?"

"In my own home?" She turned and glared at Alice. "Some privacy, please."

Alice nodded. "I'll leave you both to it."

"You don't have to go," Bob said.

But I really want to, Alice thought. "I'll check on Sam." She hurried out of the kitchen and went upstairs. She stopped at the top and tried to catch her breath. *That was embarrassing. I feel like I've been caught in the act. Although it was nice of Bob to suggest that I didn't have to leave the room. Whether he likes it or not, Christine is his wife and the house is still half hers. I don't want to be involved in their divorce.* She went into Bob's bedroom and quickly changed into jeans and a hoodie. When she came back out into the hall, she could hear shouting coming from the kitchen. She hurried into Sam's bedroom and closed the door behind her.

He was sitting on the floor, a toy car in each hand. But he wasn't playing; he was just staring into space. Alice crept over and sat on the floor next to him. "Can I play?"

He dropped the cars and turned to her. "Is Auntie Christine going to make you leave and send me back to Granny's?"

Alice wanted to weep for the poor little soul – and for herself and Bob. *We've all been through so much – why can't life just let us be?* She pulled Sam into an embrace and planted a kiss on his forehead. "No, sweetie. Auntie Christine just came back to talk to your Uncle Robert for a few minutes. You're not going

145

anywhere, and I'll still be coming to see you. All the time."

"Promise?" he whispered.

Alice began to rock him back and forth. "I promise, sweetie," she murmured.

After a few minutes Alice crept over to the door and eased it open. There was silence. She turned and smiled at Sam. "I'll be right back." She went into the hall. Just as she closed the door behind her, Bob came up the stairs, Christine in tow.

He pointed to the third bedroom. "Your stuff's in there. Boxed for your convenience. You can have your solicitor talk to my solicitor about everything else."

"I've just found out that my husband is committing adultery. I've got everything I need."

"You expect me to believe you've been faithful to our wedding vows all this time?"

"Ah, but can you prove it?" She looked Alice up and down. "Robert, darling, I thought I'd drummed a bit of culture into you. She's homely, but could you not have done any better?"

"Just get your stuff and get the hell out of my house!" Bob yelled.

"It's my house too!" Christine yelled back.

"Bob!" Alice snapped. She pointed at Sam's bedroom door. "Little ears..."

"Bob?" Christine scoffed. "You hate when people call you Bob."

"No, *you* hate when people call me Bob. We like it."

Christine turned and glared at Alice. "Be careful, dear. You might think you're sitting pretty here, but he'll screw you over one day too. Just like he's trying to do to me. He did it to Peter, his first business partner.

He even screwed over his own dead sister."

Alice's jaw dropped.

Bob groaned.

"Don't say I didn't warn you." Christine stormed into the third bedroom. Bob shrugged at Alice and followed Christine. Alice went back into Sam's room and resolved to stay there until she could be sure Christine had gone.

When Alice heard the front door close and a car drive away, she knew the coast was clear. She asked Sam to get dressed, brush his teeth and meet her in the kitchen in five minutes. She crept downstairs to find Bob on the sofa, his head in his hands. She went to him and put her arms around him. He was shaking. "Are you OK?"

"I'm either going to lose my house – or my business. I can't afford to buy her out of both." He raised his head and looked her in the eye.

She'd never seen him look so vulnerable, and wished there was something she could do to help. But she was broke. She'd got half of the marital assets in her own divorce, but she soon burned through it after she lost her job. And earning minimum wage meant there wasn't much left after rent, her gym membership and paying for her mobile phone. Perhaps there was some way she could help Bob with the business – make some savings or move some money around. As successful as he seemed to be, he didn't have any formal financial or business training. She had a long list of accountancy qualifications, a master's degree in Actuarial Science, and an MBA. Usually she didn't like to talk about her academic achievements; some people made fun of her for being so smart. Even her ex-husband had been intimidated when she passed her second master's degree with distinction.

"Why don't I come with you to work tomorrow? Let me see what we have to play with before solicitors get involved."

"You mean, like cook up a new set of books?"

"No. Nothing illegal. Just to get an idea of what sort of money there is in the business. See if there's enough to make Christine a decent offer."

"What about work? And don't you have that application form to do?"

She frowned. Yes, she did need to earn a wage, but there was nothing to say it couldn't come from Bob's business. "Hmm, how about you hire me on a consultancy basis?"

"Can I afford you?"

"I'll take minimum wage plus one pound per hour, and there can be some benefits in kind that we don't have to declare to the tax man..." She narrowed her eyes at him. "But I need to know two things first. What Christine said about you screwing over your business partner, and the other thing... Is that as horrific as it sounded?"

"When I told you that Christine and I had branched out into other types of cleaning, that wasn't entirely true. We needed work to keep us going until I lined up some new business. I knew the clients – I'd wooed them in the first place. I knew how Peter priced the jobs, so I undercut him. Stole the contracts right out from under him. It wasn't personal; it was just business."

It was unscrupulous. But things like that happen in business all the time. It wasn't *that* despicable.

"And the thing about my sister." He hung his head, looking ashamed. "Christine and I had sex at the wake after her funeral. We got bored making small talk with family and sloped off to create our own entertainment."

She smacked him on the arm, horrified. "How could you?"

"I wasn't the same man back then. I was selfish. Christine and I didn't care about anyone but ourselves. Rebecca's death didn't really hit me until a few days after the funeral, when I saw how exhausted my mum was. I knew I needed to do something. And I've changed since then. I've tried really hard to be a better person, to be a good role model. If you can see past the despicable man I used to be, I'll show you what a good man I can be."

"I can already see a good man." She leant in to kiss him, but he pulled away. "What's wrong?"

"Christine wasn't happy about you being here. You heard her – adultery. She's probably going to try to twist things, implicate you in our divorce."

Alice sighed. It wasn't ideal, but she was sure she could handle it. "Let's just look on the bright side. Adultery gets you a quicker divorce. But call your cousin tomorrow and talk it through." She planted a kiss on his lips. "Now, stop moping. You promised Sam and me breakfast. Afterwards, we're going shopping for new things for his bedroom. Let's put your credit card through its paces. After all, Christine can't get half of what's already been spent."

On Monday morning Alice phoned her temping agency and told them she wouldn't be available until further notice. She intended to spend at least a few weeks making herself familiar with Bob's business and accounts. After dropping Sam off at Pauline's, Bob drove them to his office at the Meridian Trading Estate, just south of the Thames. Alice winced as they pulled up at the back of a dreary-looking building. Maybe it was because it was a rainy June day, but the place looked depressing as hell. The large roller-shutter door was open, revealing an open space bustling with activity. Alice recognised a few faces among the chaos. Kristof was giving out orders to a group of people, while others were hurrying around gathering supplies and equipment and packing them into the six Christine Cleans vans. Bob greeted a few people as he led Alice in.

"This is the yard," he said proudly. Alice looked around at the piles of equipment, machinery, boxes of cleaning supplies and PPE. The walls were plastered with health and safety notices. Nothing looked organised.

Then he led her through another door into an open-plan office. There were a few desks littered with paperwork, more noticeboards and a reception desk, behind which sat an older lady. Bob ushered Alice over to meet her. "Miriam, this is Alice."

Miriam looked between Alice and Bob and raised her eyebrows.

Bob blushed, "Yes, that Alice. But she's here as a consultant for a temporary project. And Alice, this is Miriam – she's the real boss around here." He winked.

Miriam's cheeks reddened. "Nice to meet you."

"You too," Alice said with a smile.

Bob pointed to a door in the corner. "That's my office. I'll get you settled, then make some coffee. Want one?" he asked Miriam.

She held up a cup. "Just got one."

Bob nodded, then led the way into his office. Alice's

eyes widened when she saw the piles of paperwork surrounding the computer, the empty Coke can, the plate with crumbs, and three unfinished cups of coffee. She swallowed. "Please tell me there's order to this ... chaos."

"Of course there is."

She rolled her eyes as she sat down behind his desk and pretended to crack her knuckles. She pointed to his computer. "Fire it up." She made a point of looking away as he keyed his password into the PC. "First things first. Is Christine Cleans a partnership or a limited company?"

"Neither. I'm a sole trader."

"Sole trader? And Christine, she's..."

"An employee."

Alice gawped at him. "You two don't have a formal business arrangement?"

"No. Didn't think it was necessary. Is that a bad thing?"

"Yeah, for Christine. Where do you keep your P45s?"

He squinted at her.

"Unfortunately, you're going to have to let her go."

"I can't do that."

"Of course you can. She hasn't turned up to work in over a year. At the very least you should start the disciplinary process, then let her go. Now that that's settled, I'm going to check out your accounts, see what you have in the way of assets so I can get a better idea of what the business is worth. Who looks after the money here?"

"Me, for the day-to-day things. I have an accountant for tax returns and pensions. You know ... even though I've googled it, I still don't know what actuaries do. But I didn't think it was this kind of stuff."

"It's not. But accounting isn't complicated."

He hung his head.

"I'm sorry. This is bread and butter to me. Just get me your ledgers and show me the files I'll need on the computer and let me see what I have to work with. And I'll need to see your personal finances too, at some point. Current accounts, savings, investments."

He winced.

"What? Last night you were asking me to move in with you, and today you won't even show me your bank statements?"

"Only if you show me yours." He perched on the desk next to her and ran his hand down her cheek, but she shooed him away.

"This is a place of business. Just go about your day as if I'm not here."

"I'll be in the yard if you need me." He gave her a peck on the cheek and left her alone in the office.

Alice had been working for about an hour when there was a knock at the door. "Come in," she called.

Miriam opened the door. "Robert asked me to tell you that he had to take some supplies out to site, and then he's got a quote in Basingstoke, so he won't be back until after lunch. He'll bring you a sandwich."

"OK. Thank you." Alice turned back to the computer, but Miriam lingered at the door. "Is everything OK?"

"I know it's none of my business, but you and Robert – I think it's lovely. He told everyone about the divorce a few weeks ago, but I already knew. You don't work for someone for nearly ten years without getting to know their habits. He was acting differently, very quiet, spending lots of time with his nephew. And there was no sign of *her*; she always used to be swanning in to show off whatever new coat or bag she'd just bought. Made us call her Mrs McKendry, as if she'd forgotten she used to work with us. Honestly, I don't know how he ever put up with her. You should have heard the way she spoke to him sometimes. As if he was her employee. She walked all over him. It was an odd marriage."

Alice winced. Bob had told her that everyone probably thought he was a pushover; seems he was right.

"I'm sorry. I'm speaking out of turn. All I wanted to say was that no one's loyal to Christine here. We're all very fond of Robert. He's not always been the easiest man to work for, but since he turned forty he's been like a different man. Much more laid-back. He's actually taking weekends off and he's given more autonomy to Kristof and the other supervisors. It's nice to see. I wondered if he'd met someone." She beamed at Alice. "I'll get you some coffee." She hurried out of the office and closed the door behind her.

Alice sat back in her chair and thought about the day before. Bob had been quite firm with Christine. He wasn't a pushover; he just had a way about him. He didn't make a fuss where it wasn't warranted, and he didn't dwell on things or linger on the past. *That's probably a good thing, because if he thinks too much about my past, he might change his mind about being with me.*

*

Alice spent the next few days making herself familiar with the business. She made a few notes about how it could be restructured to make it more efficient, and there were a few financial loopholes that Bob's accountant wasn't taking full advantage of. Totally legal ones, of course. She was going to get stuck into every aspect of the business, and had found ways to involve Miriam and give her more responsibility. Her initial idea for a subtle rebrand went down a storm with Bob and Kristof, who both much preferred the name Pristine Cleans. She knew she would have to drum it into everyone that none of these changes would take effect until after the divorce was settled. Bob's business was doing well, but with Alice's plans and a lot of hard work, it would do even better.

Alice loved spending the days with Bob and the others at the office. Every night after work he drove her home before picking up Sam. She spent her evenings either at the gym or lounging around with Tamzin, but she finished most days with a few drinks alone in her room. She felt a little guilty at first, as she had promised herself that she'd never drink alone. But she reasoned that plenty of people drink when they're by themselves – like a glass of wine while having a bath, for example – and that didn't mean they had a problem. Plus, she wasn't using alcohol in a negative way to drown her sorrows; it was a treat, a reward for a hard day's work.

Just before lunch on Friday, Bob returned back from site with gourmet coffee and doughnuts for Miriam and Patsy, who was doing her weekly clean and tidy of the office and the yard. Bob brought an Americano and an apple turnover in to Alice. He set them on the desk then stood behind her chair and massaged her shoulders. "How's your head now?"

Alice rubbed her temples. She'd got good at knowing

just how much to drink so that she would wake up without a hangover, but she'd overdone it the night before and couldn't hide her heavy eyes or shake her lingering headache. "All better." She forced a smile.

"Good." He kissed the top of her head, then pulled up a chair to the other side of the desk. "Do you think we'll get out of here early tonight, boss?"

She didn't look up but nodded.

"Because Sam's been asking about you all week. I thought we could get a takeaway, a movie, then have an early night. And not just for Sam..." He raised his eyebrows at her, but she didn't even look up. "Earth to Alice."

She finally looked up. "Sorry. Yes, that sounds good."

"You really love that stuff, don't you?"

"Yeah. It's a shame your accountant doesn't. Where'd you hire that hack? I've spent all morning correcting his careless mistakes. You're losing a ton of money on the expenses he isn't claiming. And he really should have advised you to incorporate years ago – it's much more tax-efficient. Put him on notice, tell him you're bringing everything in-house."

"In-house? You can do that stuff?"

"No offence, but this is hardly a multinational corporation. But I'll show you my qualifications and I can get you some glowing references, if you want." She stuck her tongue out at him. "Once I'm done with this, I'm going to need your last mortgage statement. I need to find out how much equity there is in the house – maybe we can make Christine an offer using that as collateral. I don't want you to worry about the minutiae. Just give me the information I ask for and I'll steer you right. After all, I'm going to need that roof over my head too."

"What?"

She giggled. He'd often told her how he'd changed for the better since he'd met her, but it was nice to have that reaffirmed by Miriam and some of the others who had known him a lot longer than she had. Spending the week at the office had given her the confidence to make the decision to move in with him. Although she knew that if she did, she wouldn't be able to continue her night-time drinking. It wouldn't be a problem to stop, but she'd wait until closer to Tamzin's wedding to give it up.

"I've decided to move in with you. But gradually, like you suggested. See how we go."

"This calls for a toast." He held up his paper coffee cup. Before Alice could lift hers to clink against it, he set it back down again. "Um, if you're going to be moving in with us, it's probably time to introduce you to my parents."

His parents? An image of Dylan's parents flashed before her eyes. She'd had a great relationship with them. Well, until the divorce. The chance that she'd get that lucky twice was low. "Is that really necessary?"

"Yes. Sam's been telling them about you, and they're dying to meet you."

She bit her lip.

"What?"

"How do you think they'll react when you tell them I'm a recovering alcoholic? Unless you've told them already?"

"No, I haven't. And I was thinking of not telling them."

She sighed. "Which is it? You're ashamed of me, or you think they won't approve?"

"I think ... they're of an older generation, and not as open to things as they should be. Plus, it's none of their business."

"It becomes their business when I move in with their grandson. I think you should tell them."

"Maybe not straight away."

That Sunday they arrived at Bob's parents' house for dinner. Alice did a final check of her hair and make-up before getting out of the car. Her stomach was doing somersaults, but she tried to pull herself together. *You're nearly thirty-three. You shouldn't be nervous meeting other grown-ups.*

Bob took her hand and led her to the front door. "They're going to love you." He had barely opened the door when Sam pushed in front of them and ran in. They followed him to the living room just in time to see him bounce onto the sofa beside Bob's father, who pulled him into an embrace without taking his eyes off the TV.

"Dad, this is Alice."

There was no answer.

"Alice, this is my dad, Robert. And it seems he hasn't got his hearing aid turned on."

"He never does, Robert." His mother sighed as she entered the room. She was a short, thin woman with flushed cheeks. She made a beeline for Alice and held out her hand. "You must be Alice. I'm Peggy." She gestured to her apron. "I usually make more of an effort with my appearance, but I only found out you were coming about twenty minutes ago via text. Robert, you could have warned us that you were bringing Alice today."

"You look great, Mum." He kissed her on the cheek.

Alice shook Peggy's hand and they both glared at Bob.

"I apologise for my son. You'd think he was a teenager, the way he behaves sometimes. What if I hadn't made enough food? I'd have been embarrassed."

"You always make enough to feed an army."

"I'm sorry, Alice. Not much of a welcome for you. It's no trouble to set another place at the table."

"It's OK. Alice can have Sam's place. Sam, you can eat in the living room. Adult chat is boring."

"Thanks, Uncle Robert." He grinned.

"I hope you don't let him eat in front of the TV every day."

"Not every day, Mum. But sometimes at the weekend."

"Well, dinner's almost ready, so let's go through." She went over to the sofa and kissed Sam on the top of the head, then whacked her husband on the arm. "Dinner. Now. And turn your bloody hearing aid on."

Peggy ushered Alice into the kitchen and pointed to where she was supposed to sit.

As Alice sat down, Robert senior made his way slowly into the kitchen. He was tall and frail-looking. Bob had told Alice that he'd been quite ill. He sat down and looked directly at Alice. He screwed up his face. "Christine, what on earth have you done with your hair?"

"Robert!" Peggy snapped. "It's Alice. Robert's new girlfriend."

"Oh yes, now I remember. I'm sorry, Alice. My son brings so many women to dinner that it's hard to keep track." He winked at her and she giggled.

Peggy reached over and took the child's beaker away from Alice's place setting and put a wine glass in its place. Then Alice noticed the glasses of red wine in front of Robert senior and the other place setting.

Peggy picked up a bottle of wine from the sideboard and held it out for Alice's approval. "I hope red is OK. We don't have any white."

Alice threw Bob her best 'I'm going to kill you' look.

He held up his hand. "No wine for us, Mum. We're on a detox."

"Top me off, would you, Peg?" Robert held up his glass.

Bob frowned at him. "You should detox too. You shouldn't drink so much."

"I've had a double bypass, son. I doubt a few glasses of red are going to see me off. If you prefer white, Alice, Peg'll get some for the next time you come."

"Please don't put yourselves out."

"It's no bother, my dear," Peggy assured her.

"I don't drink at all."

"Are you Mormon?" Peggy enquired, then her eyes lit up. "Or are you pregnant?"

Alice groaned. Unfortunately, that was the most common assumption made about her sobriety, and the one that hurt the most.

"Mum!" Bob snapped. "Why the hell would you say that?"

"Why else wouldn't she be drinking?"

Alice couldn't put up with it any longer. It was bad enough having to sit and watch other people drink; it would be impossible to keep up the pretence that she didn't drink in the long term. They needed to know. She took a deep breath and went for it. "Actually, Peggy, I'm a recovering alcoholic."

Peggy's jaw dropped. "I'm so sorry, Alice. I'll put this away." She grabbed her own wine glass, set it to the side and glared at Bob. "Robert, you could have told us. I'm completely embarrassed." She hurried over to Robert senior, who was about to take a sip. He tried hard to stop her taking his glass away, but failed.

"I didn't think you were going to try and force wine down her throat, Mum. But it's OK, you two can have a glass of wine with your meal. I'll get Alice and me some of Sam's cordial." He squeezed Alice's shoulder on his way past to get the juice. Then he handed his father back his glass.

Robert senior was more than pleased to get his wine back. He took a large gulp while looking at Alice. "You don't look like an alcoholic."

"Dad!" Bob scolded. "What a thing to say. What's an alcoholic *supposed* to look like?"

He shrugged.

"Well, a little less like the lovely Alice here, and a little more like that." Peggy pointed to Robert senior, who had already sunk half the glass.

Alice wanted the ground to swallow her up. *How could he not have told them? I've only been here ten minutes and I've been mortified twice.*

Thankfully Peggy seemed to notice Alice's embarrassment and changed the subject. "So, Alice, what do you do for a living?"

"I'm an actuary."

"That's fascinating!" Robert senior declared. "My cousin's daughter married an actuary..." He took another sip of wine.

Alice sat forward to hear the rest of the story, but that was it.

Bob tried to fill the silence. "Alice is working for me at the minute. Helping me get the business in order for the divorce."

"Sleeping with your employees again, son?" Robert gave him a thumbs-up.

Alice groaned.

"I'm sorry about my dad, Alice. He ... er ... well, we think his brain got starved of oxygen after his heart attack." He tapped on his temple. "Not much of a filter there, I'm afraid. No, Dad, it's not like that. We met before she worked for me. But as soon as I found out how good she was, I had to have her." He smiled at Alice.

"The divorce is finally happening?" Peggy breathed a sigh of relief. "Good riddance to that heartless woman. And welcome, Alice. Tell me more about yourself. Do you have any children?"

"No, I don't."

"Oh well, maybe if things go well with you and Robert, I'll finally get another grandchild. That cold-hearted wife of his said she never wanted any. I'll bet she was just barren."

And I'm out of here! Alice leapt up from the table. "Please excuse me, where's the bathroom?"

"I'll show you." Bob stood up and Alice followed him out of the kitchen. "It's up the stairs and first door on the left."

She put her finger over her mouth to shush him, then pointed up the stairs. "Follow me," she hissed.

He followed her upstairs and into the bathroom.

"Remember I told you about that dinner with my family that was the most embarrassing moment of my life? Well, it's just been trumped. Let's just tell them I used to sleep around – get that out of the way too. I could kill you, *Robert*. You could have saved me some embarrassment."

"I'm sorry. We're not one of those families that tell each other everything. But you're right – I should have told them about your sobriety. Maybe they wouldn't have been so insensitive. The other stuff – well, that was just unfortunate. My mum doesn't know your medical history. She wouldn't usually say something so horrible; it's just that she despises Christine for walking out on me and Sam." He reached for her hand but she pulled it away. "Alice, please. She didn't mean any harm. Come down and have something to eat. Mum does a great roast beef." He tried to catch her eye, but she was still sulking. "I promise it will go better when I meet your parents."

"You think you're meeting my parents after this? Not a chance. Now get out. I need a minute." She pushed him out of the bathroom and slammed the door. She took a few deep breaths and tried to compose herself. *Yes, that could have gone better. But it's out of the way now, and they didn't seem too horrified. I know Peggy didn't mean any harm about the baby stuff. Best to forget about it.*

Alice made her way back downstairs, but stopped outside the kitchen when she heard her name. She held her breath and strained to listen.

"...but she's an alcoholic, Robert."

"Recovering."

"Nonsense. What happens when she starts drinking again?"

"She won't."

"How do you know that? Lydia's husband is a recovering alcoholic and he's always drunk."

"Lydia who?"

"My hairdresser. What if she puts Sam in danger?"

"Your hairdresser?"

"Alice!"

"What makes you assume she would do that? She dotes on Sam. And he adores her. She's good for him."

Peggy sighed. "I've no doubt they like each other. She seems nice and it's a bonus that she has no children of her own to favour over Sam. But you don't have to settle for the first woman you meet after Christine."

"I'm not settling, Mum. I love Alice. She's doing really well putting her life back together – and mine and Sam's. Please spend some time with her, get to know her before you judge her. You'll soon see why I love her."

"Give the girl a chance, Peg. The little mite can't get enough of her, and if she can put up with this one's bullshit, then she's OK in my book. And at least I won't have to share my booze."

"Thank you, Dad. But no more jokes. Just be normal. Well, as normal as you can be."

Alice wasn't a bit shocked that Peggy felt the way she did. She tried to put herself in her place. How would she feel if someone she loved was dating an alcoholic, recovering or not? She knew she had her work cut out with Peggy to show she was worthy of Bob and Sam; hopefully she would come around in time. Robert senior, on the other hand, seemed reasonable enough. His irreverence was refreshing.

Just then Sam joined her at the door, and wrapped his arms around her leg. "Are they talking about me again?" he whispered.

His eyes were full of sadness. A child that age

shouldn't be worried about such things. Alice ruffled his hair. "No, sweetie, they're talking about me."

"What did you do?"

"Nothing. Your grandparents are just deciding whether or not they like me."

"If they do, do I start calling you Auntie Alice?"

"You just call me Alice, sweetheart."

"Can I call Uncle Robert Bob? Like you do."

"You'll have to ask him."

He shook his head vigorously.

Alice smiled. "Do you want me to ask him?"

He nodded.

"OK. We'll ask him together later. Right now, I've got to try your granny's roast beef. Is it nice?"

He nodded and headed back to the sofa.

Good. Maybe the afternoon's salvageable after all.

Chapter Thirteen

Over the next three months Alice gradually took control of the accounts of Christine Cleans. Even though she knew she wouldn't work for Bob permanently, she negotiated herself a proper salary – not quite the £49,000 she'd been on previously, but more than enough to cover her expenses and set a few pounds aside for savings each month. Plans for the restructure and rebrand were well on track. Alice booked Miriam onto a few training courses to learn new skills so that she could take on more responsibility in the office once Alice had taken a step back. Miriam readily accepted the challenge and was more than pleased with her pay rise and additional few days' annual leave in recognition of her tenure and dedication. Kristof and the other supervisors continued to schedule and prepare for the jobs each morning, which left Bob free to concentrate on drumming up new business and spend more time on existing jobs, liaising with contractors, and ensuring quality control.

As Bob had suspected, Christine tried to use his relationship with Alice to expedite their divorce. He didn't contest her counter-petition, and admitted to adultery so the divorce could proceed and Alice could remain an unnamed co-respondent. Even though this meant that things would move quite quickly, Bob feared that the finances wouldn't be so easily settled.

On Alice's birthday, which she shared with her eldest niece, her brother David threw a family barbecue. Fortunately, her parents were away on their summer holiday and couldn't attend. Alice jumped at the chance to introduce Bob and Sam to her brother, sister and their spouses. She was thrilled at how well Sam got along with her nephew and two nieces, and there was even talk of a family holiday to Disneyland Paris the following summer.

Alice was spending every weekend at the house with Bob and Sam and moving her things in gradually, as they had agreed. Most weeknights she stayed at the flat with Tamzin. Cameron was still based in Edinburgh, so Alice was picking up his slack with the wedding preparations, as well as making the most of her nightcaps. She knew that when she moved in with Bob permanently, she would either have to give up again or tell him what she had been doing. Both scenarios filled her with dread.

The first Saturday in October was Tamzin's hen night. The plan they had come up with went well, and Alice enjoyed the day with the girls at the spa. Bob had bought Tamzin a surprise gift of half a dozen bottles of champagne, some non-alcoholic fizzy wine, and chocolate-covered strawberries, and Alice was green with envy that she couldn't sneak a glass of the good stuff. At dinner time, however, she managed to nip down to the restaurant early – under the guise of decorating the table – to secure herself a large gin and tonic, disguised as lemonade, to enjoy with her meal. Any more than that and Bob might notice when she arrived back in the room.

After dinner, the eleven-strong crowd of hens gathered in Tamzin and Natalie's room for a final make-up check and some pre-clubbing shots. Alice watched as they filled and refilled their glasses without a care in the world. She'd never felt so alone in a crowd and was more relieved than jealous when the phone rang to say that the taxis had arrived. She waved them off with a smile and was about to close the door to Tamzin's room when she noticed a bottle of Jägermeister on the coffee table. The evening had been torturous, so she thought she deserved at least one more drink. She poured and downed a shot quickly, then picked up her key card and made her way to the door, where she paused and glanced back at the bottle. *Bob won't suspect, and he'll be too busy enjoying the latest addition to my sexy underwear collection to notice...* She turned back and had three more shots.

The following afternoon, Bob pulled his car up in front of Tamzin's flat. He didn't have to look into the back seat to know that she was sleeping; her snoring was a dead giveaway. He made a face at Alice.

"It's such a shame to wake her." She giggled.

"A shame? I can't wait to get her the hell out of my car. It's a miracle she didn't puke over the upholstery."

"She did enough of that last night. She doesn't usually drink so much."

"Let's just get her inside and head home. My mum's bringing Sam back soon."

"Oh, I was going to stay here tonight."

"But Sunday's my night to have you."

"I can't leave Tam alone when she's hungover like this. And I'll be here all week. We've a few last-minute things to do for the wedding."

He pouted.

"In a week I'll be living with you permanently. You'll be looking for excuses to get rid of me."

"Never going to happen. I can't wait to have you all to myself."

"Not all to yourself – you're forgetting my other man. You know I really missed him bouncing into bed with us this morning."

"I didn't … the little cock-blocker," he grumbled.

She slapped him on the arm, but giggled. The sex they'd had at the hotel that morning and the night before was the most adventurous they'd had in a while. They were able to let loose without worrying that Sam might wake up or hear them.

There was a groan from the back seat. They turned to see Tamzin trying to lift her head. She squinted at them.

"Ah, the blushing bride," Bob joked.

Tamzin stuck her middle finger up at him. "You can go off some people, you know."

After Bob left, Alice made Tamzin some tea and topped her up with paracetamol. She snuggled down on the sofa beside her. "How are you feeling now?"

"Better now that the room's stopped spinning. But it was totally worth it. Such an epic hen. Thanks, girl. I know it wasn't easy for you."

Alice smiled. The few drinks she had been able to sneak had helped. "It wasn't too bad. I'm feeling better about the wedding now too. I was dreading it, but with Bob there, I'll be OK. Right, I'm going to head to the gym. Want to come?"

"I hate you," Tamzin sneered.

"Ha-ha! You'll miss me when I'm gone."

"I know. But I'm glad that you're going to live with Bob. You're welcome, by the way."

"For what?"

"Talking you into seeing him. Just call me your fairy godmother. And speaking of mothers, have you told your parents that you're moving in with him yet?"

"No. If I tell them, they'll insist on meeting him. Mum's not entirely thrilled that I'm seeing someone. She thinks I'm making a mistake."

"Did she say that?"

"No, but she implied it by her tone. Why can't she just keep her nose out of my life?"

"Because she's your mother. Believe me, you'll miss her when she's gone."

Tamzin's mother had died after a long battle with ovarian cancer when Tamzin was just nineteen. Alice sighed and gave Tamzin a hug. "I know. I'm sorry. It's going to be tough on Saturday without Lilly. But remember what she made you promise..."

"To be the happiest, prettiest bride ever."

"And that's exactly what we're going to give her. So, a few early nights are in order. Reverse the damage this hen night has done."

"Is it even possible?" Tamzin groaned.

"Possible, but it might be tricky. We're going to need lots of cucumbers."

Alice thought about what Tamzin had said. It was probably time for Bob to meet her parents. But she didn't want to commit to dinner, which would take at least an hour, so she told her parents they would stop by for a coffee one evening that week.

They stood on the doorstep of Alice's family home. She placed her hand on the door handle then turned to Bob. "Remember, best behaviour. My mum isn't very happy that I'm with someone, so be as charming as you can. Oh, and discretion is paramount. They don't know about my little slip the night we met." *Or all the other ones since.*

"Oh, so all your talk about being open and honest only applies to me?"

"I have to pick my battles. Let's go in."

Bob followed her in through the hall and into the living room. Alice's dad was reading the sports section, but jumped up when he saw them. Bob stopped in his tracks. Even though Alice's dad was in his sixties, he still possessed the build of a boxer and that, combined with his height, made him a dominating presence.

"Hello, my baby." He held his arms out to Alice and almost dwarfed her in his embrace.

"Hi Daddy," she cooed, and gestured to Bob. "This is Bob."

They exchanged a firm handshake.

"It's nice to meet you, sir."

"Ah, call me Stephen. Take a seat and make yourself at home."

Alice pointed Bob to the sofa, and they sat down beside each other. Stephen relaxed back into his chair.

"Where's Mum?"

"She thinks it's going to rain, so she's taking the washing in off the line."

"There's not a cloud in sight."

"You know your mother ... she had one of her feelings."

Alice groaned, but nudged Bob when her mother came into the room. They stood up. "Hi, Mum." Alice gave her mum a peck on the cheek and pointed to Bob. "This is Bob. And Bob, this is my mum, Amanda."

Bob flashed his most charming smile. "Pleased to meet you, Mrs Patterson."

"Yes, it's nice of Alice to finally introduce us. Are you an alcoholic too?"

"Mum!" Alice snapped.

"No, Mrs Patterson, I'm not."

"Thank goodness for that. I know there's a danger that people who have similar habits can gravitate towards each other and form co-dependent relationships. They're not healthy. Do you drink at all?"

"No. I used to drink occasionally. But now I don't."

"Good. Less temptation for Alice."

"Mum, would you *please* stop?"

Bob put his hand on Alice's knee. "I assure you that your daughter is in safe hands with me and Sam. We take very good care of her. And she does of us."

"She told us about what happened to your sister. I'm so sorry for your loss." She wrung her hands. "Your poor mother must be heartbroken. I nearly lost my daughter once; it was the worst experience of my life. Alice seems to forget that her actions affect the entire family. My other children were distraught for their sister. Was it awful for you?"

He nodded. "Yes. It was."

"And did you feel the need to turn to alcohol or other addictive substances to get you through that difficult time?"

"Mum!"

"Amanda!"

"No, Stephen. I need to know what kind of man my daughter is dating. And Alice needs to know that there are other ways to cope with depression than drinking."

Alice groaned and leant into Bob. "This is worse than

when I met your parents," she whispered.

Stephen overheard her comment and tried to change the subject. "So, Bob, that's a nice car you drove up in. Your business must be doing well."

"Thank you. And yes, things are going well at work. Especially since Alice came on board. Your daughter is working all kinds of magic."

Alice made a slicing motion across her throat for him to stop talking. She hadn't told her mum that yet. But it was too late; her mum already looked incensed. "Working for Bob. That's your new consultancy job?"

"It was only meant to be temporary, but we work really well together. And I suppose I'd better tell you that I'm going to be moving in with Bob too... Well, I suppose I already have."

"Moved in?" She let out a long sigh. "Stephen, Bob, may I have a quiet chat with Alice for a moment?"

"Why don't you show me that car of yours?" Stephen stood up and beckoned Bob to do the same.

"Um..." Bob looked at Alice.

It might be better if he isn't here for this, Alice thought. God knows what she's going to say. She nodded to signal that it was OK, and Bob and Stephen went out to the car.

"You're moving in with him. Are you sure that's a good idea?"

"Yes, Mum. I've been practically living with him for the past few months anyway. Tam's getting married on Saturday and it just seemed like the right time to make it official. Nothing's really changing."

"Everything is changing. By moving in with him, you are committing yourself to a man and a young child. Are you ready for that, emotionally?"

"Yes. I love Bob and I love Sam and we're going to be a family."

"I know that you've always dreamed of having a family. And no one was more upset than me when we found out you couldn't have children. I'm worried that you're latching on to Bob because he has a child. You're thinking that you can be the boy's mother and you'll all live happily ever after. Life isn't like that, and you know it. And don't get me started on the fact that you're working for him too. That makes you beholden to him for everything. What happens when you relapse, and he can't cope with that?"

Alice rolled her eyes. "Who says I'm going to relapse?"

"You know you will. The odds are against you."

"You don't know what you're talking about, Mum."

"Alcoholics always relapse!"

"How dare you make such a generalisation? I've met people at group who have been sober for decades."

"And how do you know you're going to be one of them? You're still fragile. The first bad thing that happens to you could push you over the edge."

Alice's blood was boiling. *She hasn't got a clue. I don't have a problem any more. I can control it. I'm one of the lucky ones. Not that she would understand.*

"Bob will be thrown into a situation that he won't know how to deal with. And just like Dylan, he will leave you and you'll lose your home and your job, all over again."

"Dylan didn't leave me because of my drinking!" she yelled. "He left me because he's a selfish bastard! That's why I *started* drinking – to drown the pain and the loneliness that he left behind. Bob's not like him. Look what he's done for his nephew! And for me. He goes out of his way to make me happy. And I know if I have another slip, he'll be there for me. He'll get me through."

"Another?"

Oh shit. Alice remained silent.

"Did you say another slip? When did you slip?"

She hung her head. "A few months ago. When I found out that Dylan was having a baby with that woman. It was only one night. And Bob was there for me. He helped me get through it and out the other side."

Her mother sighed and gave her that look of disappointment that only parents can give. "You know as well as I do that he can't help you. You have to help yourself."

"Please stop spewing that online psychology course. It's pure crap."

"It's not crap, Alice. Bob seems like a nice man, but I don't think you should be with him. With anybody. Everything seems perfect now, but really — it's like a Grimm's fairy tale. It'll end in disaster. And do you really want to cause that boy any more turmoil?"

Alice knew that she could argue with her mum until she was blue in the face. There was no point. She'd never change her opinion of Alice.

"I know I'm a disappointment to you. You're so proud of David and Elizabeth. I'm sorry you can't be proud of me."

Her mum remained silent. After a few seconds, Alice laughed.

"What's so funny?"

"That's the part where you were meant to say, 'No, Alice, I'm not disappointed in you'."

"I'm not, darling."

"Then why don't you ever say it?"

Amanda shrugged and didn't answer.

Outside, Bob and Stephen had already run out of things to say about Bob's Jaguar and retreated to the garage, which had been converted into a boxing studio. Bob looked around at the equipment, and laughed when he saw a mini punching bag in the corner. "A bit small for you, isn't it?"

"It's for the grandkids. I really encouraged my girls to take part when they were younger, for self-defence at the very least, but they soon tired of it. And David was more interested in golf gloves than boxing ones. Thankfully the grandkids are all keen. Might get someone to carry on the Patterson boxing name."

"But an actuary, a solicitor and a surgeon – you must be very proud of them."

"Yes, I am. David and Elizabeth both worked very hard to get where they are today. But there's something special about Alice; she's not like the other two. From a very young age we saw she was different. She was naturally smart, but pretended she wasn't. She was unhappy at school and found it very difficult to make friends. As a result, she suffered from anxiety and depression in her teenage years. It was worrying. But when she got to university and was surrounded by people as smart as she was, she came into her own. She met that Dylan, and he seemed perfect for her." He cracked his knuckles. "He was driven. He had a plan, and Alice bought into it. We didn't think it was a bad thing. For the first time in her life she was really happy, so we stopped worrying about her and … look what happened." He narrowed his eyes at Bob. "As you can imagine, we were taken aback when Alice said she'd met someone else. And when we found out about your nephew, we had mixed feelings. But I'm confident that my daughter knows her own mind. And when she says she loves you, I believe her. But you need to make me believe that you're with her for the right reasons."

"The right reasons?"

"Because you love her too. Not because you're lonely and need someone to help you raise that child."

Bob looked him in the eye. "I assure you, that's not what this is. I love her deeply."

"And you're going into this with your eyes wide open? You remember that Alice has a sickness that is never going to go away. I'm not naïve; I know about the cycle of addiction and that she'll probably relapse one day. When she does, you can't use that as an excuse to break up with her."

Bob shook his head.

"I'm not saying that you can never break up with her. But if you do, you do it for the right reasons. And do it compassionately. Honestly. She's a smart girl and she'll understand. And if she doesn't and she chooses to drink again, that won't be your fault. As long you behave in a civilised manner. Not like that waste of breath she used to be married to."

"I love her. I want to make her happy. Hopefully she'll never feel the need to drink again, but if she does, I'll be there. And I have you guys for backup. Right?"

"Of course." Stephen shook Bob's hand. "Do you like boxing?"

"Um, it's OK."

"Football?"

"Yes."

"Then you and I are going to get along just fine. I can't say the same about Alice's mother, though – you've got your work cut out for you there. Amanda and Alice have been fighting like cat and dog since Alice said her first words."

They heard the front door slam, and looked over to see Alice storming towards the open garage door. "Shit. They've been at it again." Stephen held his arms out to Alice then pulled her into an embrace. "She'll come around. I'll talk to her. We love you."

"I know you love me, Daddy. But she hates me."

"Your mother doesn't hate you. She's worried sick about you." He turned to Bob. "If you two are planning on raising that child together, there's something you both need to know. Parenting is hard."

Bob and Alice nodded in agreement.

"Ah, and you have no idea yet exactly *how hard* it is. At the moment it's probably exhausting and all-consuming, but this is the easy part. Every minute of the day you know where the boy is, who he's with, and what time he'll be back. You can relax because you know he's tucked up safe and sound in bed every night. You comfort him when he's sick and you kiss his scraped knee to make it better. Now you two may be all grown up, but you're still your parents' kids. We worry about you all the time. And when something happens to you, or if you're sick, we can't kiss it and make it better like we used to. That kills us. Alice, the night we got the call that you'd had an accident and been taken to hospital, we rushed there as fast as we could. We couldn't believe what we found."

Alice shuffled her feet.

"Not only were you in a critical condition, but we found out that you had done it to yourself because you had been drinking. And you'd lost your job, you had a drink-driving conviction. You were an alcoholic. We are your parents and we had no idea what was going on in your life." He took Alice's hand. "Your mother blames herself for not noticing how badly your life had spiralled out of control. It's not you she hates; it's the fact that she can't make it all better for you. Remember that." He kissed her on the hand and passed her over to Bob. "Now off you go. It was nice to meet you, Bob. Come for Sunday lunch soon. And bring your nephew – I want to see what he's made of in the boxing ring. Take good care of my daughter."

"I will." Bob shook his hand, then helped Alice into the car.

Alice stared out of the car window. *What was I thinking, bringing Bob to meet her? I should have known better. She thinks she knows everything, but she doesn't know me. I won't relapse, not in the way she thinks. I had one little slip where I drank more than I should. I've been better since then. I have a healthy relationship with alcohol now. I know when to stop. In fact, I just won't drink again. No problem!* She relaxed into her seat and smiled over at Bob.

"I like your dad. And I think he likes me. Your mum will come around in time. It's like your dad said: she's not angry at you, she's angry for you. And I don't mean to take her side, but she's right."

"About what?"

"Rain. Look at that dark cloud. There's going to be a downpour."

"Pfft," Alice scoffed.

But as the tiny droplets of rain grew bigger, so did the feeling of dread in the pit of Alice's stomach. *No more drinking. No problem.*

Chapter Fourteen

The day of Tamzin's wedding finally arrived. The bridal party had gathered at her family home to get ready. Alice was the perfect maid of honour. She fussed around making sure that everyone and everything was ready on schedule. After a final practice run with the flower girls, she topped up everyone's drinks. The bride and bridesmaids were having mimosas and the father of the bride was drinking Bloody Marys. Even though Alice had vowed to stop her secret drinking, she sneaked a large measure of vodka into her orange juice. It was her second one, but they were medicinal. She usually felt anxious in social situations, and needed the alcohol to relax.

When it was nearly time to go, the bridal party posed for photos outside the house. Neighbours had gathered to watch the festivities and to wish Tamzin all the best for her big day. Alice noticed her mum among them. Dutifully, she excused herself and went to say hello.

"You look stunning, darling. Your father will be gutted that he missed seeing you in your dress."

"There'll be plenty of pictures. And he *was* invited."

"One of his young lads has his debut fight tonight in Birmingham. He needed to be there. And you know how I hate weddings."

Alice rolled her eyes. *Yeah, you prefer funerals.*

"Where's Bob?"

"At home. Girls only — well, apart from Geoff. Bob's going to make his own way to the church."

"Oh. I was hoping to see him. You two left pretty

quickly the other evening. I didn't get a chance to say goodbye."

"Don't worry, he's not going anywhere. But I hope the next time you see him you'll go a bit easier on him."

"I'm sorry, Alice. I know it doesn't always come across properly, but I just want what's best for you. Be careful, is what I meant to say the other day. I love you, darling." She gave Alice a firm hug.

After a few awkward seconds, Alice pulled away and raised her eyebrow. "Did Dad put you up to this?"

"He's always been better than me at talking about his feelings. It's his hippy upbringing."

"Nanna and Grampa are not hippies. They're just more open-minded than your parents. Poor Elizabeth still has to pretend she's a spinster around Gran instead of celebrating being married to an amazing woman. It's the twenty-first century, for God's sake."

Amanda tapped Alice on the arm. "Language, darling!"

"Sorry, Mum." She saw that the wedding cars had arrived and checked her watch. "I've got to get Tam to the church on time. Bye."

"Have a good day, darling."

Alice organised Geoff and Tamzin into the first car. She tucked Tamzin's dress in as neatly as she could, then blew her a kiss. "This is it. Are you nervous?"

"Terrified."

"Don't be. Joel just texted. Cameron is at the church already. And I'll be right behind you. See you there." She closed the door and then climbed into the second car with the other bridesmaids.

Alice flashed a smile at Natalie and Cora, Tamzin's distant cousin who hadn't been at the hen night and who she hadn't seen since they were kids.

Cora grinned and opened her clutch bag. "How about one for the road?" She produced a silver hip flask and offered it to Alice.

"Oh, no thank you," Alice said quickly.

"It's OK." Cora offered again. "Go ahead, there's plenty to go around."

"I'll have a sip." Natalie reached for the flask. She took a drink and handed it back to Cora, who offered it to Alice a third time.

Alice bit her lip. Another drink would go down quite nicely, would relieve a bit of the tension that was already building. She smiled and held her hand out for the flask.

"Alice," Natalie gasped. "Do you really think that's a good idea?"

Cora looked between them. "Um, is there something I'm missing?"

Alice sighed. "I had a bit of a problem with alcohol last year."

Cora's eyes widened. "I'm so sorry. I wouldn't have brought this if I'd known."

"It's OK. I was going through a really difficult time back then, but I have it under control now. I can drink if I want to." *And I want to.* She held out her hand out for the flask again, but Cora seemed reluctant to hand it over. Alice beamed at her. "It's fine, honestly. I drink all the time." She took the flask and had a sip. The brandy burned the back of her throat, but it tasted great. Just what she needed.

The girls passed around the flask until it was empty. Between that and what they'd had at the house already, they all had a good buzz on by the time they got to the church. Natalie pulled Alice aside as soon as they got out of the car. "Listen, I know we've never really gotten along, but Tamzin told me everything that happened. She was sick with worry about you. Are you sure you know what you're doing?"

Alice gave Natalie a warm smile. She had to make sure she didn't run to Tamzin and tell tales. "I'm fine, honestly. Come on, it's Tam's big day. Let's be friends. Please?"

"OK. I suppose we could be friends for one day."

"And don't mention this to Tam; she'll only worry unnecessarily. We want our friend to have a great day, don't we? She'll be thrilled we're getting along." Alice held her arms out for a hug, but Natalie pulled away and pointed over Alice's shoulder to Bob, who was hanging around outside the church.

"There's your boyfriend. Hug him."

"I'll be right back." Alice hurried over to Bob and wagged her finger at him. "What are you doing? Everyone's supposed to be inside when the bride arrives."

"I had to see you first. You look spectacular!"

"Thank you." She curtseyed and he leant in towards her. Just as he was about to meet her lips, she remembered the brandy in the car. What if he could taste it or smell it on her? She pulled away and pointed to her lips. "Watch out for the lipstick." She blew him a kiss instead. "Now get inside, so I can get my best friend married."

"Only if you promise to catch the bouquet."

"I'll try my best." She giggled.

Alice couldn't take her eyes off Tamzin during the ceremony. She looked stunning in a second-hand vintage ivory fish-tailed dress that, if she had bought brand-new, would have cost nearly as much as her honeymoon cruise. Alice was so happy for her. She glanced back at Bob. He was looking straight ahead, but as if he knew she was looking, he looked over at her and smiled. He mouthed "I love you" then looked back at the altar. She couldn't help grinning when she remembered what he'd said outside the church. And that wasn't the first time he'd hinted at marriage.

She glanced back at the altar and suddenly had a flashback to her own wedding day. She had stood exactly where Tamzin was standing. Cameron was where Dylan had stood, and he was staring lovingly at his bride, just as Dylan had stared at her. A feeling of dread washed over her. What if Cameron turned out to be like Dylan? What if he broke her best friend's heart? Tamzin had already been through so much heartache losing her mum so young, she didn't deserve to be hurt again. Alice's chest was suddenly tight, and she thought she couldn't get a breath. She closed her eyes and tried to focus, but Geoff tapped her on the arm. She opened her eyes. He was pointing towards the lectern. It was time for Alice's reading. She'd nearly had a coronary when Tamzin had asked her to do it. But Tamzin had done so much for her, she felt she couldn't say no. Geoff had stepped out into the aisle and was holding his hand out. Reluctantly she let him help her up.

He whispered into her ear, "Stop shaking. You'll be fine."

She flashed him a nervous smile and crept towards the front of the church. She could feel everyone's eyes boring into her as she walked. A few of Tamzin's guests knew her or knew of her – the poor girl who had been driven to drink after her husband divorced her because she couldn't have children. She could almost hear the pity. She stepped up to the lectern and took a deep breath. She tried to recall a quote about not worrying over things you couldn't control. She couldn't remember the exact wording, but the sentiment was the same. She glanced at Tamzin, then at Bob. They were both smiling. They had faith in her, even if she had none in herself, and they would always be there for her. She felt herself relax, then looked at the reading in front of her. It was just a few lines.

After the ceremony, everyone arrived at the hotel for the reception. The guests mingled in the hotel garden, watching the official photos being taken. Alice noticed Bob standing on his own and felt bad that she couldn't keep him company, but she was in the wedding party and was needed for the photos. She excused herself for a second and hurried over to him.

"You were fantastic – so calm and confident. I didn't know my girlfriend was such a good public speaker."

Alice blushed. *The brandy helped.* "Only when someone tells me what to say. Are you OK? I noticed you haven't been mingling."

"I only know you and the bride, and I've only met the groom once. I should have brought Sam – at least I'd have had someone to talk to. Do you mind if I check in and hide in the bedroom until dinner?"

"Go ahead. You'll be sitting with Natalie and her husband Lionel. I must warn you; Lionel is the most painfully boring man I've ever met. And I know lots of accountants!"

Bob grimaced.

"The speeches start at half five, so be down for then. OK?"

"OK. And just like in the church, you'll do great." He blew her a kiss and headed off.

Alice panicked. *My speech! What was I thinking, agreeing to do it?* Tamzin didn't know about it, so she could still back out. But she'd rehearsed it countless times and was confident that she could get through it without crying. And she had done OK with the reading in the church. *But I had a drink before the church. That's probably why I was able to relax. Maybe I should have a drink before the speeches too. Just one, for Dutch courage.*

She looked around for the waitress who was making her way through the crowd, handing out champagne. Alice checked to see if anyone was watching. People were either focused on the bride and groom or engrossed in their own conversations. She made her way over to the waitress and took a glass from the tray. "Thank you." She took a long drink. The bubbles exploded on her tongue then the cool liquid trickled down her throat, quenching her thirst.

"You're welcome. Your dress is gorgeous, by the way. And the bride is stunning."

"Isn't she?" Alice took another gulp. The champagne flute was nearly empty. "Actually, she hasn't had a glass yet. She must be parched after all that smiling for the camera. I'll take one over to her." She finished her glass and put it back on the tray, picking up another in its place.

She headed over to Tamzin's dad, who was standing on his own by the water fountain. He welcomed her with a beaming smile but frowned when he saw the glass in her hand.

"Don't worry, Geoff. I got this from the bar. It's the alcohol-free stuff Tam ordered for the pregnant ladies and the alcoholics. How are you holding up?"

"I'm all right. Lilly's been gone for so long, I'm used to doing things without her. I'm trying to convince myself that this is just another day. What about you? You seemed shaky in the church earlier."

"Just nerves about the reading," Alice lied.

"Why? You were great. And you've been such a help today and the last few weeks. We couldn't have done all this without you."

"Anything for Tam. She's been such an amazing friend to me. I don't deserve her."

"You've been an amazing friend to her too. And to me. We couldn't have got through that year without you. You two might not be blood, but you're sisters. And you always will be. Right. I'd better go and mingle. You do the same, and we'll reconvene at the top table."

Alice took another long sip of champagne. The bubbles were doing their job, making her feel warm and gooey inside. But her glass was nearly empty. *I suppose I could just drink enough to maintain this buzz all day... I'll stop again tomorrow.* She scanned the garden for the waitress.

After the photos, Tamzin asked Alice to check that everything was perfect in the function room before the guests moved inside. Happily, she obliged and headed off to fulfil her duty. She scanned the room. It looked great. Covers on all the chairs, presents on display at the side of the room. The cake took pride of place in the bay window. The tables were set beautifully with a vase of bright autumn flowers in the middle, a wedding favour at each place setting, a jug of water, a bottle of fizzy water, and bottles of red and white wine open for the guests to enjoy.

Alice looked up to the top table, where she would be sitting. There was wine at it too. But even if she had wanted any, it would be impossible; she would be in full view.

Just then the bartender arrived to set things up behind the bar. She scurried over. "Hi. Maid of honour duties meant I haven't had a drink all day. I'm gasping. Could I possibly get a gin and tonic? I'll get you some money when my boyfriend comes down with my purse. I'm good for it."

"No worries." He reached for a fancy gin glass.

"Ugh, I hate those things. Just give me a plain one – a water glass will do. Plenty of ice, no fruit, and don't be stingy with the measure." She winked.

He smiled at her as he tilted the bottle to refill the optic, making her drink a very generous double.

"Thank you." She took her drink over to the top table and put it at her place setting. If she sipped it, it would last through the speeches and she could maintain her buzz. And it looked just like all the other water glasses on the table. Except that her water was fizzy. She reached across the table for a bottle of fizzy water and set it beside her glass.

Once all the guests were seated for dinner, the best man, Joel, who was also the master of ceremonies, invited the father of the bride to make his speech. Geoff stood up and addressed the room.

"Good evening, everyone. It's my pleasure to welcome you all here today, to help celebrate the wedding of Tamzin and Cameron. And I'm sure you'll all agree that the bride looks stunning."

There was a round of applause, a few cheers, and a wolf whistle.

"And my daughter tells me Cameron looks quite good too."

There was some laughter and another wolf whistle.

"It's hard to believe that my little girl is married. But as the saying goes, I don't feel like I've lost a daughter, but like I've gained a son − finally − as I've been outnumbered by women since the day Tamzin was born. As most of you know, my late wife and I were only blessed with one daughter. But about twenty-eight years ago when the Pattersons moved in next door, we unwittingly gained a second one. Tamzin and Alice became inseparable, never one without the other. Lilly and I were delighted with 'our girls', as we called them, and in her final few months it gave Lilly tremendous comfort to know that Tamzin would always have a sister to turn to." He raised his glass. "Tamzin, your mother would be so proud of the woman you have become. We remember her today, not with a heavy heart, but with a smile on our faces. To Lilly."

"To Lilly," everyone chorused.

Alice choked back her tears and took a sip of her drink, while Tamzin got up from her seat and kissed her dad on the cheek. He waited for her to sit down before he continued. "Now, let me tell you what a little diva Tamzin used to be…"

Tamzin groaned.

After Geoff had told a few embarrassing stories about Tamzin, he handed the microphone back to the best man.

"Now, in a break from tradition, I am going to hand

you over to our maid of honour, who would like to say a few words. Ladies and gentlemen, give it up for Alice!"

Alice stood up to a round of applause, but before Joel handed her the microphone, he chanted into it, "Who the fu—"

Cameron jumped up and grabbed the microphone from Joel. Subdued laughter rippled around the room; the guests clearly weren't sure if they were supposed to be laughing.

Alice's cheeks were burning. Joel was such an idiot. As if she wasn't feeling self-conscious enough already. Thank God for gin, she thought as she drained her drink. She took the microphone from Joel, who looked miffed that his joke had been spoiled.

She glanced down at Bob. He gave her a thumbs-up and she smiled and gave a loud sigh into the microphone. "It's OK, Cameron. I hate that Tamzin's getting all the attention, so I paid him to say that. Thanks, Joel, you can pick up your twenty quid after the first dance."

A wave of laughter spread through the room.

"I'm going to be brief. I just wanted to congratulate my best friend on finding and marrying the man of her dreams. And I'm sure you'll agree they make a fantastic couple."

She initiated a round of applause. "I remember the phone call I got from Tam when she was on her way home from her first date with Cameron. She said she was crazy in love and she was going to marry him. I told her she was just crazy. But when I met the man who swept her off her feet, I was the one who felt crazy for ever doubting her. And I was so proud to stand up with her today when she married her true love. We've had some dark days together, and some, like today, that were brighter than the sun. Unfortunately, I now have to step aside and let Cameron be your number one, but I do it gladly and wish you both a long and happy marriage." She raised her glass. "To the bride and groom."

"To the bride and groom," everyone roared.

Tamzin and Alice hugged. When Alice looked over to Bob, he had a huge smile on his face.

Alice, relieved her speech was over, stared at her empty glass. She was feeling tipsy and was impatient for another drink. Tamzin was gazing lovingly at Cameron, who was mid-toast, professing his undying love to his new wife. Alice smiled as she listened, but she suddenly felt nauseous. Maybe it was all the alcohol on an empty stomach, or maybe it was because the fairy-tale marriage they were entering into could end in disaster, like hers. Panic set in as she worried about all the ways it could go wrong. Geoff's wife died, leaving him a young widower. The best man, Joel, was already on his second wife. She was divorced. Bob was in the process. *Bob!* She tried to calm herself. *I'm all right. He won't let me down. He promised.* She looked over to his table, but saw an empty chair. *Where is he? How could he go to the loo during the speeches?* She spent the next few minutes wondering where he was until the speeches were over and dinner was being served. Natalie, who had been seated at the table with Bob, made her way to the top table and whispered into Alice's ear. "Bob got an important phone call. It was a work emergency and he had to take off. He said he's sorry, but he'll phone you as soon as he can."

Alice frowned. "A work emergency?"

"That's what he said." She shrugged and headed back to her table.

Alice was miffed. How could Bob leave the wedding for a work emergency? They only had one job on today and Kristof was on call. Surely he could handle anything that came up? She checked her phone; she had no missed calls or messages. She glanced at her empty glass.

All through the meal, Alice watched the bar, hoping to catch the eye of the bartender who had served her earlier. She was getting increasingly agitated, both by her lack of a drink and by Bob's absence. She'd tried phoning and texting him, but when she still hadn't heard from him, paranoia set in. He had been sitting at the table with Natalie. *Did that spiteful cow tell him about the drink I had in the car? Is that why he took off?* She had to find out.

As she made her way through the tables, she was stopped, more than once, by guests congratulating her on her toast or commenting on how beautiful she and the bride looked. Her cheeks were sore from smiling by the time she got to Natalie. She pulled her to one side. "What did you say to Bob when you were at the table with him?"

"Nothing. Just chit-chat. He was only beside me for a few minutes before the speeches started. Then his phone started vibrating in his pocket. He listened to a voicemail and then he left."

"So you didn't tell him about me drinking brandy in the car?" She tapped her foot as she waited for a response.

Natalie gasped. "I knew you shouldn't be drinking."

"You don't know anything."

"I know if Tamzin finds out she'll be devastated."

"Then keep your mouth shut and your nose out of my business."

"Tamzin's my business too. So watch yourself tonight, because I'm going to be watching you."

"Just like you watched out for Tam on her hen night?" Alice spat.

"I don't think you're in any position to judge." Natalie matched her tone.

Just then, Natalie's husband intervened. "Um, people are looking."

They looked around and saw that they were indeed on the receiving end of a few disapproving looks.

"Alice, Geoff is looking for you. He's panicking because the DJ has lost his playlist."

Alice sighed and looked back at Natalie. "I'm sorry. Today has been harder than I thought it would be. Don't worry. I won't upset the bride." She hurried off to find Geoff.

After Alice had rescued the DJ and the first few dances had gone off successfully, she slumped down onto a chair. She felt terrible. She counted what she'd had to drink that day. Two large vodkas and orange, a third of a hip flask of straight brandy, three glasses of champagne and a very large gin. Yup, her buzz was gone and a hangover was setting in already. She needed sleep – or another drink. She lifted her phone to check the time and saw a text message from Bob.

I'm so sorry. I won't make it back to the hotel until late. I'll text when I'm on my way. I'll make it up to you. Love you. x

The text incensed her. What the hell was he playing at? He knew how difficult this wedding would be for her, and he had promised to be there for moral support. She looked around the room. She knew some of Tamzin's family and a few of the other guests, but everyone was drinking and dancing, enjoying themselves while she was miserable. She felt like she was back at school, separated from the crowd, unable to join in because she was different. But since Bob wouldn't be back until late, it wouldn't hurt to have another drink, would it? But she couldn't do it at the wedding. Tamzin had said that once the evening reception was under way, her maid of honour duties were over, and she didn't mind if she and Bob sloped off. Well, Bob has already sloped off, Alice reasoned.

She found Tamzin and Cameron and said goodnight. She was planning to go up to her room, have one more drink from the minibar, perhaps a double, then go straight to sleep. Bob would get back and be none the wiser and she'd wake up refreshed and hangover-free, ready for breakfast. The minibar was so expensive, anyway; she couldn't possibly drink any more than that. Then she panicked. If she took anything from the minibar it would be charged to the room and would show on the bill. Bob was paying. New plan: she'd go to the hotel bar. No one from the wedding would be in there, so she could have one or two drinks using the cash in her purse, then head upstairs.

Alice practically inhaled her first double gin and tonic and was nursing her second while she scrolled through the pictures of the wedding she'd taken on her phone. A few of Tamzin and her dad, Tamzin and the bridesmaids, then she stopped at one of her and Bob that Natalie had taken. It was a great picture. They both looked gorgeous in their wedding attire, Bob had his arm around her waist, and they were grinning like Cheshire cats. Alice took a deep breath. That had only been taken a few hours ago; how far he'd fallen in her estimation since then. Abandoning her at her best friend's wedding – for what? She tried to ring him again and it went straight to voicemail. *He said he'd text when he was leaving, so he's not driving and could have answered. Where the hell is he and what exactly is he doing?* She put her phone on the table and had just let out a long sigh when she heard a voice beside her.

"What does a pretty lady like you have to sigh about?"

She looked up to see a man standing beside the table, pointing to the seat beside her.

"Is it because you're too pretty to be all on your own? May I join you for a drink?"

She rolled her eyes. She knew exactly why he wanted to sit with her. She looked like an easy target. Spinster bridesmaid sitting on her own in the bar drinking while the wedding reception was in full swing down the hall. But it wasn't as though Bob was keeping her company.

"I don't see why not. But only for a few minutes. I'm finishing this and then heading upstairs." She pointed to her glass, which was only about a third full.

"Aw, I'm sure you'll join me for another."

"I'm not supposed to talk to strangers."

"I'm Justin, and I'm buying."

She smiled at him. "I'm Alice, and I suppose I could have *one* more."

About two hours later, Bob arrived back at the hotel. He scanned the function room for Alice and, when he couldn't see her, he approached Tamzin. "How's the blushing bride?"

She threw her arms around his neck. "Grrreat! It's been an epic day."

He returned her hug. "I'm glad. I can't see Alice. Do you know where she is?"

"Oh, she felt awkward 'cause everyone was starting to drink and let their hair down. She went up to bed. Hey, where did you slope off to when there's a bridesmaid up in bed all alone?"

"I'd better get up there. Enjoy the rest of your night." He held a smile on his face just long enough to turn away from Tamzin and make his way to the door.

When he got into their room, it was in darkness. He crept over and turned on the lamp on the bedside table. He expected Alice to be sleeping, but the bed was empty and freshly made. He looked over at the bathroom door. It was closed. He knocked lightly before popping his head inside. It was empty. Where was she?

He went down to the reception desk. "McKendry, Room 203 – did my girlfriend pick up her key card?"

"Just one moment, sir." The receptionist checked the computer, then the pigeonholes. "No. Her key's still here."

"Where could she be? We're with the wedding. She's one of the bridesmaids." Then he felt a tap on his shoulder.

"Excuse me."

Bob turned to the man standing in line behind him.

"I've just come from the bar. There's a woman dressed like a bridesmaid in there. But if she's your girlfriend, you'd better hurry."

"Why?"

"She's wasted, and she looks like she's about to get off with some guy."

Bob rushed to the bar and immediately spotted Alice in a booth in the corner. A man was cuddled up against her, his arm around her. She was resting her head on his shoulder, smiling, while he stroked her knee and whispered into her ear.

Bob stormed over. "Get your fucking hands off her!" He grabbed Justin by the collar and dragged him out of the booth.

Justin shrugged free of Bob's grip and squared up to him. He was at least a head taller than him, a few years younger, and a lot better built. He glared back at Bob. "What's your problem, man?"

"You're my problem. That's my girlfriend."

They both looked at Alice, who had propped herself up against the back of the seat. She was struggling to keep her head up and was squinting at them, a confused look on her face.

"We were just having a few drinks. She didn't say anything about having a boyfriend."

"A few drinks? Look at the state of her."

"I'm fi-ne." Alice hiccupped. She tried to stand up from the table, but slumped back into her seat.

"She can't even stand up straight. Was that your plan?"

Justin cocked his head. "I don't like what you're implying."

"I don't like the way you're trying to prey on a vulnerable woman."

"Vulnerable?" Justin scoffed. "The little slut's been gagging for it."

Bob threw a punch at Justin, who only just managed to dodge before aiming his own punch towards Bob. It landed perfectly on his jaw. Bob stumbled backwards, then regained his footing. He was preparing to swing at Justin again when a woman screamed "Stop it!" and someone pulled him backwards.

It was Natalie and her husband. Lionel held Bob back while the bartender ran over and stood in front of Justin. "What the hell is going on here?" he asked.

Justin held his hands up. "He took a swipe at me first. I swear I only hit him in self-defence."

"He was trying it on with my girlfriend." Bob pointed to Alice, who was slumped over the table, sobbing.

Natalie sat down in the booth beside Alice and put her arm around her. The bartender looked at Justin, then at Bob. "I've been keeping an eye on them. They've been laughing and joking for ages; she certainly didn't look like she was complaining. But I saw her stumble back from the bathroom a while ago and I already told this guy that I wouldn't be serving her any more drinks. Now, is this misunderstanding over? Or do I need to call the police?"

Justin shrugged.

Bob rubbed his throbbing jaw and sighed. "It's over."

Justin grabbed his stuff and hurried out of the bar.

"Is she OK?" Bob asked Natalie.

"She's hammered."

"OK, Alice, let's get you upstairs." He held his hand out to her, but she cowered behind Natalie.

Natalie patted Alice's arm soothingly. "Come on, Alice. I'll take you up." She looked over at her husband. "Go and make sure Tamzin doesn't come out of that room. She can't see her like this. Bob, give me a hand."

Lionel hurried off to make sure the coast was clear, while Bob and Natalie tried to get Alice to her feet. Too drunk to protest any further, Alice allowed Bob to wrap his arm around her waist, and clung to him as he helped her out of the bar, through reception and into the lift. She looked half asleep. He propped her up against the wall and kept his arm around her waist, holding her steady as the lift jolted.

"Was she drinking at the reception?"

"I didn't see. But I know she had some brandy in the car on the way to the church. She told me it was fine ... that she didn't have a problem any more. But after you left she interrogated me – she was worried I'd told you. I wish I had. Maybe she wouldn't have ended up like this."

"It's not your fault." He sighed.

"Aren't you angry?"

"I'm livid," he said coldly. "But let's just get her to bed. Not a word to Tamzin."

"Of course not. And once we get Alice settled, I'll go down and explain. Ask the staff not to mention it in the morning."

"Thank you, Natalie."

Natalie didn't hang around. Once they'd got Alice into the room she took off, leaving Bob to deal with Alice. He watched quietly as she fiddled with the strap on her high heels. How had this happened? She was fine when he left. And what did Natalie mean when she said that Alice told her she didn't have a problem any more? He knew there was no love lost between the two of them, but in the short time he had spent in Natalie's company, he had found her to be pleasant and friendly.

He went over, knelt in front of Alice and took off her heels. Then he sat down beside her. She turned to face him. Her make-up was streaked and her eyes red and puffy from crying. "Do you hate me?" she asked quietly.

"No. I don't hate you." He kissed her on the cheek.

She leant against his shoulder. "I hate me."

He remained quiet. There really was nothing to say.

He sat with her for a few minutes, then went over to the dressing table, picked up a complimentary bottle of water and poured it into a glass. He brought it over to her. "Drink this, then we'll get you into bed. We'll talk tomorrow."

Chapter Fifteen

When Alice woke the next morning, she was alone in bed. She lifted her head and scanned the room. Bob was still dressed in his suit. He was sitting on the floor, his back against the wall, staring at her. He was pale, his eyes were heavy, and a nasty bruise had appeared on his chin. Their eyes met, but neither said a word.

Alice put her head back down on the pillow and closed her eyes. Her head was pounding, she felt sick, and she remembered more than she wanted to about the previous night. She lay still, knowing that very soon Bob would want to talk, and they'd fight. Then he'd probably break up with her.

She couldn't bear to face him. She couldn't bear to face herself.

After a few minutes, Bob got up from the floor and sat on the bed beside her. He touched her cheek. "How are you feeling?"

She shrugged. "I'm not sure yet."

"I'll send down for some proper coffee."

"I'm sorry," she whispered. Then braced herself.

He remained silent.

She was confused. She had been expecting more of a reaction. He was too calm, and too calm wasn't good. She was sure that it was over. He would break up with her and she would have no one to blame but herself.

"Why?" he asked eventually.

"I was anxious about the wedding. About my reading, and the speech. And I wasn't prepared for how I would feel in the church. The church where Dylan promised to love and cherish me until death do us part.

I panicked when I imagined all the ways poor Tam's happiness could be destroyed, like mine was. Then … you. You knew how difficult this wedding would be for me and you just abandoned me. For a stupid work thing. I felt so alone."

"My dad had a heart attack."

Fuck! Why didn't he just tell me that to start with? None of this would have happened then. If I'd known the truth, I would have been able to stay in control.

"I told Natalie to tell you it was work because I didn't want to worry you or ruin the day. But you were able to do that all by yourself..."

She winced. His words hurt, but he was right. This wasn't his fault for leaving her alone, or Justin's fault for plying her with drink. It was her fault. She was weak and selfish. She hadn't even asked after his dad. "How's your dad? Is he … alive?"

"He's stable. Once they got him settled, they kicked us out. I took Mum and Sam back to our place and I came here to get you and bring you home." The disappointment in his eyes was evident. "What if Tamzin had seen you?"

"She didn't."

"She could have. Anyone else at the wedding could have walked into that bar and seen you. Didn't you think about that?"

Alice hung her head in shame.

"I saw you. You were all over that guy. And his hands were on you. How do you think that made me feel?"

"Mad?"

"I must be. And I have an awful feeling that if I hadn't stopped you, you would have slept with him."

"No," she pleaded. "I wouldn't have. I swear."

"Let's pretend I don't know how you used to behave with men when you were drunk. Let's say I believe you. That guy thought he was on a promise. What if he wasn't the type of guy who takes no for an answer?"

"He was. I told him. He knew."

"How many victims of date rape have thought the same? A few more drinks and he could have lured you to his room or followed you back here. You could have been hurt – or worse."

"No. I was in control."

"You're deluded!"

"I wasn't deluded. I can control it now. I just forgot myself and got carried away."

He squinted at her. "What are you talking about?"

"Nothing," she said quickly. As far as he knew, this was the only time she'd had a drink since the night they met. She could get away with it. All she had to do was convince him it was a one-off, beg his forgiveness, then never have another drink. She could do it. She had to.

"No. Not nothing. Natalie said you told her in the car when you were drinking brandy that you didn't have a problem any more. What did you mean by that?"

"She must have misheard."

"Did I mishear too?"

"No. It was just one day. Like the day we met. And now I'll stop. Like I did that time. I swear, no more. I don't want to lose you."

"You won't lose me. But I'm worried sick about you. I was up all night thinking about the mistakes I made. I was so caught up in falling in love with you that I forgot about your addiction. I thought you were stronger than *it* was. Turns out, I know nothing. And when was the last time you went to a meeting? *We* don't even talk about it any more. Things have to change. Listen, I know I'm not perfect. I'm going to let you down, piss you off, but I need to know you won't hit the bottle every time I do. We are not going to sweep this under the carpet like we did last time. We have to confront it head-on."

She nodded. "I'll go to meetings again. I promise."

"And we need to talk about it. All the time."

"All the time. So, do you still love me?"

"Of course I do. But I'm still mad at you, and at myself for letting this happen. And when we get home and I get my dad sorted, we're going to come up with a new game plan." He kissed her on the lips, then stood up. "I'll phone down for that coffee. We'd better get showered and changed."

She groaned and pulled the sheet over her head.

He ripped it off her. "Your maid of honour duties aren't over yet. You need to make yourself look presentable and get downstairs for breakfast. Act your ass off so no one knows you're hungover. You've organised the limo and the big bubble fest at noon to wave the newlyweds off on honeymoon, remember? You don't want to miss that."

She dragged herself out of bed and headed for the bathroom, but stopped beside Bob and wrapped her arms around him. She smiled to herself when he did the same. She'd done it. Averted disaster. She just had to stick to it this time. No more drinking. The all-too-familiar feeling of dread pooled in Alice's stomach.

Before they entered the breakfast room, Bob reached for Alice's hand and squeezed it tightly. "How are you feeling now?"

"Not too bad. I think I'm more upset than hungover."

"You'll feel better after a bite to eat."

He held the door for her. Just as she was about to step into the room, Justin stepped out. Bob's grip on her hand tightened as the three stood there in silence. Alice was mortified. She couldn't look Justin in the eye. Images flashed into her mind of how shamelessly she had flirted with him the night before. Justin stared at the bruise on Bob's chin.

"It was self-defence, mate."

Bob just nodded and held out his hand for Justin to shake. He did, then turned to Alice. "Are you OK?"

She nodded.

"Good. I'm sorry. I didn't mean you any harm. Enjoy your breakfast." He scurried off.

"There you are!" Tamzin called from across the room. She looked gorgeous in a silk dress, her hair tousled from the million clips she'd had in it the day before. She waved them over. "Sit next to us." She stood up and gave Alice a big hug. "Everything you did yesterday was perfect. Thank you so much."

Alice forced a smile. If only Tamzin knew about what she'd done the night before. She could have ruined the whole day.

Tamzin was about to hug Bob when she noticed his bruise. "What happened to you?"

He rubbed his chin. "Cut myself shaving."

Tamzin nodded, then screwed up her face. "What?"

"It happened at work. You just didn't notice last night when we spoke."

"Oh, OK. You found her, then. And you both look exhausted. What naughtiness have you been getting up to?"

Cameron nudged her. "Boundaries, wifey."

"*Bound*, more like," she joked. "Oh, there's Natalie and Lionel. The waitress said it was OK to pull that table over, hubby. Come sit over here!"

Natalie and Lionel smiled as they joined the expanding table. Tamzin hugged them both and before Natalie sat down she went over and hugged Alice. "You OK?" she whispered into her ear.

Alice nodded. "Yes. Thank you."

"Oh, look at that. My girls finally getting along." Tamzin clapped her hands with delight. "I wish my dad would hurry up and come down, then I'd have all my favourite people to share breakfast with."

Just then the waitress arrived with Bloody Marys for the bride and groom.

"You're an angel. Could we get five more of these, please? But virgin for these two." Tamzin pointed at Alice and Bob, then took a gulp of her drink. "Ugh, I needed that. You're so lucky you don't drink any more, Alice – hangovers are the worst."

Alice could practically hear Bob, Natalie and Lionel judging her. She sank lower in her chair.

On the way home, they were both quiet. Alice stared out of the window, going over everything in her mind. She was worried that Bob's reaction to the whole thing hadn't been severe enough. Yes, he had tried to punch Justin, but she would have felt better if he had screamed and shouted at her. She wouldn't hold it against him, and at least he would have vented instead of keeping things bottled up. But she was beginning to realise that that was Bob's style. Like when Christine left him, or with his new role as a parent, he just seemed to accept things and move on. Every few minutes she initiated a bit of small talk, about the scenery or the quality of other people's driving. Bob always responded politely, which made her even more paranoid. Was he being *too* polite?

He pulled up outside the house and switched off the engine. He turned to face her. "My mum and Sam are in there. I can't deal with everything at once."

She nodded.

"I texted and told her that you had food poisoning. Can I ask you to play along? Just go straight up to bed and lie down. I'll come up in a bit."

That sounded reasonable enough; one more lie wouldn't be too hard to tell. She nodded again.

He reached across and squeezed her knee. "Don't look so worried. I love you and we can get past this. We've just got a lot of talking to do."

"I know."

"But for the next few hours, my dad has to be my main focus." He got out of the car and went around to the passenger side to help her out.

She smiled when he took her by the hand. "I love you, too."

Alice went straight upstairs, but couldn't help overhearing Peggy ask, "Where's Alice?"

"She went up to bed. She's still not feeling well."

"Oh, the poor girl. Pink chicken should be a hanging offence. I hope she reported it to the management. And what happened to your face?"

"Oh, nothing. There was a scuffle at the hotel, I tried to break it up. Got this for my trouble. Any word from the hospital?"

"I spoke to Dad himself this morning. The

cantankerous old fart told me to leave him alone. Said he's enjoying the peace and quiet."

Alice couldn't help laughing. She really liked Robert senior, and hoped he'd make a full recovery. The most intense feeling of guilt washed over her. She should be down there with Bob, Peggy and Sam, helping them through this difficult time. Bob shouldn't have to lie and split his attention between his family and his hungover girlfriend. Why did she fall apart when he needed her most? And she could have easily made a fool of herself in front of Tamzin and ruined her wedding. *Mum was right that day. I don't think about how my actions affect other people. Why am I so selfish?*

She went into the bedroom and lay down. She was still hungover, but tomorrow she wouldn't be, and that would be day two again. No more drinking with work people at lunch or at the end of the day. No more buying bottles and sneaking them into the house to drink when Tam wasn't around. *Shit! There's still that last bottle I brought here from Tam's. I didn't get a chance to get rid of it.* She glanced over at her side of the wardrobe. The bottle was hidden in a shoebox, inside a bigger box, which she had pushed to the back of the wardrobe and placed some shoes neatly in front of it. She had to get rid of it. *I'll wait until he leaves to go to the hospital to see his dad.* She pulled the duvet over her head and snuggled into her pillow. There was something about hiding away under the covers that made her feel safe and comforted, as if nothing could hurt her. She didn't mean to, but she fell asleep.

When she woke it was 7 p.m. and the house was quiet. She went downstairs to confirm that there was no one home. After checking quickly out of the window to make sure Bob's car wasn't there, she hurried back upstairs to retrieve the bottle. Time was of the essence. She had no idea when he had left or when he would be back.

She pushed the shoes to the side, slid out the big box and took out the smaller shoebox. She took off the lid and there it was. About a third of a bottle of Tesco's own-brand gin. She contemplated drinking it. *It's not enough to get me really drunk, but it would take the edge off this hangover. And it won't matter if he can smell it on me; he'll assume it was from last night.* The bottle shook in her hand. *No. I can't. I'll pour it down the sink, then wrap the shoebox in a few plastic bags and hide it at the bottom of the bin outside. I'll cover it in rubbish; Bob will never see it.*

She set the shoebox on the bed and slid the bigger box back into the wardrobe, then rearranged all the shoes neatly in front of it again. She had just straightened up and reached for the shoebox when she heard the front door close, then footsteps on the stairs. In a panic, she grabbed the box and was holding it, wondering what to do with it, when Bob stuck his head round the door.

"You're up." He pushed the door open. "I came up earlier but you were sleeping, so I let you be. We all went to the hospital, then I took Mum and Sam back to her house. He's going to stay with her for a few days. She wants the company, and I thought we could use the time to talk."

Alice nodded and tried to stop shaking so the bottle wouldn't rattle around in the box.

"You OK?"

"Yeah. I'm just hungry. I haven't eaten anything since breakfast."

"Me neither. I should have brought something back. I'll nip out again."

Perfect. I'll have time while he's out.

"What do you fancy?"

"Anything. You choose. I'm not overly hungry."

"But you just said you were."

"Did I?"

"Yes. You're exhausted." He pointed to the box. "Do you want me to put that in the attic with the rest of them?"

"No. Um, I was just going to put this … in the bin."

"I'll do it on my way out." He held out his hand, but she pulled the box away from him.

"No. I'll do it."

He rolled his eyes. "Why are you so bloody stubborn? Gimme the box."

He'll want to break it down for the recycling. He'll see the bottle. He'll know what I've been doing... She sat down on the bed and cradled the box against her chest. *Who am I trying to fool? I won't be able to stop drinking. I'm dreading trying. Bob deserves better, and I don't deserve him. Mum was right. I've ruined everything.*

Tears were flowing down her cheeks when she handed the box to Bob. "Please don't be cross. It's … left over … from before."

He took it cautiously and opened the lid.

Alice waited. And waited. But he didn't speak.

Bob finally looked up at her. His eyes were desolate. He took the bottle from the box. It shook in his hand as he brandished it in front of her. "You brought alcohol into this house?"

She didn't answer.

"Last night wasn't the first time, was it? How long has this been going on?"

She remained silent.

"How long?" he yelled. "How many times?"

Alice trembled as she tried to come up with another lie to explain the bottle. But even if she could, she knew she couldn't hide her drinking from him now that they were living together. The only way she would be able to stop – again – would be to admit that she had a problem and ask for help. Whether help would come from him or not was a different problem. She wouldn't blame him if he broke up with her. Perhaps he wouldn't mourn their relationship as much if he knew how pathetic she really was.

"I've been drinking for months."

He slumped onto the bed beside her.

"I thought I had it under control. I had one or two each time, then stopped. I did. Every time. I was testing myself to see if I was normal again. The odd time, I drank more than I should, passed out. Lost time. Woke up with a hangover."

"Your headaches ... I thought you might need glasses. I never even suspected a hangover. How stupid am I?"

"You're not stupid."

"Aren't I? And where was I when you were doing all this drinking? And Sam. Were you drunk when you were with us?"

"No," she said quickly. "Never. Not when I was with you or Sam. I didn't need it then." She suddenly remembered the hen night. She'd had no need to drink that night either, but she had done it anyway. "Just one time. At Tam's hen night. Everyone else was drinking. I felt lonely, left out."

"Lonely?" he scoffed. "How could you be lonely in a group of people? How could you be lonely knowing I was down the hall waiting for you?"

"You don't understand."

"You're damn right I don't," he snapped. He took a deep breath to steady himself. "And what happened yesterday?"

"I was worried about the wedding so I had a few, just to steady my nerves, like I told you. Then when I thought you'd abandoned me for something stupid at work, I thought I could have a few more. I'd sleep it off and be OK this morning."

"So you were drinking before I left?"

"Yes. Just a few. But then I couldn't stop myself. I didn't want to."

"You want to drink?" He unscrewed the lid from the gin and offered her the bottle. "Go ahead."

She shook her head.

"What's the problem? Drink."

"No," she said quietly.

"Drink!" he yelled, forcing the bottle into her hand.

Tears streamed down her face as she examined the bottle. It was touch and go whether or not the gin would have actually made it down the sink. She wanted to drink it, but what good would it do? It wasn't enough. It wouldn't be enough until she had passed out and couldn't see the disappointment on his face any more, or forget the way he'd looked at her when he saw her with Justin.

Justin. This is all his fault! She threw the bottle at the wall. They flinched when the bottle smashed into tiny pieces and gin and splinters of glass flew back at them.

"You happy now?" Alice screamed.

"Far fucking from it!" he shouted back. He looked her in the eye. "You've been lying to me. For months. And you dare stand there and ask me if I'm happy about it? Everyone told me I was making a mistake being with you. My friends, my mother, *your* mother. Even y*ou* warned me to stay away from you." He could see she was shaking but he continued to shout at her. "But no! I thought I knew better. That you were better than the booze. I took you into my home, made you part of my family. All because I thought you loved me."

"I do love you," she pleaded.

"How am I supposed to believe you after I've just found out what a fantastic liar you are? I didn't even suspect – because I trusted you!" His gaze darted around the room. "Where's the rest of it?" He stormed to the wardrobe and flung the doors open.

"There isn't any more."

He didn't relent. He rifled through her shelves and hangers, then kicked away the shoes and pulled out the big box. He emptied the contents onto the bed and scanned them quickly. He did the same with another box. When he didn't find anything he got down on his knees and looked under the bed.

"I said, there isn't any more."

When he looked up at her, she froze. The look in his eyes was frantic. She thought she'd seen him angry the night before when he tried to punch Justin. But this was nothing like that. She thought he was going to explode.

"You've said a lot of things." He got to his feet and went to the dresser. He pulled open her underwear drawer and rummaged through it. He slammed it closed, then did the same to the next drawer, and the next one. When he didn't find anything, he grabbed the dresser and shook it violently, rattling all of Alice's make-up and perfume bottles, which were arranged neatly on the top. He swiped his arm across the dresser, sending everything crashing to the floor. He turned round and glared at Alice. "How could you do this to me if you loved me? How could you do it to yourself? I... I can't look at you right now." He stormed out of the bedroom, slamming the door behind him.

Alice wasn't sure whether to follow him or let him go, so she stood and surveyed the mess on the floor. Everything was broken. Nothing could be salvaged or fixed. Including her relationship and new life. Her hands were shaking as she rubbed her aching temples. *What have I done?* She sank down onto the bed and tried to clear her head, but it was no use. The smell of gin mingled with her perfumes was making her nauseous. She had to get out of the room but couldn't bear to face Bob.

She picked up her mobile from the bedside table and hurried downstairs. She grabbed her handbag and coat and headed to the front door, not knowing where she would go, or what she would do when she got there. She reached for the handle but froze when she heard Bob behind her.

"I need to know if you really love me, or if that was a lie too."

She took a deep breath. Without turning, she said, "I do love you."

"Then don't go."

When she turned to face him, a tired smile crossed his face, almost distracting her from his red, swollen eyes. Grateful, she slid her arms around his waist and rested her head on his chest. She could feel his heart pounding against her cheek: it was just as fast as hers. She screwed her eyes closed and held him as close as she could.

"I love you too," he whispered.

They stood in the hallway with nothing but silence between them.

After a few minutes Bob led Alice into the living room, and they sat down on the sofa. He cradled her hand in his. "I don't understand why you can't just stop. I have. I haven't had a drink in months. It's easy. I just don't do it."

"It's not that simple."

"Why? Explain it to me."

"I can't. My therapist said that most addictions stem from an underlying problem. I had depression and anxiety when I was younger. They came back full force when I found out I couldn't have children. I felt so inadequate, like my life suddenly had no meaning. And the one person in the world who should have been there for me felt the same. I begged Dylan not to leave me, but he threw away our twelve years like they meant nothing to him. Like *I* meant nothing to him. He rejected me, and I felt like nothing. Alcohol helped drown out some of the pain in my heart and the noise in my head. It made me not care that my life was falling apart. Losing my job and my driving licence should have been enough to make me stop, but it didn't. I didn't care about my personal safety. I put myself in danger over and over again by getting drunk and going home with strangers. You were right about Justin…"

Bob clenched his fists.

"He could have been a predator. Any of the men I

slept with could have been. I wasn't thinking about the risks; I was desperate for love, for validation that I was still a woman. The reason I didn't end up hurt or dead was blind luck. Then there was my accident – again, I was lucky that my roommate was home and I didn't bleed to death on the bathroom floor. And yesterday at the wedding, I sat at the table and I drank in front of you. In front of Tam. Like I was invincible and nothing could go wrong. Then last night..." She began to cry again. "I nearly threw away everything I've ever wanted. If you hadn't been there to witness it, or find that bottle upstairs, I'd have got away with it. Then I'd have done it again. And again. Because I just can't stop." She looked up at him. A tear was rolling down his cheek. She wiped it away and cupped his face in her hands. "I do love you." She kissed him softly on the lips. "I want to stop, but I know I need help. Will you help me?"

He pulled her close, and they sat together in silence.

After a while, Bob went upstairs to clean up the mess in the bedroom while Alice went to make something quick and easy to eat. They sat at the kitchen table in silence and watched their scrambled eggs and toast go cold. They didn't say a word to each other until bedtime.

"Neither of us is going into the office tomorrow. I'm going to fire up the laptop to see what's scheduled and give Kristof a call to make sure he can handle everything. You go up. I won't be long."

She knew Kristof would already have organised everything for the morning but nodded and went upstairs to bed. Bob didn't come up for a long time. She assumed he wanted to be on his own for a while, and couldn't blame him. Everything was such a mess, when two days ago it had been perfect. *But it wasn't perfect. That was just another lie I told myself.*

After about two hours of tossing and turning, she heard Bob coming up the stairs. Quickly, she turned onto her side to face the wall and pretended to be asleep.

"Alice?" he whispered. She didn't answer. He undressed and got into bed, where he lay facing her. He placed his hand on her hip, and caressed her gently. Alice sighed. His touch was so comforting – it was his way of letting her know he loved her. She rolled over to face him.

He ran his fingers through her hair. "I'm sorry I shouted at you."

"I'm glad you did. I hate the silent treatment."

"Nothing about our way forward is going to be silent. There's going to be a lot of talking. But it's going to be OK. You know that, don't you?"

She didn't answer, but she hoped so.

"Try and get some rest. Tomorrow is going to be a long day."

She nestled against his chest and closed her eyes. Although she felt safe and comforted, she couldn't help worrying about what his words had meant.

Chapter Sixteen

When Alice woke up the next morning, she was alone in bed. That wasn't unusual, but today she felt uneasy. Physically, she felt fine: the hangover was gone, and it was just regret that lingered. She picked up her phone to check the time. 7.32. A text from Bob was waiting.

Just nipped out to get bread and milk. Back soon. x

He'd sent it at 6.58. Thirty-four minutes to nip to the corner shop? Was he avoiding her? Truthfully, she wanted to avoid him too. At the very least, she wanted to avoid another fight. How would they get through this? If he even still wanted to. Maybe he had slept on it and decided that he wanted to break up with her after all. If that was the case, she only had herself to blame. Perhaps she should just break up with him. It would tear her apart, but he and Sam would be better off without her. A lump formed in her throat. She shook it off and tried to gather her thoughts. *I have to be more proactive about my addiction. I'll get a timetable of AA meetings and go every day. I'll make an appointment with my GP and ask them for help. I've let my gym visits slide too. Before I met Bob, I went five or six times a week, now it's just one or two. Time to get my life back on track.*

After a long soak in the bath, Alice threw on a pair of jeans and her favourite hoodie and went downstairs. When she reached the living-room door, she heard familiar voices on the other side. She opened the door and was startled to see her mum and dad sitting on the sofa.

A silence fell. Although Alice had frozen on the spot, her stomach was doing somersaults. *What the hell is happening? They couldn't have called over unannounced; they don't know Bob's address. He must have called them.* Her surprise turned to anger. *How could he betray me like this? He knows how I feel about my mother. She's the last person I want to know about what happened.*

Her gaze darted to Bob and she got her answer. He looked guilty as hell.

"Oh, my darling. Come here." Amanda got up and held her arms out wide.

Alice glanced at Bob. He nodded encouragingly, so she approached her mum and was pulled into an embrace.

"My poor girl," Amanda sobbed. "My poor, poor girl."

Stephen joined his wife and daughter, and the three of them held each other. Bob excused himself and retreated to the kitchen.

Once they had composed themselves, they sat down on the sofa, Alice in the middle seat and her parents on either side of her. She looked from one to the other, trying to figure out what was happening. The ticking of the clock on the wall was driving her insane; she just wished that someone would say something. But her parents seemed to be waiting for Bob.

Finally Bob arrived back from the kitchen with a mug of coffee for Alice. He smiled as he handed it to her, then went to sit in the armchair. He took a deep breath. "Alice, this is an intervention."

Alice jolted up from her seat and looked towards the front door.

"Don't worry," Bob said. "There's nobody else coming. I'm out of my depth here – I didn't know what else to do. I went to your parents' house this morning and told them everything. Please sit down so we can talk."

Alice nodded and sat down slowly. She tried desperately to hold back her tears, but when her mum's grip on her knee tightened, she let her tears flow freely. "I'm sorry," she whispered. "I've let everyone down."

"Don't be sorry, baby," her dad said softly.

"I thought I had it under control. Now I know that I didn't – and I never will. I promise all three of you that I'm never going to drink again. I'll go to AA meetings again, every day."

They nodded.

"And I'll go to my doctor and ask for some counselling as well…" She noticed them exchange a guilty look. "What's going on?"

Bob held up his hand. He was clearly in charge here. "Um, the time for meetings has come and gone."

"What?"

"When you first thought that you could have a drink and stop – that was the time to go to a meeting. When you started to drink – one, then two – that was the time to ask for help. This has gone way beyond what we can manage."

"What … are you suggesting?" Her chest tightened as the conspirators exchanged another look.

"There's a rehab place. Just outside the city. They have outpatient programmes, but we think residential is better for you. You have an appointment at four o'clock this afternoon. If they think you're suitable, they have a space for you. It's a twenty-one-day programme."

Residential? Alice let out a nervous laugh. "No. I don't need a twenty-one-day programme."

"But darling, the brochure says 'The sooner you take steps to remedy it, the easier it will be to tackle the problem'."

"But there are meetings … and you know those pills you can take that make you vomit if you drink? I'll take those. You can hide them in my food. I promise I won't even try to look for them." She grabbed her dad's arm. "Please, Daddy. You can't let *her* send me back there." She scowled at her mum.

"This is a different place, baby. A private clinic. And I don't want you to worry about the money. Bob and I are going to split the cost."

"Yes, darling. Let us show you some pictures on the internet." Amanda pointed to Bob's laptop, which was open on the coffee table. "It's a 'calming, secure and confidential environment in which you can focus fully on your treatment and recovery without the distractions and temptations of outside life'. And they have a gym, lovely gardens – you'll like it there."

"No!" Alice snapped. "I'm not going, and you can't make me. Not this time!"

Bob screwed up his face. "But you loved it last time..."

Her parents did a double take. "Is that what she told you?"

Bob nodded. "Alice?"

She avoided his eye.

"She did nothing but cry for the first week. She refused to see us when we visited, and when we phoned, she hung up. Then during the second week, every word out of her mouth was an obscenity."

Stephen rubbed his temples. "The clinic said she was disruptive and uncooperative, they suggested she try a programme in another facility. But when we arrived to pick her up, she begged us to let her stay because she didn't want to start all over again somewhere else. She promised to behave, and she did. She came around, did anything they asked of her so she could complete the programme and get out of there."

Dumbstruck, Bob turned back to Alice. "Why did you tell me you loved it?"

"To sound brave." She shrugged. "I didn't want you knowing how weak I was."

"I don't think you're weak. You don't have to love rehab; you just have to do it. And you can do it again. This time you'll have me and Sam waiting for you when you come home."

"I can't..."

"You can. You just need to trust me, like I trusted you."

She scowled at him.

"All the things I've let you do with the business. Do you think I would have let you take control if I didn't trust you? Now, I need you to trust me. The next twenty-one days are an investment in your future. In mine and Sam's future too."

"And we're right behind you, darling," her mum assured her. "You have our full support and our love. No matter what happens, you'll always have those things. We just want you to be healthy and happy. I'm so sorry that I wasn't more positive about your relationship with Bob. He's a good man, and I can see how much he loves you." She smiled at Bob.

Alice looked around the room. Her parents had tears

in their eyes. She'd do anything to take away their disappointment, even if she couldn't shake the hatred she felt for herself. It was going to be tough, but they were right. She had to do it. With a heavy heart, she stood up and forced a smile. "I'll go and pack a bag."

Bob and her parents shared a hopeful look as Alice went upstairs.

Alice grabbed a bag – the one she had only recently unpacked – and threw in some socks, underwear … what else would she need? Her head was foggy. How could this be happening? Surely they're overreacting. She thought back to the first time she'd been in rehab. It was a terrifying experience. The withdrawal hadn't even been the worst part; it was the realisation of how unmanageable things had become and the thought of the uphill struggle she'd face to gain any sort of control over her life again.

She tried not to think about it, and opened the wardrobe for some clothes. The first thing she saw was her shoes, neatly lined up in front of the box in which she had hidden the gin. Hidden. Gin. That on its own was a big enough warning sign that she was out of control. And the lies. She'd lied to everyone she cared about, but the biggest lies had been the ones she'd told herself. She selected a few tops and some comfy trousers and pyjamas, then went into the bathroom to get her toothbrush and some other toiletries. *What else did I take last time? Will this be my last time, or should I make a list so I know what to bring next time? I could have a bag ready, like pregnant women do when they're close to their due dates.* She almost laughed at the thought.

She went back into the bedroom and found Bob sitting on the side of the bed. He tried to smile, but it didn't disguise his worry.

She felt a pain in her chest. She had spent the last few days thinking only about herself, and hadn't given a thought to what, or how, he must be feeling. There was no doubt in her mind that he loved her, and she loved him too. It was breaking her heart making him go through this – and what if it didn't work? She'd be subjecting him and Sam to a lifetime of worry and uncertainty. It wasn't fair. They hadn't even been together for a year yet; maybe they should cut their losses before it went any further. It seemed clear to her that they would be better off without her.

She put her toiletries into the bag and sat down on the bed next to him.

"All packed?"

"Um, yeah. I've got what I need for the next few weeks. But I want you to pack up the rest of my stuff. I'll ask my dad to come and collect it. I won't be coming back here."

"Why?"

"I think us being together is a mistake."

"What?"

"This is my life, but it doesn't have to be yours. Or Sam's. I'm not good enough for you both."

"Stop it. We love you."

"You said it yourself last night. Everyone warned you, and you should have listened. I overheard you talking to your mum that day. She thinks you're settling for me. And she might be right."

"I'm not 'settling' for you."

"Yes, you are. And do you know what? Maybe I'm

settling for you too."

"Rubbish."

"It's not. Think about it. We're not each other's first choice. If I could have had kids and your sister hadn't died, we wouldn't be together."

"But those things did happen. They don't prove that we're settling for each other – they prove that the people we were married to were settling for us!"

She recoiled.

"They didn't love us. Not properly. If they did, they would have stuck with us, not taken off when the shit hit the fan. You and I belong together. We know what it takes to make a relationship work, and we're willing to do it. It's support, compromise, and unconditional love. Knowing that neither of us is perfect and embracing that. Not trying to change each other into who we want them to be. I don't know what's going on inside that head of yours to make you think you don't deserve to be loved. But I love you. And I know you love me. So, this isn't over."

"But that fight we had last night – how can we move past that?"

"We fought because you lied to me. I thought being an alcoholic meant you got shit-faced more than the average person. I wasn't prepared for the lies. That's why I was so angry, but I know you didn't do it on purpose; it's part of the addiction. I get that now. You've been trying to do this all on your own. That's why you're beginning to struggle. It's reset time. You need to go to the clinic and get your head straight. And I need some time apart from you to take stock and prepare myself to support you properly." He checked his watch. "It's nearly time to go. I wanted to take you, but your mum has insisted."

"No!" Alice snapped. "She'll make a scene. You take me, or I'm not going."

"But..."

"Are you afraid of my mum?"

"A little."

The journey seemed to take forever. Alice kept her head down and tried to block out the memories from last time. The withdrawal, shame and embarrassment. At least she wouldn't have to detox this time. That was one plus. She looked over at Bob and smiled. He was another plus – and so was Sam. Even her parents were in a better, more understanding place. They'd been here before. She sat back and looked out of the window. But just as she did, the car turned off the main road onto a gravel driveway that wound through woodland for what seemed like miles. Eventually it opened up into a car park. Bob parked and turned off the engine. Alice suddenly couldn't breathe.

As if sensing her panic, he put his hand on her knee and squeezed. "It looks lovely."

She didn't answer.

He took off his seat belt and turned to face her. "I can't pretend that I know how hard this is for you. But I have faith in you. I know you can do it."

His words gave her some comfort. He was right – she'd done it before, and the hard way, resisting at every turn. This time, if she could throw herself into it, pretend it was a test or project at work, she'd breeze through it. She took a deep breath and undid her seat belt. "I'm ready."

They walked hand in hand across the car park to the front door of the converted Grade II listed Georgian manor house. She felt like she had arrived at a spa when she compared it to the hospital she'd been in previously, but when they were greeted at the door by a portly woman dressed in a white coat and holding a clipboard, the illusion was shattered.

"You must be Alice," the woman said cheerfully, then turned to Bob. "You're Bob, and I'm Ursula, one of the coordinators. It was me you spoke to on the phone."

Bob shook her hand. "Thanks for seeing us at such short notice."

"It's usually the way here. If you want to come with me into the office, I'll have a quick chat with you both, and then you can go, Bob."

Alice shrank back against Bob's shoulder.

"Don't worry, Alice, you're in good hands here." Ursula showed them through the elegant reception area into a bright, airy office and offered them a seat. "Alice, all I need to know right now is why you're here."

Alice looked at Bob, who nodded reassuringly.

"Um, I'm here because ... I don't want to drink again."

"Good. That's what we want for you too. Bob told me that you have been in a programme before. Can you tell me about it?"

She shrugged. "Um, I was referred after an accident ... that happened after I'd been drinking. It was about a year and a half ago. I hated every second of being in that place. But I got through it, and managed to stay sober for two hundred and forty-three days before I had my first slip. It was a single binge-drinking session. I was able to stop the next day."

"That's good."

"Not really. Because I only managed to stay sober for

sixty-five days that time." She looked at the ground when she realised she hadn't told Bob how long it had actually been going on. "I'm sorry." Her voice wobbled.

"It's OK, Alice. Just be honest."

"I thought I could handle one or two drinks. And I could. So I did that a couple of times. Then it became more than one or two. I have drunk to excess several times over the past month or two. All the time, I managed to hide it." Her gaze darted to Bob.

He reached for her hand and gave it a squeeze.

"Then the other night, I kept drinking. I didn't stop. I just didn't want to. I could have lost everything that night. Bob found out. He also found alcohol I had hidden in the house. And now I'm here because ... I don't want to drink again."

Ursula scribbled something on her notepad. "All right. We can offer you a place here to help you get back on track. We will tailor a treatment plan specifically for your needs. Now, I'll step out and give you a few minutes to say goodbye." She left the office, closing the door behind her.

Alice felt a weight on her shoulders. Her eyes welled with tears. Bob pulled her into an embrace and softly whispered into her ear. "It's OK. You're in the best place, and I'm always at the other end of the phone. There's visiting on Saturday. It's only five days away."

"OK." Her voice wobbled.

Bob stood up and led Alice to the door. When she saw Ursula, who was waiting in the hallway, Alice wrapped her arms around Bob. When he tried to pull away, she wouldn't let go. She clung to him like an infant being left with a childminder for the first time. Ursula had to peel her off him, then kept her arm firmly around Alice while Bob walked to the door.

"Please don't leave me here," Alice cried.

Bob hesitated and looked at Ursula.

"Just go," she said. "I'll look after Alice."

He choked back his tears and hurried out of the door.

Tears streamed down Alice's face. She was shaking so much, she thought she was going to vomit.

Ursula placed her hand on Alice's arm. "Come on, I'll show you to your room. You can have a few minutes to yourself to settle in."

Alice was on autopilot as Ursula led her down a corridor and up two flights of stairs. She was pointing things out as they went, but Alice couldn't hear a word over the beating of her heart. When they reached her room, Ursula placed Alice's bag on one of the two beds. "This is your bed. Your roommate has a class at the moment, but you'll meet her later. You two should get on well together."

Roommate? Alice recalled her roommate from the last time she was in rehab. She'd had an awful habit of narrating everything she was doing, that had almost sent Alice insane. "Can't I have a room of my own?"

"Your boyfriend asked for one, but we don't have one available. When we do, we'll move you over. Although you might find you enjoy having a roommate. Someone to talk to, share your experiences with, share the process of recovery. She's quite quiet, keeps herself to herself. Now..." She pointed to Alice's bag. "I'm really sorry, but I have to check your bag. Make sure there's nothing in there that might hinder your recovery."

"Go ahead." Alice watched Ursula – a complete stranger – go through her belongings. It was so embarrassing. Why couldn't the ground just swallow her up? There was nothing in her bag that shouldn't be, but that didn't stop her cheeks from burning.

"Everything looks in order here. Why don't you settle in and I'll come back and get you in about ten minutes." Ursula left, closing the door behind her.

Alice sat down on the bed. She was still shaking, but she tried to calm herself with a few deep breaths while she looked around the room. It was a generous double with ample natural light. Two beds, two chests of drawers, two writing desks with chairs, all Scandinavian oak, which perfectly complemented the original features of the room and the more contemporary additions, like the pop art on the walls. She got up from the bed and peeked into the bathroom. It was over-the-top luxurious in chrome and marble, with a roll-top bath and a walk-in shower. She shuddered when she thought of the price that her dad and Bob must be paying for this, and promised herself that she'd pay them back. Every penny.

Back in the bedroom, she looked out of the window at a perfectly landscaped lawn, exploding with the reds and oranges of autumn, and a stone path leading into a forest. The trees looked to be hundreds of years old. There were a few people out walking, and a woman sitting beneath a huge tree, reading in the evening sun. The place was stunning. It was such a shame Bob wasn't there to share it with her. But then again, she wasn't there on holiday. However fancily they tried to dress the place up, it was still a hospital.

Just then the door opened. Alice turned around to see a young woman enter the room. She was short, painfully thin, with long, straggly blonde hair, pasty skin and sunken eyes. The most disturbing thing about her appearance was her age. Alice estimated that she was no older than sixteen.

The girl rolled her eyes when she saw Alice at the window. "I thought I'd have the place to myself for a few days at least. You'd better not snore like the last one."

"I don't think I do. I'm Alice."

"My name is Alice, too. What are the odds?"

"I'd say slim at best."

"Gotcha!" the girl exclaimed. "My name's Fleur. But I really wish I had a normal name like yours."

Alice let out a laugh. No one had ever been jealous of her name before.

"So, did you detox for long?" Fleur asked.

"No."

"Good – that shit's hard on you. I'll never get used to it."

Never? Alice winced. "How many times have you done it?"

"This is number four. Drugs and alcohol."

"Four? How old are you?"

"Nineteen."

Alice couldn't stop her jaw from dropping. There was no way this waif of a girl was nineteen.

"I know. I get that a lot. I've been drinking since I was eleven."

Alice opened her mouth to speak, but nothing came out.

"I know what you're thinking. Where does an eleven-year-old get alcohol? Boarding school, that's where. Drugs, too, lots of drugs. Do you want to get better, Alice?"

"Yes."

"Good. Then stay away from me. I don't want to be here, and I'm probably going to start drinking and using again as soon as I leave. I always do."

"Why?"

"Because I want to."

"Then why are you here in the first place?"

"My dad sticks me in here every now and then so he can look like a responsible parent. Tight bastard won't even spring for a private room. He says the company will be good for me. I only stay in this shithole because he threatens to cut off my trust fund. He doesn't give a toss about me."

"But don't you give a toss about yourself?"

"Yeah. I want to be happy. Getting fucked up makes me happy."

The door opened and Ursula came in. "Hi, Fleur," she said with a smile. "I see you've met Alice already. I want you to be nicer to her than you were to Toni."

"Phoney, more like."

"Fleur!"

"What? Nothing about that woman was real. The boobs, the hair colour, the teeth... Even the posh accent she tried to put on."

Ursula shook her head and turned to Alice. "If you're ready, I'll show you around before dinner."

"Have a good time, Alice. Ursula's a hoot. I'll save you a seat for dinner."

Alice nodded and followed Ursula out of the room.

Ursula gave Alice a tour of the clinic and explained some of the ground rules. "You're free to leave at any time, but we ask that you come and talk to someone before you do. If after that you still want to go, we won't try to stop you, but we will ask that you let us call someone to come and get you. We really don't want you leaving here by yourself. You can keep your mobile phone with you, but social media is a no-no. It's really bad for your mental health. Reserve your phone for calling friends and loved ones, but try to limit it to your free time. Meals are three times a day, and healthy snacks are available between certain hours. Tea, coffee and water are always available. You'll have a structured routine and schedule of activities aimed to keep you occupied and help break the addiction cycle. Tomorrow after breakfast you'll get your timetable. It will consist of exercise, counselling – one-to-one and group sessions – leisure activities, talks by guest speakers, and family sessions."

It was a lot to take in. Alice just nodded.

"How are you feeling, physically?"

"I had a hangover yesterday, but today I'm just tired. Anxious. Depressed."

"All normal feelings. You have an appointment in the morning with the doctor for a physical – it's nothing to worry about. And you'll be assigned your counsellor for the one-to-one sessions. Ah, and here we are at the canteen, just as dinner is being served. I'll leave you to eat. Can you find your way back to your room afterwards?"

Alice nodded.

"I'll collect you there at eight and show you where we do the evening meditation. Enjoy your dinner." She scurried off.

Alice looked around the canteen. It was busier than she had expected, with a real mix of people, sitting in small groups. Some were at tables alone, including Fleur, who Alice spotted hiding away at a table in the far corner of the room. She picked up a tray and joined the queue for food.

At bedtime, Alice couldn't wait to phone Bob. She got her mobile from the drawer and was surprised to see a text from Tamzin. It was a photo of her, relaxing in a hot tub on the deck of a ship, drinking what looked like a cocktail out of a pineapple.

Just cruzin'.

Alice smiled to herself, but her smile soon faded when she thought about how easily she could have ruined her best friend's big day. There was no way she would ruin Tamzin's honeymoon by telling her what was happening, so she sent a text exclaiming that she was insanely jealous. Then she phoned Bob.

He answered quickly. "Hi, how are you?"

"Um, OK. I think. It's really weird. Familiar, yet totally new. Any news on your dad?"

"He's still improving. They say he may get out in a few days. Mum says she's delighted, but I think she's secretly enjoying the break from him."

Alice laughed. "And how are you?"

"Now that I've heard you're OK, I'm doing better. I must admit that after I left you, I drove about a mile down the road and I had to pull over. I cried like a baby. It took everything I had not to go straight back there and bring you home."

They talked for a few minutes: she described her room and the grounds, and told him about Fleur. Then Bob put Sam on the phone for a quick chat. They had told him that Alice had had to go away for a few days, but there was nothing to worry about. They said goodnight and ended the call. Alice felt hopeful. She resolved that she was going to kick ass in rehab. For real, this time.

Too exhausted to call them, she texted her mum and dad, telling them she was settling in and she would phone them tomorrow. She received a reply from her mum almost immediately, telling her that she loved her and that she was proud of her. A tear formed in her eye. Alice couldn't ever remember her mum saying that before. Her mum was obviously making an effort to improve their relationship, and Alice resolved to do the same. Then a notification popped up in her messaging app. 'Family' was the title of the group. It had four other members. Her mum, dad, brother and sister. She let out a long sigh. *Mum's told the others. What must they think of me?*

Immediately two more messages popped in.

Big hugs from the five of us. Will speak to you later in the week! Love, Dave

We love you, sis! Liz & Katie

She couldn't stop the tears from rolling down her cheeks. She wasn't surprised at her sister's concern – she was very close to her and her wife – but her brother's message choked her up. He had been quite indignant during her first stint in rehab, and she thought he considered her a burden to the family.

She settled into bed feeling more hopeful than ever. Tomorrow was going to be the first day of the rest of her life.

Chapter Seventeen

The next morning, after exercise, breakfast and her check-up with the doctor, Alice went to her first group therapy session, which was being led by the resident psychologist. It took Alice longer to find the room than she had given herself time for, and everyone looked over at her as she hurried through the door.

"Sorry I'm late," she said, and made her way to the only free seat in the circle.

"You must be Alice. I'm Arnold, and you're just in time." He gestured to another man in the circle. "This is Manny, and it's his first day too. He was just about to tell us why he's here."

Alice nodded to Manny and sat down.

Manny was probably the oldest person in the room. Although he looked haggard, he was dressed in nice clothes and looked pleasant and approachable – more like someone's grandfather than an addict. It was a few seconds before he spoke.

"I'm Eric Manson, but everyone calls me Manny. I'm fifty-nine and addicted to painkillers. Well, it started out as painkillers when I hurt my back. Got tramadol from the doctor. But I took them all and I was still in pain. My GP wouldn't give me more. Told me just to take ibuprofen – like they did any good. I mentioned it to someone at work, and he gave me something. Said it was just the same as tramadol. Before I knew it, I was paying him for them. I didn't know what they were or where he got them. He'd only give me three or four, never more than that. Sometimes I felt different after taking the pills, but I didn't care as long as they did the trick. Every so often he would run out and I'd go a day or two without a fix. It was like being in hell. Then he'd call to say he'd got some, but they cost a little more. They always seemed to cost more, but I kept paying. I didn't even think I had a problem until my wife suggested going on a foreign holiday. I was terrified. I couldn't go on holiday. Where would I get the pills? I couldn't take them with me. What if she found them, or Customs did? What if what I was taking was illegal? The closer it got to the holiday, the more frantic I got. I thought about hurting myself so I couldn't go. I was going to trip myself up. Hope to break or sprain something. I knew it would hurt, so I took an extra couple of pills. But just before I was about to do it, I had a brilliant idea. We couldn't go on holiday if we didn't have passports. I had to get rid of them. You should have seen the look on my wife's face when she arrived home unexpectedly, just in time to see them in flames in the wood burner." He hung his head. "Luckily for her, my bag was already packed. She kicked me out. My son took me in. Tried to help me detox, but it turns out that cold turkey isn't so good. I got really sick and ended up in A&E. From there I went to medically assisted detox. The whole time, I didn't think I was really an addict, but the last four days proved otherwise. I thought I was going to die. I still feel like crap."

Arnold grimaced. "Thank you, Manny. That was very honest." He initiated a round of applause. "Your story is very familiar to me personally. I'm glad you found your way here. OK, Alice, do you want to tell us about yourself?"

She was still taken aback by Manny's story. "That's a tough act to follow."

There was a laugh. Manny nodded at her.

"Um, OK. This isn't my first time in rehab. I was in a place like this before. I know what you mean about the detox, Manny. I didn't have to this time, but last time was brutal. I had the DTs, flashbacks, paranoia. I was in a terrible place, both mentally and physically. This time I'm here as more of a circuit breaker. I was sober for a while, but I stopped going to meetings. Stopped talking about my addiction. I was slipping back into old habits, thinking I could drink and then stop. Doing it in secret. Lying to my friends and family. I never want to come to a place like this again. I want it to stick this time."

Arnold smiled. "I love your attitude. Relapse is part of the recovery process. Not to use you as an example, Alice, but rehab isn't the answer to all your prayers. It's one of the many steps you have to take to learn how to live *with* your addiction without giving in to it. Today we're going to do another mindfulness exercise. We just started these yesterday, so Manny and Alice, you haven't missed anything you'll need for today's session, but if you could stay behind afterwards, I'll go over what we did yesterday."

The catch-up chat after the group session meant that Alice and Manny missed lunch. All that was left in the canteen when they got there were tuna sandwiches. Manny declined, but Alice wolfed hers down and they both went to meet their counsellors for the first time.

Alice's counsellor was Clara. She was a recovering alcoholic too. She'd been sober for twelve years and a counsellor for seven. Alice took to her straight away and didn't hold back in filling Clara in on her past: depression in her teenage years, marriage, infertility, divorce, addiction and relapse. Before she knew it, two hours had passed and she hadn't taken a breath. She took a long sip of water while Clara tidied up her notes.

"That was a great first session." She got up from her chair and took something from a shelf. She offered it to Alice. It was a spiral-bound journal with a glossy beach scene on the cover. "Take this. I want you to write in it every day — your thoughts, feelings, hopes for the future. And any fears that you have."

"I'm worried about Sam, to be honest."

"The little boy?"

"Yes. I don't want him to think that I've gone for good. Like his mum. Even Bob's wife went away and didn't come back."

"It's tough when children are involved. You can't shield him from this as much as you would like to. It's important that he knows there's something going on. That there's a reason everyone's acting so strangely. You don't have to be totally honest with him about everything that's happened, but he needs to know that you're not well and that you need help to get better. And maybe not this week, but he should come with your boyfriend for a Saturday visit to see that you're well. Then you can reassure him yourself that you'll be home soon."

"Are children allowed to visit?"

"Of course they are. But only as long as it's helpful to your recovery. Children of addicts sometimes come to family group too, if they've seen their parent drunk, been witness to any upsetting incidents or been adversely affected by their behaviour. I don't think that's necessary in your case. Sam can come as a regular visitor. Once you are ready."

Alice grinned. "I'd love to see him."

"Then we'll see how it goes. I'll see you tomorrow – and don't forget about your journal."

"I won't."

Ursula was right when she'd said they liked to keep everyone busy. Alice went straight from her one-to-one to an arts and crafts class. She couldn't understand what was supposed to be therapeutic about drawing a bowl of fruit, but she did it anyway because that was what was required of her. In the end, she was proud of the start she had made. She would continue her drawing in the next session.

After that, Alice had an hour of free time before dinner. She went outside to explore the grounds and recce a potential route for a good run the next morning. She walked around the house, but that didn't take long, so she timed herself as she walked down the driveway to the main gate and back. It was about two miles, give or take. Depending on her mood the next morning, she'd run it two or three times.

Her stomach was rumbling when she got back to the house, so she headed straight for the canteen. She chose lentil curry, white rice and naan bread. Looking around for somewhere to sit, she spotted Fleur at a table, talking to another girl. Alice smiled to herself. Fleur gave the impression that she was a loner, but Alice was beginning to suspect that was a coping mechanism of some sort. Either way, Alice hoped to find an empty table. She'd talked so much already that day. But then she realised that perhaps that was something she'd missed in rehab the first time: camaraderie and support from her peers. Manny was at a large table with one other man, so she made her way over to them.

"Do you guys mind if I join you?"

Manny indicated that she should sit down beside him, then pointed to the other man. "Simon, my roommate. Simon, Alice. It's her second time in rehab. She's a veteran."

"Ha! I wouldn't say that. So, what have you guys been up to?"

"Just telling Simon about my kids. My daughter is just as appalled as her mother is, and they won't even pick up the phone to me. But my son hopes to make it to family group next week."

"I hope he does. Last time I was in rehab, I was the one shutting my family out. It really does help with recovery to have them involved."

"You married, Alice?" Simon asked.

"I live with someone. Bob. But we're not married."

"Any kids?"

"Um..." She used to hate being asked that question, but this time she wasn't sure how to answer. Bob was Sam's uncle, so did that make her Sam's aunt? Or step-aunt? She was the closest thing he had to a mother figure, so was she allowed to call herself that? She scratched her head. "It's complicated. Bob is the legal guardian of his nephew; we all live together. I dunno, it works. I think."

"Well, if it works, good luck to you all," Simon said. "OK, I've got to go. Nice to meet you, Alice. Later, Manny." He picked up his tray and walked away.

"I'm gonna go too. Try calling Vera again. She won't talk to me and it's killing me – worse than detox. She's my life." Manny looked distraught.

Alice reached over and patted his shoulder. "She'll come around."

"I hope so." He took a deep breath and pushed back his chair to stand up. "Will I see you at the lecture later? It's on liver cirrhosis."

"What else would I be doing on a Tuesday night?"

He made a face. "I'll save you a seat."

That night, before bed, Alice went out into the garden to phone Bob. She wrapped her coat around herself to shield her from the nip in the autumn breeze. She walked down the stone path into the trees and was surprised to find a stream meandering along. There were a few benches dotted along the bank, and quaint street lamps that had already flickered on. She sat down to make her call. She filled Bob in on her busy day, and in return he told her about his day and Sam's. He also mentioned that, in the interests of moving forward, he had told Kristof and Miriam where she was. They were both shocked but sent their best wishes and assurances that they could hold the fort until she returned.

"Tell them thank you. And bring me my laptop when you come on Saturday. I can work on the new pricing matrix while I'm here."

"Absolutely not. With no disrespect, the business has done OK for twenty years; we can muddle through without you for a few weeks. Oh, you'll never guess who turned up at our house this evening."

"Christine?"

"No..."

"Then who?"

"Your mum."

"My *mum*?"

"Yeah. She said she'd been 'stress cooking' and thought she would bring over some meals to keep us going. She brought two chicken and ham pies, an enormous lasagne and a lamb stew. Does that mean she likes me?"

"I think you've won her round. You'll have to teach me how you did that."

"I had to introduce her to Sam. I hope you don't mind."

"Of course not. How'd it go?"

"Great. Your mum was really good with him. But he kept forgetting her name, so he just called her Alice's mummy. He misses you. I miss you."

A lump formed in her throat. "I miss you guys too."

There was silence for a few seconds until Bob spoke. "I do love you, Alice. A lot."

"I know." Her voice wobbled. She was on the verge of tears but didn't want Bob to hear her cry. "OK, I'm going to hang up now. Sleep tight. I'll phone tomorrow night. Love you."

"Love you too."

He hung up and Alice succumbed to her tears. She just wanted to go home.

Chapter Eighteen

Over the next few days, Alice settled into a good routine. Up early for a run and a shower before breakfast. Group, workshops, individual therapy, meditation, more exercise, lectures. In her free time, she retreated to her favourite spot by the stream in the woods to write in her journal. It was a great way to release negative thoughts and clear her mind, as well as to set and monitor her recovery goals and begin planning for her future.

The days passed quite quickly. Before she knew it, it was Saturday and Bob was arriving for a visit.

Alice chewed her nails as she waited by the front door. She was dying to see Bob, but she hoped there wouldn't be any awkwardness between them. She still thought his reaction to her relapse had been too good to be true. Yes, they had argued, and he'd been angry, but he had still been loving and supportive. She didn't think she deserved it.

When she saw his car, she bolted out of the door and across the car park, eager for him to get out of the car. When he did, she threw her arms around his waist and hugged him tightly. He kissed the top of her head, then took a step away from her and looked her up and down.

"You. Look. Great." He pulled her against him for a proper kiss.

All thoughts of potential awkwardness left her as she melted into him. It was the best kiss she'd ever had. *And one of the longest*, she thought as she finally pulled away from him. She tucked her hair behind her ears and tried not to blush.

He was blushing too. "I wasn't sure what to expect, but you look good. Happy."

"Thank you. I feel good. I hate to admit that my mum was right, but this is exactly what I needed. I think, last time everything was still so raw. So new. I didn't have time to process it. I'm hopeful about this time." She ran her hand down his arm. "You look great too."

He took her hand and led her around to the boot of the car. "I brought you something." He presented her with a bouquet of crudely designed crepe paper flowers and a handmade card.

She held them to her chest. "Oh, these are amazing. Tell Sam I love them."

"Er, Sam didn't make them all. We stayed up until after ten last night to make them. Sam was like a bear this morning."

"And where is my little bear today?"

"At Pauline's. And he's having a sleepover with her two tonight. He's ridiculously excited. When I leave here, I'm picking my dad up from hospital and taking him home. I'll stay there tonight, help Mum get him settled in. I'll pick Sam up on my way home tomorrow."

She sighed. "I feel awful that you have so much on your plate. The business, Sam, your parents. I should be helping you, not adding to your problems. And I still feel like I need to beg for forgiveness. I thought I had everything under control. I'm so sorry."

"You don't have to say sorry. Being here shows me you're sorry. Just don't lie to me any more. If you're struggling, talk to me. You're always telling me how easy I am to talk to."

She nodded. "You are, and I will."

"Good. So..." He looked around the car park. "What

do we do now?"

"We could get a cup of coffee."

"Sounds great."

"Then I'll show you my room."

He cocked his head. "I'm allowed in your room?"

"Yes, but we have to keep the door open."

"Screw the coffee, take me there now." He took her hand and let her lead him inside.

They lay side by side on Alice's bed, holding hands, not talking, just enjoying being close to one another. They had been lying there for a few minutes when Bob rolled over to face her. "I almost forgot. Look at me – do I look any different?"

She scrutinised him. He hadn't had his hair cut; he was badly in need of one, actually. His shirt was familiar and he'd shaved as usual.

"No. I'm sorry."

"Last time you saw me I was married, and now I'm nearly not. I got my decree nisi."

"That was quick."

"I know. And I know you put a lot of work into drafting that settlement for Christine, but she rejected it."

"What? It was more than fair."

"That woman is so bloody stubborn. She's refusing to settle for anything less than half. Honestly, I think I might just give it to her..." He watched Alice for a reaction.

She nodded. "If that's what it takes to finalise your divorce. At the end of the day, it's only money, right?"

"Right. The least of our worries at the moment." He gestured around at their surroundings. "I know this is temporary and you'll be coming home soon. But it doesn't stop me missing you."

"I miss you too," she whispered.

He leant over her and ran his hand across her cheek, then down her neck and brushed against her breast. He began nuzzling her neck.

"Stop it." She giggled. "The door is open."

"And don't mind me..."

Fleur trudged into the room and over to her desk. "Just getting my phone."

Alice frowned. Fleur's father was supposed to come today; he can't have shown up. She got up and beckoned Bob to do the same. "We were going to get some coffee. You're more than welcome to join us."

"No, thanks. I know how much you were looking forward to seeing your boyfriend. I can guard the door if you two want some *proper* alone time." She winked at Bob.

Alice glanced at him and giggled when she saw his cheeks turn pink. "We'll be out in the garden if you need us."

After a quick coffee and a walk around the gardens, Alice brought Bob down to the stream to show him where she went to make her calls and write in her journal. They snuggled together on one of the benches, talking and kissing, until it was time for Bob to leave.

Alice walked him back to the car. She leant against the driver's door to prevent him from opening it. He sighed. "I really have to go. My dad is waiting."

"OK." She pouted. "But you're coming back on Tuesday for family group, right?"

"I'd say I'm looking forward to it, but it doesn't sound appropriate."

"It'll be fine. You don't even have to talk if you don't want to. At least you won't be here on Thursday when my mum and dad come. She'll probably tell Arnold how to do his job. It's going to be excruciating."

"I thought you said they wouldn't allow visitors who could be detrimental to your recovery."

Alice groaned. "Sorry. I'm exaggerating. I have to give Mum a break. I know she loves me really, but she hides it well." She laughed. "You'd better go. I hope everything goes well with your dad. Call me later and let me know. And when you see Sam tomorrow, give him this from me." She wrapped her arms around Bob and squeezed him really tight. Bob pretended to fight for breath and broke away from her. He kissed her quickly then got into the car.

Alice waited until he had driven off before she wiped a tear from her eye.

"Hey," a voice called from behind her.

She turned to see Manny rushing towards her.

"Was that your guy? He has great taste in cars. Women too." He nudged her.

She tutted.

"Oh, come on, but if I was thirty years younger..."

"And not married."

His face fell. "Am I, though? I still can't get Vera to answer the phone. I know she's read my messages because of the ticks, but she's never replied. I haven't heard from her at all since I got here."

"Really?"

"Yeah. The last thing she said to me was that I'd broken her heart. The lies, the money, the fucking passports. I begged her to forgive me. I promised her the world as penance. She told my son to get me help, but I thought she'd offer me some sort of support – you know, like your guy supports you."

"Bob's different."

"What?" He recoiled. "You think your boyfriend's a better person than my wife?"

"No. I'm so sorry. That's not what I meant. What I meant was... Well, how long have you and your wife been together?"

"Thirty-nine years."

"Wow. And has it been a happy marriage?"

"Mostly."

"And how long has she known about your addiction?"

"Eleven days."

She clicked her fingers and pointed at him. "That's the difference. Bob has known about my addiction since the day we met. I was honest with him about it and he wanted to date me anyway."

"Yes, because you're smoking hot."

She clipped him on the shoulder. "Stop joking around. This is new to your wife. She needs time to process the fact that her husband has had a drug problem for the last year, and she didn't even notice. My mum was the same with me the first time I was in rehab. She's only beginning to come around now. Hopefully once your wife comes to terms with what's happened and she sees how determined you are to get better, she won't throw away all those good years because of this bad one."

"You're very wise for someone so young."

"Meh, I've been in and out of therapy since I was a teenager. There's only so much psychobabble you can ignore before it starts to sink in."

They began to laugh, but then Fleur walked past. Alice frowned.

"What's your roommate's story?" Manny asked.

"Her dad was a no-show today."

"Ouch. I didn't get any visitors either – maybe she and I should form some sort of support group."

Alice laughed, but it wasn't the worst idea she'd ever heard. At least it would be a distraction from feeling lonely and left out. "Sit with us at dinner and suggest that to her. I wonder how they're going to disguise tofu this evening. I'd give anything for a dirty burger."

"Mmm." He drooled. "And beer-battered onion rings."

"Not for me! I'm an alcoholic."

"Shit. You really can't have those?"

She tutted and shook her head.

"Tofu it is then."

They headed off towards the canteen.

Family group on Tuesday was focused on improving communication skills between the patients and their loved ones, using role-playing exercises. Once their initial feelings of awkwardness had passed, Alice and Bob participated fully in the group session.

Afterwards, Alice walked Bob to the door. "Well, what did you think of your first taste of therapy?"

"Let's just say, I didn't hate it. That's got to be something, right? And I would do it every day if that's what it takes to get you better."

"Thank you. And isn't it great that Arnold has given the go-ahead for Sam to visit this Saturday? I can't wait to see him."

"I don't know how many times I've assured him that

you're coming back, but I don't think he believes me. It will do him the world of good to see you." He checked his watch and sighed. "I'd better go."

"Go? You're allowed to stick around for half an hour for some private time."

"I'd love to, but if I don't leave now, I'll get caught in traffic and be late for Sam."

She nodded. "OK. I'll call you later."

"Love you." He kissed her and hurried out of the door.

"Love you, too," she called after him. She was about to turn away, but the door opened again and Bob rushed back into reception. He gathered her into his arms.

"I just need one more." He kissed her hard, and for a long time. She was breathless when he let her go. "Bye," he whispered, then hurried off.

She was taking a minute to compose herself when Manny, who had been watching from across reception, came slinking up beside her. "That looked steamy."

Alice couldn't help but grin.

"He seems like a nice guy. You must be really special, Alice. I felt totally crap in there. I was the only one who didn't have someone."

"I'm sorry your son couldn't make it."

"I guess he got held up." He tutted. "And what am I going to do about Vera? How can I convince her I'm getting better if she won't even talk to me?"

"I don't know."

His shoulders slumped. "I'm just going to stop."

"Stop what? Rehab?"

"No. Stop calling, texting. Maybe that will get her to talk to me."

"I don't think so. What if she thinks you've given up?" Alice racked her brains. There had to be another way. Perhaps he could write to her? They'd been encouraged to keep a journal as part of their therapy, and this included drafting letters to themselves and loved ones. The letters were cathartic and were never meant to be posted, but Manny could do a version to send to his wife. He just had to be careful what he wrote. "What do you usually say to her?"

"I say sorry and tell her that I love her. I ask her to call me."

"How about … changing what you say to her? Tell her positive things about what you're doing here. What you have learned. What you talk about in therapy. What you miss about *her*. She's going through a hard time too. Have you asked how she is?"

"No." He frowned at her. "You're not really a patient, are you? You work here undercover."

"What a depressing job. I don't know how they do it. It's definitely a vocation." She clapped her hands. "Let's turn things around. What are you doing between now and dinner?"

"I was going to watch some TV."

"No TV. You're coming running with me."

He shook his head. "Nah."

"Come on. Exercise helps – it's not a myth. Why do you think it's built into our daily timetable?"

"I'm glad you said that. I thought you'd forgotten we'd already exercised today."

"That wasn't exercise. It was a few stretches. Go and get changed, meet me back here in ten."

For the next few days, Alice tried to whip Manny into

shape. They ran laps of the grounds every morning before breakfast and joined in with yoga in the evenings after dinner. In their down time, they got together and talked at length about their feelings, fears, and hopes for the future, although Alice made sure she kept some time free each day to retreat to her bench in the woods to write in her journal.

After yoga on Friday night, Alice returned to her room to find Fleur frantically packing her bags. Alice thought that was weird, because she had a few more days to go.

"What are you doing?"

"I just can't take it any more. This place. These people. You!"

"What have I done?"

"Nothing. You're doing everything right. You're going to do well when you leave here. At least you have a life to go back to."

"So do you."

"Not a life like yours. I saw your mum and dad here yesterday, crying because they had to leave you. Your phone is constantly beeping with messages from that boyfriend of yours. I've been here for sixteen days. I haven't even had one call or text from my dad. Even if hell froze over he wouldn't visit tomorrow. It's a cert that I'm going to start using and drinking again anyway, so what's the point in delaying it?"

"Don't you have any friends you could turn to?"

"I used to have a wonderful friend." Fleur sounded wistful. "She was like a sister to me. We did everything together, as far back as I can remember."

That seemed hopeful. "Yeah, like what?"

"Get fucked up and party. But she got shoved into

rehab too. Difference is, it worked for her and now she's boring as hell. Bitch told me she doesn't want to hang out with me while I'm using, so I ghosted her ass."

Alice thought of her own friendship with Tamzin. She had tried to cut Tamzin out of her life when she began to comment on Alice's drinking. She had been awful to her. When she was in recovery, she was terrified that Tamzin would never forgive her, but that wasn't the case. Best friends would usually forgive; they just had to be given the opportunity to do so.

"Maybe you should give her a call now. You're in rehab, you're doing well. I'll bet she'd love to talk to you."

"I don't think so." Fleur zipped her bag closed and threw it over her shoulder. "You'll probably be long gone when I get back. It was super knowing you, Alice. Good luck." She made her way to the door.

"You're just leaving? Shouldn't you talk to someone before you go?"

"I just did!"

And with that, Fleur was gone.

Alice thought about running after her, but she didn't know what else to say. The main door was always monitored, and Fleur would be challenged by a staff member. They'd know what to do.

Alice went into the bathroom and started to get undressed. She had taken her top off when there was a knock on the bedroom door. Ugh! She pulled her top back on. There was another knock — more frantic this time.

"Give me a minute!"

Alice hurried out of the bathroom and opened the bedroom door, expecting to see Fleur with her tail between her legs, but Manny burst into the room and scooped her into his arms. He spun her around. "She texted. She texted me!"

"Vera?"

"Yes! She said she'll come and see me tomorrow. I can't believe it!"

"Oh, that's great," Alice said flatly as Manny set her back onto her feet.

"What's wrong? I thought you'd be more excited for me."

"I am. But Fleur just walked out. She's going back to her old life. I tried to talk her out of it, but..."

"Oh, Alice." He put his arm around her. "You can't help everyone. You're obviously meant to be *my* guardian angel, not hers. Come on, we need to celebrate. I'll buy you a hot chocolate."

"But it's free."

He rolled his eyes. "I'll push the button on the machine for you. Will that do?"

"It'll have to."

Chapter Nineteen

The next morning, Alice and Manny were so excited about their impending visitors that they cut their exercise short so they could get ready. Alice had heard from Ursula that Fleur had refused to speak to anyone and had demanded to exercise her right to leave. She left in a taxi not long after 8 p.m.

Skimping on exercise turned out to be a bad idea as it made the morning drag, but it was finally time for visitors to start arriving. Alice and Manny were waiting in reception watching the door. He jumped out of his seat when he saw his wife arriving.

"There she is. Wish me luck." He hurried off towards the woman, who had a face like thunder. Manny reached out to hug her, but she took a step backwards, keeping him at arm's length.

Alice was so busy staring at the incredibly awkward reunion and feeling awful for her friend that she didn't notice her own visitors had arrived. All of a sudden Sam was beside her. He threw his arms around her leg. "Alice!" he cried with joy.

"Hello, my gorgeous boy." Alice leant down to him, placed her hands on his cheeks and locked eyes with him. She peppered his forehead and nose with kisses and they hugged each other tightly.

Bob looked on. A tear formed in his eye at the sight of them. "I want in on that hug." He engulfed them in his arms and they hugged until Sam struggled free, leaving Alice and Bob free to kiss.

"Yuk!" Sam cried, making Alice and Bob laugh. They pulled away from each other.

"Come and see what I've got for you." Alice took them by the hand and led them up to her bedroom.

Bob laughed when he saw her room. Alice had made a fort out of Fleur's empty bed. Inside was the latest copy of the *Pokémon* magazine, a carton of juice and a packet of Haribo. "Why don't you chill in your fort and give Uncle Bob and me a chance to talk? Then in half an hour, we'll go outside. I heard a rumour there's another boy coming, and he's bringing a football. We can all have a good kick-about."

"OK." Happily, Sam climbed into the fort.

Alice and Bob sat down on her bed.

"How'd you get the contraband?"

"I asked my mum to bring it when she came for family group on Thursday. It went better than I thought. I think we're turning a corner."

"That's good. There are real positives this time."

"There's just one more problem. Tam. She's getting home from honeymoon tomorrow. She's going to want to see me, and I'm going to have to tell her what happened. I'm dreading it."

Bob put his arm around her. "Don't worry. She had a perfect day. A perfect honeymoon, from what you've told me. Why don't you say it all kicked off the day after, keep the memory perfect for her? I'll play along."

"I don't know if I should: it's a lie. I can't tell lies. My recovery has to be about truth. No matter how painful it is."

"As long as you're true to yourself, and to me and Sam, a little white lie to your best friend so she can keep a perfect memory of her wedding day isn't the end of the world."

"You might be right."

"I think it's the right thing to do, but it's your decision. But just tell me what you decide. I don't want to put my foot in it by saying the wrong thing." He nudged her. "And speaking of weddings... I'll be an eligible bachelor again soon. I think we should talk about marriage."

Marriage? She squinted at him. He'd mentioned it casually before, but she'd assumed he was joking and hadn't given it much thought.

"Please don't think I'm proposing. It's just that we've never really talked about it and I wanted you to know that if it's something you want to do in the future, that's fine with me. And if you don't, that's also fine. I could take it or leave it."

Well, that could never be mistaken for a proposal. "That's good to know." She blushed. "Right, I didn't ask you to bring Sam so I could talk to you all afternoon. Let's go outside now. I've found a tree I know he'd love to climb."

They spent a lovely few hours together in the garden, playing football, climbing the tree, and the catering staff brought out bowls of ice cream for Sam and the other children who were visiting. It was almost like a normal Saturday afternoon in the park. Until it was time to leave. Alice walked them back to the car. Even though she wanted to go home with them so much it hurt, she tried to stay upbeat for Sam. She showered him with kisses then strapped him into his car seat.

Bob gave her a lingering kiss. "I'll see you on Tuesday. I love you."

"Love you too. You too, Sam," she called into the back seat. She waved as they drove away, then went back to her room, alone.

Alice was dismantling the fort when she found the *Pokémon* magazine Sam had forgotten. She flicked through it and smiled at his attempt at the word search. Then she saw a drawing he'd done in a blank space near the back of the magazine. Three stick figures, one tall, one medium and one small. She assumed it was meant to be a picture of the three of them. It was the cutest thing she had ever seen.

At that moment, she realised that she did want to marry Bob. Sam would never be her son, but he was a McKendry. And if she married Bob, then she would be too. They would be a proper family – well, as close to proper as she was ever going to get. And she couldn't wait.

Then she thought about Tamzin. Bob was right. She didn't need to know exactly how she had relapsed, just that it had happened. Her recovery was going well, so Tamzin had no reason to worry about her, and Alice didn't want to give her one. She felt her stomach growl, which prompted her to check the clock. It was dinner time.

In two minutes flat she arrived at the canteen and was relieved to see that there was no queue. She selected the lasagne, hoping it was actual beef, not Quorn again, a slice of garlic bread and some chips. Salivating at the sight of the food on her tray, she scanned the room for Manny, hoping to sit with him. She was eager to hear how things had gone with his wife. She couldn't see him, but spotted his roommate at a table with another guy. "Hey, Simon, do you mind if I join you? Where's Manny?"

Simon's face fell. "He's not coming."

"Why?"

"Things didn't go too well with his missus."

"Oh no." She groaned. "What happened?"

"He didn't say. But she only stayed for a few minutes. I saw her storming out. He's in a bad way, just wants to be on his own."

"No. That's not right. He can't just sit up there by himself. I'll go up, convince him to come down. He really should eat something." She pushed back her chair to stand up.

Simon stood up too. "It's OK, I'm finished. I'm heading back up there. I'll tell him you're looking for him and send him down."

"OK, thanks." She tucked into her lasagne and tried to think of something positive that she could say to Manny when he came down. But she could think of nothing.

After Alice had finished her meal, there was still no sign of Manny. She'd eaten quickly on account of her hunger, but he should have been down by now. She headed up to his room, knowing she had her work cut out for her.

As she approached the top of the stairs, she heard a commotion. She quickened her pace. When she turned the corner to Simon and Manny's room, she saw a group of people in the corridor. She ran towards them and saw Simon among them.

"What's going on?" Her gaze fell on his hands. They were blood red.

In a panic she tried to push past one of the clinic doctors, but Simon grabbed her by the arm. "Don't go in there!"

"I need to see him." She tried to pull away, but he held her firmly.

"No. You don't."

Just then, Ursula arrived with two paramedics. She showed them into the room then turned to the small crowd. "Everyone please, go back to your rooms."

When no one moved, Ursula sighed. "Then can you all please go down to the day room. I need to keep this area clear."

Alice and Simon looked at each other. Without a word, they turned and made their way downstairs.

As word of the incident spread around the clinic, more and more people gathered in the day room to wait for news. Simon was speaking to Clara, and a few others were whispering among themselves. Alice wrung her hands. *If I hadn't convinced him he could win his wife back, she mightn't have come, and this wouldn't have happened. She must have said something awful to prompt him to do this...* She tried to recall anything he might have said to suggest that he was so vulnerable, but she couldn't think of anything. Guilt washed over her when she realised that, while she had been having a great afternoon with Bob and Sam, Manny had been facing such turmoil.

The room fell silent when the ambulance siren started, and everyone shared concerned looks as the noise faded into the distance. Not long after, Ursula arrived at the door accompanied by the general manager. He gave a sad smile. "Manny has a faint pulse. We're all praying that he pulls through."

Never overly religious, Alice tried to recall the Lord's Prayer, although she doubted her prayers would do Manny any good. She stayed in the day room for a while – not because she wanted to talk, but because she didn't want to be alone. It was almost eleven when she got back to her room. Too drained to undress, she climbed into bed and pulled the covers up over her head, thinking that there was no way she would sleep. But she fell asleep quite quickly and slept for hours.

A knock on the door woke her. She lifted her head to see daylight trying to break through the crack in the curtains. She was checking the time when there was another knock.

"Hello?" she called.

The door opened and Ursula popped her head through. "Alice, you have a visitor." She stepped back to let Bob into the room.

Alice welled up immediately. "What are you doing here?"

He approached the bed and knelt down beside her. "When you didn't call me at the usual time, I tried calling you. When I couldn't get through, I started to worry. I rang the office and they said there had been an incident but you were safe, and they'd get you to call me in the morning. But I couldn't sleep a wink worrying about you. I had to see you, so I dropped Sam to Pauline's for an hour."

Alice looked over his shoulder at Ursula, who was still at the door. "Any news of Manny?"

"Yes. We had word from the hospital. He's going to be OK. But he won't be coming back here. He needs more specialist care."

"Can I go and see him?"

"That's not a good idea. It may sound selfish, but you have to focus on your own recovery. And that continues today. So, take a few minutes with Bob, then have a shower and some breakfast. Arnold wants to meet you out by the big tree at ten. Sharp. Got it?"

"OK," Alice said quietly.

"I'll be outside if you need me."

Alice watched Ursula go, then focused on Bob. He was still kneeling beside the bed, holding her hand. She couldn't believe he'd come so early on a Sunday morning just to check on her. She felt a pang of sadness when she thought about Manny, and Fleur, and wished they had as much love and support.

Bob got up from the floor and sat on the bed beside her. He pulled her into an embrace. "I can't stay long. I just wanted to check that you were all right."

She nodded. "I'll be fine. I'm so relieved Manny's going to be OK. It's made me realise, yet again, that I'm so lucky to have you. After everything I've done, you still want to be with me when you should be rueing the day we met."

"Of course I don't. Listen to me, Alice. What's happening here – it's for the best."

She made a face at him.

"I didn't understand addiction. I had no idea how easily things could fall apart. Now I'm beginning to understand that it doesn't go away just because you've been to rehab or a few meetings. It needs to be kept at the forefront of your mind, not swept under the carpet. And we can do it, Alice. I have faith in you. In us. Will you end up in a place like this again? Who knows? But you're not going through this alone. You have a family who love you, and we're never going to write you off."

She wiped away a tear. "I'm going to prove to you that I'm good enough."

"Stop it." He groaned. "You *are* good enough. Too

good, in fact. The way you've opened your heart to me and Sam – you've given us the best parts of you. I wish you could love yourself as much as we love you."

"I'm trying."

"That's all I ask." He planted a kiss on her cheek and stood up. "I'm sorry – they said I could only stay a few minutes. I'll be back for family group on Tuesday. Call me later. I love you."

"I love you too."

He waved as he left, then closed the door behind him.

Alice glanced at the clock. It was nearly eight and she wasn't meeting Arnold until ten. Breakfast and a shower would only take a few minutes, so she had time for a bit more shut-eye. She lay down and cuddled into the pillow, but the door opened and Ursula bustled in. She pulled the sheets away from Alice. "You're not hiding in there."

"Please, I just can't."

"You usually go for a run before breakfast. Routine is important. So up and at 'em. The exercise will clear your head."

"But I don't feel like it."

"No buts. This is exactly the time to get up and shake it off, not wallow. Your attitude to your recovery has been fantastic so far. You have to keep that momentum going. Forwards, not backwards."

Alice started to cry. "It's just all so hard."

"I know." Ursula put her arms around Alice and let her sob on her shoulder. "You know, Alice, I never wanted to work in a place like this. Six years ago, I lost my job in a nursing home and this was the only job I could get that would pay my bills. I kept applying for jobs and swore to myself as soon as I could get back to another nursing home, I'd run out that door and never look back. But when that day came, I just couldn't leave. Not because I love it here or have delusions that everyone who leaves here is going to make it. It's because I believe in hope. Sometimes everything seems hopeless, but hope is always there. I've seen utter heartbreak and so many lost causes. But you, my dear, are not one of them."

Alice squeezed Ursula's hand. "You really think so?"

"I know so. Now, get yourself out of that bed. And off you go."

A short run was all Alice could manage, but after a shower she did feel much better. She headed to the canteen craving comfort food. Her usual breakfast of fruit and cereal wasn't going to cut it. Instead, she opted for a bagel with bacon and cream cheese, and a large cup of coffee.

At 10 a.m. Alice went outside to meet Arnold. She sat on the ground beside him and leant against the trunk of the enormous tree. "I really want to go and see Manny."

"That's not a good idea. Not at the minute, anyway. He has a long road ahead of him. And you have yours. Do you want to talk about what happened last night?"

"How could his wife do that to him? Give him hope like that and just take it away?"

"You have no idea what they said or what went on between them. No one does. Whatever it was, she has her own struggle. She has to come to terms with what's happened too. She rushed to the hospital as soon as she got the call."

"Did she?"

"Yes. And both of his children. They were all there with him when I left."

"That has to be positive, right?"

"It's certainly not a bad sign." He sighed. "It was a huge shock for you. I just want to check you're OK. I know you two were friendly."

"Some friend I was – I didn't see the signs. I had no idea he was suicidal."

"None of us did. I'm sure you've been guilty of putting a smile on your face when you're crying on the inside."

She nodded.

"We all have. I saw a huge smile on your face yesterday when you were out here playing football with that little boy of yours. Was that smile real?"

"Yes." She couldn't help grinning. "Completely authentic."

After lunch, Alice went back to her room and lay down on the bed. She had no sooner closed her eyes when there was a knock at the door. That had better not be Ursula, she thought. The door opened slowly and one of the housekeepers popped his head around the door. "You OK if I come in and change the sheets? You're getting a new roommate."

Alice groaned. She would have preferred a few days on her own. "Do we know who?"

"No. She's coming from detox in another facility. She'll be here this afternoon."

"OK. Thanks." She grabbed her phone to catch up with her texts from Bob, her mum and sister, and sighed when she saw a few missed calls and three texts from Tamzin. That meant she was home from honeymoon, and she couldn't wait to tell Alice all about it. Her stomach churned at the thought of speaking to Tamzin, but she had to, sooner rather than later.

The housekeeper was soon done, and Alice was left alone. She called her friend.

Tamzin answered quickly. *"Finally!* I've been calling you all morning. It was so weird arriving home and you not being here. Can you come over later? I'm dying to tell you everything."

"Um..."

"Oh, or I could come to you. If Bob doesn't mind."

"Um, no, he wouldn't mind. But I'm not at home." She braced herself and just went for it. "I'm in rehab again."

There was silence.

"Tam? You there?"

"If this is your idea of a joke, it's not funny."

"It's not a joke. I'm really here."

Tamzin's voice was shaky. "What happened?"

"I started drinking again."

"When?"

"Months ago. I've been keeping it a secret from you, from Bob, from everybody." Confessing was easier than she thought it was going to be. "I thought I could handle one or two. Turns out I couldn't. Bob found out and he called my parents. They all got together and shipped me back to rehab. But I don't want you to worry. I'm doing OK. It's so different to last time, because I *want* to be here. I feel like I'm really benefitting from it, and that's not bullshit."

There was silence again.

"Tam? Say something."

"I don't know what to say."

"Do you hate me?"

"No. I just... I'm stunned. I can't believe this is happening."

"Me neither. I'm so sorry to drop this on you. It's the last thing you need when you just got back from your honeymoon. How did it go?"

Tamzin tutted. "I can't tell you about my honeymoon over the phone. I'll have to come and see you. And while I'm there, make sure you're not bullshitting me about your recovery. I don't go back to work until Wednesday – when can you fit me in?"

"I'll have to clear it with them. I'll let you know. So, you're not mad at me?"

"I'm mad as hell, Alice," Tamzin said sternly. "And how did Bob take it?"

"About the same as you. Although he did cry a little. Can't you spare a few tears for your best friend?"

"I'm saving them for when I see you. I'm sorry, I've got to go. Cameron said something about making lunch, and now there's a really funny smell coming from the kitchen. Text me and let me know when I'm allowed to come. Oh, and the address might help too."

"Bye, Tam. And thank you."

"Don't sweat it, girl. Bye."

Alice ended the call. She could just imagine Tamzin running to Cameron to tell him what had happened, then the two of them discussing her for the rest of the day.

Relieved to get the call out of the way, Alice lay back down on her bed. Maybe she could have a few minutes to herself before her new roommate arrived.

Chapter Twenty

The next week passed without incident. Tamzin had visited the day after they had talked on the phone, and again a few days later. Alice's therapy was going well, and she was feeling hopeful about the future.

She was getting along well with her new roommate, Maya. She had been very quiet at first – understandably so, as she had spent a difficult few days in detox. But once she had begun to adjust to her circumstances, she and Alice found they had a lot to talk about. Maya was a few years older than Alice, and she was married with two children. But her job as a live music producer took her away from home quite often, and she had become addicted to late nights and parties – and the alcohol and drugs that went with them.

Alice's last day arrived in no time. The morning was just the same as the others – exercise, breakfast, group therapy – and she finished her latest masterpiece in arts and crafts. After lunch she had her last one-to-one with Clara. Although the sessions were exhausting and sometimes very emotional, Alice felt she had made some great advances, and was able to work through many of the deep-rooted emotional issues that made her want to drink.

At the end of the session, Clara closed her notebook and set it on the table. "I'm sad to see you go, Alice, but I'm happy that you're leaving in a better place than when you came. How do you feel?"

"Nervous. I know I've done this before, but it's still daunting."

"That's why aftercare is so important. You know that rehabilitation doesn't end when you walk out that door. It's a long-term process that requires constant diligence and dedication. You have your recovery plan, which you are going to follow to the letter. If at any time you're struggling, or feeling like things are becoming unmanageable, my door is always open."

"I know. Thank you for everything."

"Oh, and I want you to have this." Clara handed her an A4 hardback journal with a beautiful sunrise on the cover. "I've had it for a long time. I thought it was too pretty to write in, so I was keeping it for something special. But I want you to have it. And to fill it."

"Thank you." Alice took the journal and made her way to the door. "Thanks for everything, Clara."

"You're welcome, Alice. And good luck."

As Alice left the office, she checked the time. She still had to finish packing, but she had an overwhelming urge to visit her spot by the stream one last time. She went outside, hurried down the stone path into the woods, and perched on her favourite bench. She closed her eyes and listened to the wind blowing through the trees, and the faint sound of the stream as it trickled past. Although she was glad to be going home, part of her felt sad to be leaving here, and the safety of the clinic. But as daunting as it was, it was already more positive than last time, as she had Bob and Sam to go home to. Alice knew that her recovery was ultimately up to her, but she felt a bit more confident knowing she had their support and the support of her family and friends.

She stared down at the journal on her knee. Clara was right – it was almost too pretty to write in. The warm sunrise, bringing with it a new day, full of hope and possibility, was the perfect metaphor for her recovery. She flicked through the blank pages and imagined that the journal was her future. She made a promise to herself that she would fill it with only positive things.

She closed her eyes and went over the plans she'd been making. Aftercare was included in the clinic's package, but she had decided she didn't want to return there and chose instead to schedule her outpatient therapy at their sister clinic in the city. Bob and her parents were going to continue joining her for family sessions. In addition to the outpatient therapy, Alice had downloaded a timetable of AA meetings in her area, although she planned to go back to the church hall on Sunday morning to see if Joan was there. Alice had made a connection with her during the few meetings she'd been to, and wanted to ask Joan to become her new sponsor. Hopefully Joan would agree to the challenge.

The projects Alice had been working on at Christine Cleans were almost complete. She was sorely tempted to stay in that safe, familiar environment, but there was no real need; she could do the accounts in her spare time and Bob and the others had everything running smoothly. It was time for her to resume her career. And unlike the last time, when she left rehab and hid herself away in a hotel kitchen, she was excited to get back to work and had already updated her CV and begun trawling through recruitment websites.

Just then, another patient jogged past, disturbing Alice from her thoughts. Eager to get going, she took a deep breath, had one last look around, then headed back to her room.

Alice zipped her suitcase closed and made a final sweep of the room to make sure she hadn't forgotten anything. Then there was a knock at the door. Assuming it was Bob, she rushed to open it, but was startled to see Fleur standing before her.

"Good, you're still here." She pushed past Alice into the room.

"What on earth are you doing here?"

"When I bailed the other week, I went on a bender. Ecstasy, coke, booze – it should have been awesome. But it wasn't. No matter how fucked up I got, I just couldn't get your whingey little voice out of my head." She tried to imitate Alice's voice. *"Maybe you should give her a call."*

"Who?"

"Fifi. My boring-as-hell best friend. I was coming down the other morning and I got all sappy and sentimental and started looking at some old photos. Before I knew it, I'd called her. We talked for a few minutes and then she said she wanted to come and see me. She wanted to see me, Alice. Can you believe that?"

Dumbstruck, Alice nodded.

"So, we talked. For hours. And she stayed with me and got me sober. Then she came with me to see my dad. I asked him why he wasn't supporting me, like your parents support you. He said he'd tried. And to be honest he did, at first. But when he saw me relapse, time and time again, he thought I was beyond help. But I told him that I'm really going to try this time. And he's promised to be more supportive. He brought me here today, and he promised he'll come to family group and visiting. Fifi too."

"Oh, I'm so proud of you." Alice threw her arms

around Fleur's neck and hugged her until she pulled away.

"Don't hug me, traitor. You're leaving just as I get back in. Where am I supposed to get my daily dose of positivity?"

"You'll get a new roommate. And I'll give you my number." Alice darted to her bag, took out one of her old journals and ripped off a page to scribble down her phone number. "Call me if you want to chat. Any time. Day or night."

"Like that's the same," Fleur scoffed. "How about I come out with you now? We'll party for a few days, then come back and do it together."

Alice pointed to her bag. "Sorry. I'm ready to go."

"Then you'd better hurry. I saw your boyfriend's car arriving. If you don't get out there quick, Ursula will have him."

Alice gave Fleur another quick hug, then picked up her bag and hurried out of the room.

"Good luck," Fleur called after her.

Alice made her way downstairs. Her tears were flowing freely, despite having promised herself that she wouldn't cry. But she hadn't bet on seeing Fleur. She'd said all her goodbyes that morning, so she avoided eye contact with anyone she passed. When she got to the top of the last flight of stairs, she spotted Sam sitting on the sofa beside the main door. He was playing with one of his toy cars. She wiped away her tears and quickened her pace to sneak down the stairs without him noticing her, then crept over and plonked herself down beside him.

He jumped, then turned towards her. "Alice!"

"Hello, my gorgeous boy," she cooed. She wrapped

her arms around him.

"Are you really coming home today?"

"Yup."

"Yay. 'Cause we got you a surprise. It's a—"

"Zip it, squirt!" Bob said as he arrived beside them. "Otherwise it's not a surprise."

Alice stood up and beckoned Sam to do the same. She was about to give Bob a quick peck on the cheek when she noticed Ursula standing at the door of her office.

"Don't forget, we're here if you need us. Good luck, dear. Take care of each other."

"We will. Thank you."

"You're welcome." Without another word, Ursula turned and went back into her office.

Bob picked up Alice's bag and offered her his free hand. "You ready to go home?"

She slipped her hand into his and offered her other hand to Sam. "Yes. Let's go home."

They walked hand in hand to the car. Bob put her bag in the boot and strapped Sam into his car seat while Alice had one last look at the Georgian manor that had been her home for the past three weeks. When rehab had been presented as an option, Alice hadn't thought it was necessary. But now she knew that the time she'd spent there in therapy and self-discovery would turn out to be the most important twenty-one days of her life.

She got into the car and took a deep breath. "Let's go."

Before Bob started the car he turned to her. "I wanted to make this special for you. I was going to organise a little gathering. Your family and Tamzin, and I planned to get fancy coffee and pastries. But then I thought it was too much. We should probably do something normal instead. But I didn't want you to think that I didn't bother trying to make it special."

"Normal is good. And you make me feel special without even trying. I do want to see my parents, and Elizabeth – even David. But over the next few days, and definitely not all in one go. Let's get a takeaway and the three of us can snuggle on the sofa and watch a movie. Maybe even an early night?" She winked at him. "I've really missed you."

"I've missed you too." He smiled and started the car.

As they drove out of the car park, Alice had a final look back at the clinic. She closed her eyes and prayed that she'd never have to set foot in one of those places again.

Acknowledgements

Dear reader, thank you. I'm always humbled when someone takes a chance on one of my books. I hope you enjoyed it. Feel free to pop by and say hello on your preferred social media channel.

I'd like to thank my family and friends for their continuing encouragement and support.

A big thank you to returning beta readers Jen, Mags and Lynda. Thanks to Helen for all the legal advice, more than half of which didn't make the final edit.

Thanks to Aaron and Jane for another beautiful cover.

Thank you to Jane Hammett and Louise Glynne-Walton for their editing and proofreading.

catherinemorrisonauthor

wouldbewriter

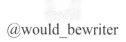

@would_bewriter

About the Author

Catherine Morrison lives in Northern Ireland with her husband and two children.

Despite graduating from the University of Ulster in 2002 with a BA in English Literature and Media Studies, Catherine did not put pen to paper until she was certain she had forgotten absolutely everything she had learned during her degree.

Little did she know in 2018, when she sat down to write her first novel, that writing would consume her completely. Since then, almost every evening when the day job is done and the kids are in bed, she sits down to write the kind of stories she loves to read.

Other Novels by Catherine Morrison

The Hook – a fun and flirty romantic mystery set in New York City.

Waiting for Saturday – a new friendship turns a married woman's life upside down.